Gerhard Oberressl

EDELWEISS
CASTLE

Death of an Interviewer

outskirtspress
DENVER, COLORADO

Edelweiss Castle
Death of an Interviewer
All Rights Reserved.
Copyright © 2015 Gerhard Oberressl
v2.0

Cover Photo © 2015 Gerhard Oberressl. All rights reserved - used with permission.

Outskirts Press, Inc.
http://www.outskirtspress.com

Paper Back ISBN: 978-1-4787-5750-4
Hard Back ISBN: 978-1-4787-5882-2

Outskirts Press and the "OP" logo are trademarks belonging to Outskirts Press, Inc.

PRINTED IN THE UNITED STATES OF AMERICA

Contents

§0

The Narrative and Its Characters

Joseph von Aybesford, an aristocrat living on his farm in the grounds of Edelweiss Castle, was in those days a member of the Brundtland commission (1983-1987). On Saturday seventeen May 2014 he was to give a television interview.

He had come to an agreement with the interviewer Xanda van Aanstryk; she would see to it that he gets sufficient opportunity to champion the cause of sustainable development.

Xanda van Aanstryk, a woman of gloomy secrets, had been overdue for some time when her young colleague Louise Chevrolet arrived and announced that Xanda had fallen ill. But she declared to be on familiar grounds; she would very much like to do the interview.

Aybesford, hesitating between sustainable development and the prompting of the beautiful young woman, decided at the last moment to let himself in for the interview. It was the day before the general election in Austria.

When the interview was under way it became apparent that Louise hadn't got a clue to the agreement between Aybesford and van Aanstryk. She had meant to shine with her knowledge of the history of the world-famous castle on the level blue rock plateau.

In the course of the conversation the elder gentleman got increasingly annoyed; so much so, that he started to get sarcastic. Upon this Louise Chevrolet lost the thread and got into floundering. Aybesford seized the opportunity to make political statements concerning the general election.

He would never have imagined it possible that this would lead to sovereignty of the little hitherto Austrian province Goodland within a week.

A reporter from Manchester, who was staying in Edelweiss at the time, smelled already the outbreak of the Third World War. It didn't come to that; but on the morning after the interview Xanda van Aanstryk was found dead. The police were groping in the dark.

In the following weeks, the Austrian press kept on and on conjecturing, that the Aybesford family could be involved in the dealings that led to the death of the woman.

Gordon Aybesford, the circumspect master of the castle, was concerned about the reputation of his name. There were also older rumors in the wind, which were to the detriment of the Aybesford family. Did these also have to do with Xanda van Aanstryk?

He made up his mind to wipe the slate clean and engaged the investigator Pierre de Fermat from Chantilly and commissioned him to get to the bottom of things relentlessly.

The enquiries of the Frenchman brought a couple of rather unpleasant surprises into the light of day; among others the uncovering of a murder from years back. Also the solution of the riddle of Xanda van Aanstryk's demise seemed to be within reach, when the investigations unexpectedly fizzled out.

It was only when Gloria Aybesford, the older daughter of the house, and Walter Nadler jun. injected themselves into the inquiries, that things moved into gear again.

For ease of reference, a list of characters follows hereafter. The characters names are cited in the order of their appearance or mention in the story. With each individual who enters the scene, his or her social grouping is drawn up and the figure's name is placed within this group. If no group relevant to the narrative can be determined, the name is placed on its own in line.

The individuals' ages are given as they were true on the morning of the day when the interview took place, namely on Saturday seventeen May 2014, that is to say, in the year of the World War One centenary.

List Of Characters

Walter Nadler Sen., 79, former castle administrator
Walter Nadler, son of Walter Sen., administrator in 2014
Tusnelda Nadler, the administrator's spouse
Walter Nadler Jr., 24, son of Walter and Tusnelda
Aunt Mitzi, lived in Alfalfa
Nelson, a friend of Walter Nadler Jr.

Lena Forster, 49, landlady of the Castle Inn
Karl Forster, Lena's second husband
Prof. Peter Forster, 29, Lena's son, mathematician
Elisabeth Forster, 30, MD, Peter's wife, forensic doctor
Heidi Forster, 23, Lena's daughter, landlady to be
Maggie, a waitress in the Castle Inn

Peter Dorset, 44, a reporter from Manchester

Franz Haversack, organic farmer and lawyer in Cowford

Rita Olivero, 33, landlady of the Fox and Hare Inn

Joseph von Aybesford, 89, an aristocrat in Edelweiss
Barbara Aybesford †, (78), Joseph's wife, died 1980
Agnes, Barbara's sister, 80, called Aunt Agnes
Jacquy de Jong, 33, Agnes' adopted son
Gordon Aybesford, 54, Joseph's son
Eleanor Aybesford, 47, Gordon's wife

Rupert, 27, MD, son of Gordon and Eleanor
Gloria, 23, daughter of Gordon and Eleanor
Melis, 12, daughter of Gordon and Eleanor
Nicholas, 12, son of Gordon and Eleanor
Claas Mabutu, 67, factotum in Edelweiss Castle
Naran Dasgupta, 73, former speaker of Government
Donald W., DJ and singer

Louise Chevrolet, 23, newscaster, Cyclamen TV station
Mr. Langer, floor manager, Cyclamen TV station
David Berraneck, senior officer, Cyclamen TV station
Mr. Wiesel, head of Cyclamen broadcasting studio
Mrs. Sigmund, secretary, Cyclamen TV station

Xanda van Aanstryk, 49, presenter, Cyclamen TV station,
Manfred †, Xanda's husband, had assumed her name
Titus, 27, Xanda's son, gardener
Selissa, 25, Xanda's daughter, owner of an antique shop
Laurens and Marike van Aanstryk, Xanda's parents

Mrs. Achmadi, secretary in Aybesford Enterprises

Etienne Friendly, 44, proprietor of Home Investigations
Xiu, Etienne's wife, owns the Chinese Restaurant Paradise
Samantha Ying, daughter of Etienne and Xiu

Melitta Stern, District Attorney, Cowford
Dalia Kalanda, DCI, Cyclamen City Police Department
Willie Dunstig, Special Constable, Cyclamen City
John Younghenry, Chief Prosecutor, Cyclamen City

Pierre de Fermat, 44, private investigator from Chantilly

Max Siegenthaler, retired sailor, lived in Avril Court
Miss Solder, student, lived in Avril Court
Larissa Bennent, 78, retired judge, lived in Avril Court
Vesna, Xanda's neighbor in Avril Court

Mateo Capota, 60, Xanda's great love
Meta Capota, second wife of Mateo Capota
Vanessa, 9, daughter of Mateo and Meta
Xavier, Capota's son of the first marriage
Roxanne, Capota's daughter of the first marriage
Aleva, short-term lover of Mateo Capota
Belinda, a friend of Aleva

Cheng Xinde, Xiu's father, proprietor of the Home Building
Cheng Jianlee, Xiu's mother
Sara Lagoons, office manageress of Home Investigations
Veronica Smith, employee of Home Investigations
Yanica Alexanru, MD, factotum in the Home Building
Pauline Buckley, employee of Home Investigations

§1

The Reporter from Manchester

In the month of May in the year 2014 Walter Nadler Jr. had become twenty-four years old. He was then a business economist straight from university and in search of a job that would give him satisfaction. For the time being, he lived with his parents. With the exception of his stays in the university town on the campus, he had never really left his parental home. Weekends and other days without classes he had always spent at his place.

On Saturday, the seventeenth of the said month, at the ninth hour in the evening, he came home and found the house empty. He noticed a slip of paper lying on the kitchen table. Scrutinizing it, he recognized his mother's handwriting. The message was to him and it read: "We are across. We got tickets for the evening performance. Pie is in the oven. Enjoy your meal! Mum."

Walter was not in the mood for eating on his own; and he wasn't hungry, anyway. So he went up to his room.

When he opened the window to let in a gust of mild May air, he noticed Heidi's Peugeot in the backyard of the neighboring inn. It's her day off and perhaps she's helping out in the inn tonight he thought, and he decided on the spur of the moment to go over and have a beer and perhaps a chat.

On entering the lobby of The Castle Inn he caught Heidi in the very act of serving a resounding slap across the freckled cheek of a stranger. The recipient of the blow looked like a queer fish over forty, cloaked in a fake Burberry coat. He was not taller than the donor of the stroke.

Walter Nadler Jr. knew Heidi Forster, the innkeeper's daughter, from the cradle. They have been growing up next-door to one another. Although she was tall and sturdy, she had grown a very attractive feminine being, with exquisite elbow-length ash blond hair that she wore in a bun though, when she helped out in her parents' restaurant.

Utterly amazed, Walter halted on his way to the bar room. "But, Heidi! Is there a problem?"

"There is a problem. Yes! This one is the problem. He has no business inside the ladies' room … and become insolent with me on top of it all. I've a good mind to forbid him to enter the pub."

Walter, slightly taller than Heidi, was a stately athletic young man. He approached them and built himself up before the delinquent and said, "What do you think you're doing?" But instead of looking the stranger in the eye, he looked fascinated at his ginger hair that was parted on the left and rather long and wavy.

All in all, his too long coat taken into account, the rebellious element looked like a character sprung out from an old movie.

The odd stranger had apparently not understood what Walter had sad, because instead of answering to him, he bowed before Heidi and apologized, explaining in very bad German and in an awkward manner how everything was a misunderstanding.

"Where do you come from?" asked Walter, switching from German to English.

"My name is Peter Dorset. I'm an Englishman."

"Heidi and Peter, splendid!" said Walter.

The three of them couldn't help laughing. Presumably only Heidi and Walter could know however that this was funny for two reasons. But the spell was broken.

Heidi knew about the fact that Walter wouldn't miss an opportunity to converse with English speakers so as to improve his command of the language.

Walter thought it was for this reason that she didn't throw out the criminal, but said, "I have work to do. In a few minutes, a lot will be going on in here," then wheeled around, and left him to Walter.

Walter Nadler Jr. thought to himself that the Englishman was not a bad fellow after all. Therefore he said, "Perhaps you have had a sip too many? Come on, have a coffee or something!" Peter Dorset accepted the peace offering meekly.

Walter led the way into the public room and made for the regulars' reserved table. During the weeks of the festival, the regulars shunned The Castle Inn; so Walter found his favorite seat unoccupied and could sit down on it.

From here, with his back to the wall, he overlooked the whole room. Through the window on his right-hand side he had an excellent view of the castle's frontage opposite the inn, on the other side of the square. The look was obstructed only partly by the fountain in the centre of the roundabout halfway between.

Walter pulled the curtain a little aside. Concert attendees

already began to step out at the moat doorway, which was some distance off the castle's portal. He drew Peter's attention to it.

"Be a dear and pour me a draft beer, Maggie, will you?" Walter said to the busy waitress who had been passing by several times already without asking. Maggie felt spurned by Walter and behaved as if he were invisible. "And a pint of non-alcoholic beer for my friend, please."

From where Walter sat he could also have a look into the dining room where tables were laid for guests who would have supper.

A lot of the concert-goers invaded The Castle Inn. People who did not want to dine were choosing themselves tables in the public room or went into the bar room.

Every year during the Edelweiss Festival, The Castle Inn was full to bursting point after the performances. Besides the proximity to the castle, people liked the inn's rustic cosiness. There were carved wood-beamed ceilings and wood-paneled walls in all the rooms. With the exception of the public room's floor, which was tiled, all rooms had varnished wooden floorboards.

Walter took two colorful beer mats from the holder and put them on the table so that Maggie, who seemed to be in a hurry, could place their drinks on them. The circular mats displayed an image of the rear wing of the castle, as seen from across the river Holly. The arced letterings *Edelweiss Castle* and *Brewery* bordered the picture on top and at the bottom.

"Cheers!"

"Good health!"

Heidi came out of a side room holding a mobile computer

in her hand. "I think you left your tablet in the women's room, Reporter," she said, approaching them. Then she put the device onto the table in passing.

"Reporter?" asked Walter Nadler Jr.

"Sort of."

Walter frowned.

"OK, not really. You see, my younger brother Boris is with a publishing company and he is always on the scout for a sensational piece of news. When we chatted early this afternoon," he indicated his tablet, "I told him about the éclat. He said I should gather as much information as I could possibly get. 'Perhaps we can bring off a coup with an early publication. You never know with these people,' he said, 'Austria was involved in the outbreak of the First World War, and the second; well, Adolf Hitler did not come from the North Pole. Maybe a Third World War is soon to come.'"

"Are you pulling my leg?"

"No not at all! One hundred years ago the Austrian successor to the throne, Archduke Franz Ferdinand was murdered and a month later a war started. Eventually thirty-eight countries around the world were involved. The war lasted for four years and seventeen million people died and twenty million got wounded."

"OK, all the papers write about it these days because of the anniversary. But what éclat are you talking about? Which éclat? When was there an éclat; and where?"

"Now you are playing the fool!"

"Certainly not! I don't know whereof you speak!"

"Well, shortly before the festival's opening ceremony this morning ... the interview!"

"The interview?"

"Exactly! The interview with the old nobleman; I think he is the lord of the castle. I chanced to overhear people talking. They said something like – it was broadcast live all over Goodland or Cyclamen or both – or even all over Austria? You must know, surely!"

Walter Nadler Jr. replied: "That's the very latest to me. I have been out of town for the last few days, on a visit to my aunt Mitzi in Alfalfa, helping her to clear the premises. Two years ago, her husband died and she is now moving into a smaller place.

When I came back, I put my car in the garage and went straight to the pub, knowing my parents were attending the show. I haven't been listening to the radio or watching TV all day long."

After a minute's pause he added: "Gordon Aybesford may be on the wrong side of fifty but I should not speak of him as being old."

"No, no, this man was definitely older."

"Joseph Aybesford? He is a man of eighty-nine years, shortly ninety, in fact. Why give an interview and what did he say?"

Walter was tempted to continue 'did he reveal his sex life?' but then thought the better of it and omitted the joke because he would have felt abashed. Joseph Aybesford was one of the elders and betters and was actually most popular with the people of Edelweiss, which was then a small rural town not far from the industrial town Cowford in the Province Goodland in Austria.

"Well, tomorrow there is the general election in Austria, isn't it?" said Peter.

"Yes. What of it?"

"This elderly gentleman must have stirred up the people to become mutinous or something like that."

"Slowly please, slowly. What is your business in Edelweiss, in the first place?"

"It's like this: I'm an engineer with Wattley in Manchester. They import the Gerber laser machine-tools. There is a big delivery due, so I'm presently for inspecting and acceptance purposes in the Gerber Engineering Works in Cyclamen City. Today being Saturday, I left my lodgings and came over to Edelweiss."

"I see!"

"I had seen the palace on top of the level blue rock plateau two years ago when I was in Cyclamen for the first time. But I could take a look at it from the other side of the river Holly only. There is far and wide no bridge whatsoever. At the time, to see the world-famous sight sufficed me, actually. This year I heard about the festival which was due to be opened this morning at eleven o'clock."

Walter nodded.

"I didn't mean to attend the opening. It was booked up anyway. For a while I watched folks arrive and go into the castle. There were some celebrities, local ones that is. Then I wandered about the town, taking a photo here and there. When I passed the tavern at the edge of the little wood, The Fox and Hare I think it's called, I heard rapturous acclamations from within. You see?"

"I see," said Walter again, although he saw not much as yet. But he expected more to come.

"I managed to peep in by a window," continued the

Englishman. "In a separate room twenty or so people were assembled before a big television. On the screen were this elderly gentleman and a pretty young woman with beautiful blond
shoulder-length hair to be seen. They were sitting opposite
one another. Obviously they were talking like in an interview.
I thought the man was at least seventy years old."

"It must have been Joseph then. He does not look his
eighty-nine."

"I had meant to have lunch somewhere anyway, so I entered the public room. After half an hour or so, the TV watch-
ers came in too."

"Uh-huh."

"They were discussing animatedly. One of the keenest en-
thusiasts was the fine-boned innkeeper woman. I can hardly
understand a word of German, let alone Austrian German. So
I did catch very little. But you could clearly see that the interview must have met their expectations. They seemed to wal-
low in an election fever. Could they be a bunch of royalists, do
you think?"

Walter tapped his forehead. "Now something dawns on
me! The thought crossed my mind back in the castle tavern
already, however I can't see what the group should have to do
with Joseph Aybesford ... no, they are not royalists, separatists
rather."

"Are they not happy with Austria?"

"They would like to change a lot of things. They are for example of the opinion, that a little country like Austria should
not show off with a Federal President who earns more than the
president of the United States of America; whereby to earn is
not the appropriate term in this context. The money that other

people work hard for, should not be squandered by politicians. You see we people around here have a will of our own. Fellow countrymen are mocking us. They call us outdated, backward or even Amish.

"That's interesting; I've never heard of that."

"We do not fall for every novelty without thinking, but we are known to be hard-working, diligent and thrifty. But with us this has nothing to do with religion as is the case with the Amish or the Hutterites. With us the respect for nature and the human kind count."

"This sounds very sensible, actually."

"We despise political economies based on growth and profit no matter what damage they do to mankind and environment. Making the odd quick profit was never at the top of our people's priorities."

Peter nodded.

"You yourself mentioned a good example a minute ago: Edelweiss Castle. The Aybesford family decided not to open their castle to the public. And in a referendum the citizens of Edelweiss voted against the building of a bridge over the river Holly, so as not to encourage visitors unduly."

"But the citizens of Edelweiss bought the vineyards beyond the river and make now visitors pay for looking at the blue rock with the white castle on the flat top of it."

"I didn't say we are stupid," laughed Walter. "You could justifiably say that Goodland practiced sustainability long before it became a well-known saying."

"This is exactly the concern of the lord of the castle, sustainable development. Isn't it?"

"Yes; I can see now, why they were so happy with what he

said in the interview."

"I thought they wanted him to be chancellor or president or something like that."

Walter burst out laughing. "This I can't even imagine."

"But with the present coalition government people seem to be particularly dissatisfied."

"No federal government ever has been according to the taste of the Goodlanders; neither is the functioning of the European Union. It is for this reason, that some years ago, spirited citizens established The Sustainers."

"The Sustainers?"

"They were at first a loose gathering of like-minded men and women. But the initially weird bunch has grown over the years, and is by now a regular political party. On the federal level however it is not as popular as in Goodland. But its popularity is growing."

"Do they have a leader; or something like that?"

"Chairman of the SDP, the Sustainable Development Party, is Franz Haversack. He is a lawyer in Cowford; but he also operates an organic farm on the edge of Edelweiss.

The Sustainers meet regularly here in Edelweiss in The Fox and Hare. There is a big ball room attached at the back of the main building where supporters from all over Goodland assemble on a regular basis."

"Is this Joseph Aybesford one of them? Do you think they want to establish an independent state?"

Walter Nadler took a long swallow of beer.

"As to your first question ... as I said before, I see no connection ... I never heard the slightest rumour."

"But the sustainers admire him."

"By all means! Sustainable development is their common bond. On the other hand, I don't think that Joseph Aybesford is in favor of the separatist ambitions. Also I cannot imagine that he fosters monarchist wishful thinking."

"But I think that he is also not in favor of the present government. What do you think?"

Walter hunched his shoulders. "Well, he is known to have been arguing the case of sustainable development for decades. He is a member of the *Center for Our Common Future*. He writes articles and travels abroad frequently. I know no particulars, though."

"Could they try to break Goodland away from Austria?"

Walter guffawed. "They cannot simply break away Goodland. But yes, I suppose it is their dream to convince the people of Goodland to achieve independence by democratic means! They claim that Goodland would be far better off on its own. But they don't know how to go about to make sufficient people give them their votes."

After a while Walter added thoughtfully: "You've made me curious. I wonder what exactly Joseph Aybesford said today. In here everybody is busy, and the guests are all not from here."

"Let's go to The Fox and Hare!"

"That's exactly what I had in mind! … Maggie! Put the beers on the cuff please! … Come on, Peter. Let's go and find out what exactly happened this morning!"

The two men quaffed down their beers and left the inn. They sauntered along Castle Avenue, savoring the mild May evening air. Chestnut trees stood at regular intervals on the green area between the road and the pavement. Since his childhood, the blossoms on them always had reminded Walter of candles on Christmas trees, especially at night when the street lights were on. Occasionally, as they went, smell of lilac escaped one of the front gardens.

"Are you well acquainted with the people in the castle?" asked Peter after a while.

"You surely have noticed the urban villa opposite the castle portal and next to the inn? We were passing it just before."

"Yes, I have noticed it. The wall around the property reminded me of The Selfish Giant by Oscar Wilde."

"There is nothing selfish nor wild about it," said Walter laughingly. "It's the habitation of the castle administrator. This position is filled by my father, Walter Nadler; and before his time, it was filled by my grandfather, Walter Nadler Sen."

"I see!"

"So we know the family. The Aybesford children, the two elder ones to be exact, the Forster children Heidi and Peter," – here they grinned at one another and Peter nodded his understanding – "and my humble self did many things together."

"Despite the differences in age?"

"Yes, in spite of it all. But Gloria, Heidi and I we are of the same age anyway. We were always in the same class at school. Also later we attended dancing classes together, we went dancing, made excursions; we still frequently do a quick game of table tennis, and so on. But I have no intimate knowledge of family affairs; neither with regard to the Aybesford family nor to the Forster family."

"Why do the Aybesfords not manage their castle themselves?"

"It's actually not the castle itself but the huge woodlands, photovoltaic plants, the big farm, a sawmill, hydraulic power plants, and I don't know what else."

"So your career is predestined, you are a made man, you are set for life!"

"There is a chance. But I want to acquire experience else-where first, possibly abroad."

When they had come into range of their destination, Walter said: "Listen, I'm warning you! Before you get meddle-some again! You will have noticed that the landlady of The Fox and Hare is very attractive. Watch out! The lady is under my protection. Some say that she is lesbian and closely connected to a police woman by the name of Dalia Kanlanda in Cyclamen City. This is nonsense. She is only waiting for me to stand on my own feet before we will get married."

"You need not worry, I'll behave myself."

"Good evening! Hello Walter!" welcomed them Rita, the black-haired innkeeper of The Fox and Hare. "When have you come back from Alfalfa," she asked, addressing Walter.

A few of The Sustainers were still in the pub. Walter intro-duced Peter to the present crowd. Some of the guests were regulars of The Castle Inn. All confirmed that Joseph Aybesford had called on the people to cast invalid votes next day.

Everyone present contributed facts, opinions and prophe-cies in a lively manner. They spoke about nothing else than the interview and its possible impact. Even if somebody wandered off the subject for once, the conversation was soon back cir-cling about the interview and the forthcoming elections.

"I think Joseph Aybesford did not deliver a set speech but acted impromptu. When Louise Chevrolet didn't know how to proceed he began to improvise," said Rita. "Essentially he said that we should reconsider our electoral behavior and for this we need a pause for reflection. So best cast invalid votes and wait and see. That's in a nutshell what he said."

"So he didn't advertise for the Sustainers?"

"Not expressly, in no way. I didn't look at it this way. But we were all very pleased, nevertheless. We could really use such a speaker. So well-spoken."

"After the interview of his father, Gordon took the same line, even sharper I think," said Jacquy de Jong.

"Gordon too gave a television interview?" asked Walter.

"No, no, he got political when he began with his speech," said Jacquy, looking at Peter Dorset. He spoke slowly so that the Englishman could understand him, he thought.

Peter nodded.

"Every year the festival is opened with a ceremony. The ceremony always starts with a speech of a local celebrity. This year it was Gordon's turn. When he was about to start his speech, unrest was in the audience, partly because Louise Chevrolet had flaked out; but more so because of what Joseph had said. So Gordon took up the theme about the election. It was broadcast live both on Cyclamen and on Goodland TV.

"What Gordon said sounded to me as if he had rehearsed it," said a young man who permanently endeavored to present his forearms in the proper light, because they were freshly tattooed. He himself admired his tattoos time and time again.

"Fiddlesticks! That's because he is more in practice to speak impromptu. And all the time he is contemplating what could be improved in the political situation in this country," said Jacquy resentfully and added: "All this may have unforeseeable consequences."

"Peter's brother speaks even of a Third World War that may evolve," said Walter amusedly. "I wonder what the impact will be. I think Peter's brother wants to write a book about the éclat and its implications."

Peter Dorset nodded approval.

"I think I'm going to write a book myself," Walter carried on. "Best to write it in English so I can sell it to the whole world. You could supply useful information from within the castle, Jacquy."

Jacquy was thirty-three years old, long and slim. He had a thin face, thinning blond hair and side-whiskers. But his trademarks were his gold rimmed glasses. He liked to speak of himself as the major-domo of the castle.

After a few beers Walter liked to bait him whenever an opportunity arose.

But Jacquy did not take the bait properly: "Are you expecting a revolution or something? In this country no changes to the better take place. Democracy does only work in an informed society. More than half of the Austrians don't know the difference between parliament and government. Just as many don't know who is in government."

Murmur of approval was to be heard from all sides.

"Out of habit they elect the same breed again and again. Unfortunately this breed gets nowhere fast. The established politicians only look after feathering their own nests; and they aid one another in getting the best positions. All you can expect is rotten compromises, meekness towards transnational companies, corruptibility and wastefulness. What the hell. People have the governments that they deserve. Instead of ..."

"Now you are contradicting yourself. Only just you spoke of unforeseeable consequences," interposed Walter.

"But I don't mean political changes for Austria. I'm

apprehensive of dire consequences for the Aybesford family."

"Don't you be falsely alarmed about the Aybesfords," said the one with the fresh tattoos. "They aspire to the reign of Goodland. No more, no less. Joseph is alright. But Gordon Aybesford is a Champagne socialist; that's what he is."

"Gordon needs for himself in one week less than what you spend in one day on beer and cigarettes," said Jacquy de Jong. He had the impression that the other – who was a Cyclamener – was only assuming an air of importance.

"You come to his defense because you are his half-brother, aren't you?"

"If you are having a try at winding me up, you are drawing a blank,"

"Time, gentlemen, please order your last drinks now! We must close a little earlier tonight; shortage of staff," announced Rita.

Walter Nadler Jr. had gone to the toilet and didn't seem to come back again. After some time Peter Dorset went outside too. On his way out, and more so on his way back into the public room, he could overhear that Walter had got into an argument with the landlady. They seemed indeed to be well acquainted with one another, because their quarrel had an intimate note.

To Peter it seemed as if Walter wanted to revive their relationship, but Rita brought in all kinds of objections. Then Walter reproached her for having relations with women.

Peter swiftly returned into the public room when he sensed that Walter was about to end the argument indignantly.

When Walter returned to the table he tried not to show his emotions but behaved in a jovial manner. "Look here," he said boisterously, slapping Jacquy on the back. "Whatever the outcome of the present situation may be; there will be reasons enough to write a book. Are you game?"

But in the meantime Jacquy had been discussing the interview and the coming elections in earnest and got annoyed at Walters's insistence. "A book! Are you joking? Half an hour ago I tried to explain to you that nothing is going to change in this country. Tomorrow the Austrians go to the ballot, or roughly sixty percent of them. Two month later, it will be business as usual. And to write about possible implications for the Aybesfords would be vulgar."

"But what if tomorrow's elections are going to make history? Look at it this way: if absolutely nothing spectacular happens in the wake of today's interview and tomorrow's elections, there is no book, anyway."

"I can't stand it any longer!" thundered Jacquy. "The book! The book! What has got into you? I never knew you to be barking mad! You were absorbed in the study of business administration for the last few years. And you are looking for a good job right now. Writing a book, and in English at that!"

"I've been thinking of writing a book before, and in English too. It's no challenge to write a book in your mother tongue."

Jacquy shook his head only a few degrees from left to right and gave Walter a scornful glance. "I'm afraid you overestimate yourself. You have no call to delve into writing English literature from one day to the next, only because of an interview in Edelweiss. It's as if I would embark on writing a book in French, only because I read the French weekly L'Express from cover to cover every week."

"Gosh! But that's a poor comparison somehow ... OK,

look here, I'm only joking! But perhaps you could keep Peter's brother informed how matters are going to develop."

"I'm not going to give information away as far as the castle is concerned, and the rest you can read in the papers."

"You have no sense of humor. It's because you stick to ginger ale even on a Saturday night shortly before a revolution."

"I think you are half in the bag already!"

"To be honest, I don't think either that anything is going to change," said Walter conciliatorily. A slight unpleasantness had come up from this dull discussion and Walter blamed himself for it. "Neither the political situation in this country, nor you, nor I, nor anything in Edelweiss is going to change."

They chattered away more in harmony until Rita announced: "Closing time!"

Jacquy gave Walter and Peter a lift. Walter gave the Englishman shelter for the night in the castle administrator's spare bedroom.

On the morning of election-Sunday Walters's mother served them breakfast. They conversed about the previous evening in The Fox and Hare. Walter had to explain a lot. He expounded what the talking last night had been about, because Peter asked on and on and said that he had caught very little.

After this they went over into the castle where they had an appointment with Jacquy. He had agreed on the evening before to show them a recording of the interview.

"You should perhaps also know," said Walter before they stepped into the castle's portal, "that Jacquy de Jong casts a covetous eye on Heidi!"

§2

The Television Interview

For the last half hour Jacquy de Jong had been alternately peeking at his watch or looking expectantly out of the window. He was on edge and on the brink of calling the interview off, when eventually the vehicle of the Cyclamen broadcasting station drove into the castle yard.

He sighed with relief; but in the next breath he tensed up again. The woman that got out of the mini bus was not the one he had expected to arrive. This was not Mrs. Xanda van Aanstryk who stalked towards the entrance of the hall but Miss Louise Chevrolet. What did it mean? Was she to conduct the interview? She was definitely number-two choice. She was still very young and only one of the newscasters.

Had Jacquy only been in the know about the agreement between Joseph Aybesford and Xanda van Aanstryk. At this juncture, he could have avoided the disaster to come.

"I'm sorry, Mr. de Jong," said Louise when he intercepted her at the hall door, "but Mrs. van Aanstryk has quite suddenly fallen ill. My boss Mr. Berraneck has been briefing me. And I am informed about the report that is on the air at the moment. I should very much like to step in."

The floor manager Mr. Langer approached them. He had known all along. He had been on his mobile without end, but had said nothing. He appeared as cool as a cucumber. He said, "The report will be on the air for another seven minutes. If need be, we could delay the opening for a few minutes. We have sufficient material to fill in. We are prepared for the unforeseen. However, Mr. de Jong, I think it important that you introduce Louise to Mr. Aybesford and ask if it is all right with him. If he wants to refrain from doing the interview, it would pose no problem."

So Jacquy de Jong ushered Miss Chevrolet into the castle chapel, where Mr. Joseph Aybesford was awaiting the events to follow. Jacquy explained the new situation to him. Aybesford took it calmly – at least outwardly. Louise seized his proffered hand and they exchanged a friendly handshake. De Jong let them alone so they could get attuned to one another.

Last summer, a crew of the Cyclamen TV station had been allowed to take shots in the castle and its surroundings. They had also wanted to conduct interviews with members of the Aybesford family, but none of them had been interested. So Jacquy de Jong, the major-domo of the Aybesford household, had to find excuses; and he was mandated to provide information about the history of both the Aybesford family and the reputable Castle.

The TV report resulting from this preparatory work was currently on the air. Last week, apparently on a whim, Joseph Aybesford had consented to give a short interview on the occasion of the opening ceremony of the festival. So the people of the TV station had suggested sandwiching the interview between the broadcast of the report and the live broadcast of the opening ceremony.

Half an hour ago Aybesford had told Mr. Langer that he did not want the interview to take place before the audience on the stage outside. He preferred the big coronation hall, where the concerts and plays where presented when the weather was bad. Consequently one camera was positioned inside the hall. At the end of the interview, the outside cameras would take over.

In about twenty minutes, Gordon Aybesford, Joseph's son, was to officially open the Edelweiss Castle Festival 2014. Outside, in the open-air arena in the picturesque castle moat, preparations had come to an end and all people had already taken their seats.

"OK," said Langer, and indicated the chapel door with a motion of the head, whereupon de Jong reached for the handle, when at the same instant the door was opened from within. Presently, Joseph Aybesford, accompanied by Miss Chevrolet came out into the hall. He, who most of the time sported a pleasant countenance, looked seriously and strode erectly, royally. In spite of his eighty-nine years, and although his impeccable mane had a silvery shimmer, he had an aroma of youthfulness about him.

He had approved of very little makeup only. He nodded to everybody around and said, "Not a moment too soon." Jacquy de Jong had installed a little television set and a recorder; meeting thus the wishes of Joseph Aybesford. I may feel like watching the videoed interview one of these days, he had declared.

After friendly opening-remarks and after the enquiry, how the man, soon celebrating his ninetieth birthday prefers to be addressed, the interviewer posed her first relevant question: "A hundred years ago, the First World War broke out. It ended on the eleventh November 1918. A consequence of this war was the collapse of the Habsburg Empire, the fall of Austria-Hungary. In the year, 1919, the First Austrian Republic was established and the nobility was officially abolished in this new, henceforth torso Austria. Your father had been the Prince of Aybesford. You were born five years later, in 1924. Did you yourself ever suffer under the loss of the title that would have come to you? Did it ever make you angry?"

Joseph Aybesford gave a charming smile: "'Official title or not, we are still the Aybesfords,' is what my mother used to say. Jokes apart, I never had any feelings about this matter at all."

"This beautiful Edelweiss Castle is in the possession of the house Aybesford since 1733, nearly 300 years. There must have come the day when you realized, that you are a member of a special family. Do you remember when this happened?"

"Actually, this happened rather late. I can still vaguely recall my first day at primary school. There were few children that I was not acquainted with. With the half of them I was already friends, anyway. We would play inside and outside the neighbouring farmhouses or in the castle's outbuildings with all the other children of the vicinity. Families were big then, and Edelweiss was a village. The way to school was long."

"You were walking all the way to the schoolhouse in the neighboring village. How long did it take you?"

"It takes a grown person twenty-five minutes to walk one way. But homeward bound, it took us sometimes two hours. In the summer months we would go barefooted. I remember one winter day. I stumped around on the ice covering of the frozen over brook, announcing: "I am Aquarius." My audience on the arched footbridge whooping. When the sheet of ice cracked, I was knee-deep in the water. I did not dare to go home. I sought refuge in one of the farmhouses. In the kitchen of the farmer's wife, I was helped to dry my clothing at the hearth."

"This sounds very adventurous."

"It was normal then. Mothers didn't bother when you were late. Nobody was in danger of getting lost. We enjoyed going through the wood, alongside the brook, between fields and over meadows. We learned a lot about nature only by walking our way to school, and more so, by sauntering the way back. We grew up like all the other children."

"Here by *we* you mean yourself and your brothers and sisters, I suppose?"

"That's right."

"But you must have realised that you were privileged."

"Yes, indeed. We were the only ones who could roller-skate through their home."

Joseph Aybesford and Louise Chevrolet both laughed.

"What is the secret of your agility?"

"I don't know if it's a secret and I don't know if it helps, but I rub my back with a Turkish towel every morning and then stretch the towel alternately pulling one end up with my left hand and down with my right hand for ten seconds and then vice versa. No repetitions."

Miss Chevrolet was not sure if he was serious or joking but she could not work up the courage to ask further. "Are there people who sometimes address you with your title, or more precisely, one of your titles?"

"At times it happens, abroad mostly, that I'm addressed

with Your Highness. I do not protest in such situations. I would feel ridiculous; as ridiculous as a TV announcer appears to me who says *pardon* after a slip of the tongue."

Miss Chevrolet swallowed.

"Many things have happened in the course of your life. What are the events that have impressed you the most? Which things will you always remember?"

"It is like this, Miss Chevrolet: for me, apart from the Big Bang, the most remarkable thing happened two and a half thousand years ago. When, after two and a half million years of Stone Age, humans were no longer satisfied by stories about gods and started to reason rationally. The arising of philosophy — *love of wisdom*, mathematics and the natural sciences, these are inexpressibly beautiful events; compared to which everything else is small, most notably the great wars or the present financial crisis provoked by greedy bankers." Aybesford spoke slowly and devoutly. "But you were speaking earlier of *being angry* ... ," Aybesford took a sip from a glass of water that had been placed before him and, becoming more agitated, he went on, "... things that make me angry are numerous:

- Greedy agricultural industries extinguish traditional seeds and promote monocultures and governments look on.

- The European Union is on the brink of becoming a bureaucratic dictatorship. Did you know that there exist one hundred and thirty thousand EU regulations?"

Miss Chevrolet was losing the thread. This man was not behaving as she had expected. She put on a constrained smile, and furtively looked at her notes.

After a moment's hesitation, Joseph Aybesford hauled himself out of the armchair a little, thereby changing his position slightly, and addressed the camera directly: "Tomorrow we go to the ballot box. Shall we again vote for stupendous tax hikes? Another round of tax increases is sure to come, if we vote for the continuation of the "grand" coalition.

Since we are a member of the EU, we have a fourth layer of Government. We have the municipalities, the Provinces and the Federal Government; and now the EU parliament. In addition there are the EU Council and the European Commission. The citizens are tired of being led around by the nose by a horde of recklessly wasteful politicians who dissipate the money of decent people. If matters are to become better, things have to be changed.

The governments of the individual provinces are closer to the people; they are not so out of touch with the will and the needs of the folk. They could maintain a body of politicians to do the work relating to foreign countries and the EU, including the federal presidency. The president of our little country pockets more money than the president of the United States of America, although his function is very limited.

We need a new beginning and must first find out together, what to do. Should we leave the EU or dissolve our federal government or should Goodland become an independent state? Important matters should be decided by the people directly, anyway.

I say, whoever is fed up with the status quo, must attend the election tomorrow, but must cast an invalid vote. Election Day is payday and not a day for confirmation of old habits. For a successful new start we need first a stalemate situation. The religion of greed and money, the global dominance of transnational companies ..."

At this point, Louise Chevrolet probably fainted, because she glided elegantly from her seat to the floor. A technician terminated the transmission by pulling a plug high-handedly. For the TV viewers an *Interruption*-lettering was to be seen. After a few seconds a speaker showed on the screen and declared that they were sorry to say that the broadcast had to be interrupted due to technical problems. They would be back presently. A recording of the last Vienna New Year's Concert was played back.

In an instant, a physician who had his GP's surgery in the castle was at Miss Chevrolet's side; and so were de Jong and Langer. Miss Chevrolet's eyelids flickered. "Just a fit of nerves," said the doctor after a brief examination. "Thank god you are here," said de Jong. "Let's lay her on the bench over there," replied the doctor.

When the commotion had settled somewhat, Gordon Aybesford who had also rushed in, was heard to say to his father, "What possessed you to speak in this fashion?"

"I don't know; it was arranged with Xanda van Aanstryk that we speak about sustainable development; the girl said she was informed, I wonder what about she was informed … anyway, it was such an opportunity!" Joseph Aybesford replied gleefully.

"But I'm the one who's now going to stand out there before the audience and do the ceremonial address," said Gordon, who seemed to be partly annoyed and partly amused.

"Don't worry, they will not know yet."

"They surely know and you know that they know. Has this been on your mind all along?"

"I toyed with the idea, but I didn't imagine I would bring it off."

The moat was humming with the murmuring of the audience, when Gordon Aybesford walked onto the stage. Some people had been watching the broadcast on their mobiles and nearly everybody knew what had gone on inside. Visitors who had come from far away were perplexed however. When Gordon Aybesford came to a stop and looked into the audience he was welcomed with cheers by some of the locals.

"Vivat!" shouted somebody.

"Back to monarchy!" shouted somebody else.

Aybesford raised both his hands. This was greeted by the orchestra with a rousing fanfare. He made a soothing gesture and said:

"Ladies and Gentlemen! Remember this is not a political event. My father gets ninety in two or three months. He is not running for parliament. Neither am I nor my wife or any of my children. The Aybesfords are not striving for monarchy. I want to make this very clear. But I take the liberty to say that the present two party coalition ridicules the hardworking population of this country and should be voted out of office."

Murmuring started again.

"I want to speak explicitly my opinion about the election tomorrow."

Instantly, the moat was silent like a morgue.

"In the last decades, the Austrian voters have made the same grave mistake repeatedly: they elected themselves a bunch of selfish representatives which they despise at the bottoms of their hearts. It's a sad case that those citizens who are least interested in politics are the stirrup holders for established parties and politicians again and again. The majority of the voters are neither acquainted with the party programs nor with the actual aims and intentions of the candidates. They vote out of tradition or small-minded ideological fixation rooted in the past. If you take the view that there is no set of suitable parties or of appropriate candidates to choose from, you could do as my father suggested: go voting tomorrow, but cast an invalid vote. Tick off all candidates and write *I thank you, no*, for example."

Only viewers tuned to the Cyclamen and the Goodland TV stations were able to watch the interview live. Soon however its impact vibrated across the whole country. The private television stations that broadcast throughout Austria exploited the juicy episode.

Mr. Wiesel, the head of the Cyclamen regional broadcasting studio got many calls which he didn't take. Consequently he got many emails and SMSes which he didn't read. He got a fright when he, more or less accidentally, became a witness of the catastrophe on TV. He was stiff with consternation and fear.

Without doubt, most of the ignored messages came from the highest quarters. He feared for his existence. The public talked of the ABC as the GBC, the government broadcasting corporation.

Only a week ago, he was in seventh heaven, when the artistic figure Conchita Wurst won with whopping score of two-hundred-ninety the Eurovision Song Contest in Copenhagen. He could kill this bloody Berraneck. Today of all days, on the eve of the Austrian general election day, the Austrian Broadcasting Corporation had provided a dubious finale for the election campaign.

§3
Eight Months Before the Interview

E-mail from Gloria Aybesford to her friend Heidi Forster: Wednesday, 11 September 2013. Hi Heidi! Long time no see, long time no say! We must sit together soon or hang out together. We must compare notes and exchange confidences, perhaps go for a run in the car?

You are surprised that I write to you in English? I'm inspired by my surroundings. You cannot guess where I'm writing from! I'm in Newport, Wales, UK. Unexpectedly I have free time on my hands and have found myself a quiet corner in an alcove in the hallway on the fourth floor of Concept House in Newport.

When you enter the building, you notice a conspicuous nameplate in the lawn. Intellectual Property Office it says on it. It's the first time that I'm with my father on a business trip. Now and then he gives me a look of commiseration. I think he took me along so it will take my mind off the trouble with Donald.

But it's finally over now! Have you heard the latest? He is now sweet on Louise Chevrolet! That's the last straw! Miss Pardon, the hussy! She knew quite well that we have been together for years. I could kill the bitch. But I will pay her back one of these days! Vengeance is sweet! And Donald can go and jump in the lake! I have thrown him out, of course.

A good many weekends and evenings I spend in my old rooms in the castle at the present time. I find it too depressing to be alone in the flat; to know that nobody is coming home makes me feel really cooped in. But I must manage to get accustomed to it. In the castle I feel at least secure; and also I don't feel so lonely even when I'm on my own in my bower. I appreciate the solace that I perceive through the presence of my family under the same roof. Time heals all wounds says mum.

It's the first time that I set foot on British soil. Although at school we took English as the first foreign language, never until this week have I had a chance to converse with or to listen to native speakers in real live, if only in shops, in restaurants and that sort of thing. Unlike you, I've never been as an exchange pupil to England. I must get along with my school English. I don't understand everything, but I think it's very exciting to be here; like a sponge, I soak up both new impressions and new expressions.

The last few days father and I spent in London. Both Carnaby Street and Barnaby Street are worth seeing. I bought two smashing belts. You can have one of them, the one you like best.

Today we arrived in South Wales. It's simply gorgeous! I think I could get used to travelling.

My father and his London patent agent have an appointment with examiners of the Patent Office. It's about a patent dispute with a Japanese Firm. But it's also about a new patent application in which my father is named the sole inventor of the main claim. Otherwise he would not have appeared in person, I think.

Before his breakdown in health, he was always full of activity. Now he has turned into a wonder in delegating affairs of business. The metamorphosis took place in the last two years. Otherwise the everyday work load would have eaten him up, I think. But he simply couldn't resist making this trip. And it's sort of no work at all, to travel around and hold talks, don't you think?

I have no business in these meetings here today, so I fill up my free time with keeping my diary up to date and reading and sending emails. I nearly left my laptop and internet modem at home. Now I'm glad, I didn't. Jacquy lent me a plug adaptor which comes in handy here. I've detected a wall socket behind a rubber plant. Apropos Jacquy! He asked me what you are doing now. Do you no longer work as a visual merchandiser? It's such a pity we so seldom see one another these days.

It is now settled that in two weeks I shall enter the Aybesford Corporation. My first station in the train of getting to know the business shall be the personnel department. Nobody expects me to take the rein one day or nobody says so, still sometimes I have a nightmare. I dream that I have to take over from my father all his duties.

Should this ever become reality, I would have to rely utterly on the management that my father has groomed up in the course of time. You too will take over the inn from your parents eventually. But you need not be so intimidated because you know already what is expecting you. I hope my bad dreams will cease once I've started working.

I ponder occasionally what hard times my father must have had, when thirty years ago he took the responsibility for the family business. He was then twenty-five years old, only two years older than we are at the present day. He had barely finished university. My grandfather had been very ill at the time. They feared the worst. Fortunately he recovered and was thereafter able to help my father to work his way into the task.

Since then, Dad has added the brewery, some engineering works and a corrugated cardboard plant to the enterprise. These days, his desk is almost empty and tidy at all times. All he is doing himself nowadays is seeing to it, that the different plants run smoothly; he achieves this by holding responsible his senior directors. He confers with them every morning, if only for ten minutes if nothing much is the matter.

I do not dare to address the topic, but I think that it was his alarming state of health that brought him to his senses. From the grim worker he has turned to a casual hobby leader, you would think. Being a mechanical engineer by trade, he sometimes may appear in one of the workshops wearing a mechanic suit in order to inform himself firsthand about a certain machine or a certain aspect of the production processes.

Now I come to the main point of this mail to you: last night in London, my father and I went to the St. Martin's Theatre. After leaving the show we thought it was such a nice September evening and we decided to go for a short stroll around town. While walking, we talked about the performance. We both have read the story earlier, so we both knew the outcome beforehand. But we agreed that it had been fun and worth seeing.

We were now closing our round and nearing our hotel in Charing Cross Road, not far from West Street, when all of a sudden we were attracted by the sound of gay music. The music was Caribbean and sounded familiar to me. It seemed to emerge from the Chinese Restaurant Paradise, which we were passing. On opening the entrance door a crack, we heard that we assumed correctly. I closed the door again. But then, on the spur of the moment, we decided to go inside.

We thought we might have a spring roll or something. We were taking seats at a table in a corner, when I beheld a dashy man of medium height. He had a braid and a Chinaman's hat. He approached us. With his blue eyes and bushy eyebrows he looked somehow unreal. He bade us a good evening, speaking with a Chinese accent. He was definitely peculiar in more than one way.

"Sir Gordon," he began. "Please do me the honour of being my guest, over there in the family booth," he carried on, making a low bow.

Never before have I seen my father so stunned. For five or six seconds he sat stock-still, visibly thinking hard. Then he said in German, keeping a straight face, "but with the greatest of pleasure, Herr Stefan."

We got up and the two men shook hands vigorously, grinning like Cheshire cats.

"How long ago was that?"

"Let me think. I left Edelweiss in 1990. That would be twenty-three years!"

"But you migrated to Canada, didn't you?"

"That's right. I had an aunt in Québec who encouraged me to come."

"You went so as to avoid the call-up, wasn't it?"

"Funny, why do you think so? Have people been talking that drivel?"

"Sorry, I may be profoundly wrong. It's been a long time."

"It was like this; I had never known my father, because I lost him in the time before my recollection starts. Then, shortly before I graduated from high school my mother died. She had a sister in Canada who came for the funeral. She invited me to come and stay with them in Sorel-Tracy which is in the province of Québec.

They had talked it over beforehand, she and her husband. They were confident, that with my French and English knowledge acquired at high school I could join the Royal Canadian Mounted Police. I liked the idea and applied for an entry visa. These were my reasons for going to Canada."

"I see, I had forgotten," said my father. Turning towards me, he said, "This is Stefan. His mother used to work under old Nadler on the big farm and they had rooms in the castle. You weren't born yet when he left Edelweiss. He has never ever returned; not even on a brief visit."

"Well, I have no more relatives in Austria," said Stefan, shrugging his shoulders. "Apropos, in Canada I have changed my first name to the French version Etienne. It's been a long time that somebody called me Stefan."

"The Franco-Canadians are a major ethnic group in North America, aren't they?"

"That's right! And what's more, in Québec French is the *sole* official language. A lot more than ninety percent of the population speaks French as their first or second language."

"Were you never tempted to change your first name again; to Stephen or Steve, now that you live in London?"

"The thought had crossed my mind, but I saw no need. As a young man in Québec I was not too self-confident. I was anxious not to stand out as a foreigner, or as little as possible.

I wanted to become a Mountie, after all."

"How fantastic a coincidence," I exclaimed, "that you should meet again tonight".

My father, touching my shoulder gently, said: "May I introduce my daughter Gloria to you."

"I'm very pleased to meet you!" said Etienne.

"Did you ride on horseback while on duty?" I couldn't help asking.

"Ah, you saw the television series and old Hollywood movies? Actually the work with the horses was discontinued by the end of the nineteen thirties already. Riding remained however as a base training for the recruits. Since 1961 the Musical Ride is part of the responsibility of the Royal Canadian Mounted Police. It is performed every year. On normal duties, the RCMP uses standard police methods, standard equipment, and standard uniforms."

"And the red serge tunic, do you still have one?"

"Same as all the other old conventions, they are only used for ceremonial occasions. But indeed, I still have a scarlet jacket. I wouldn't part with it."

"Can you give an example for a *ceremonial operation?*"

"Well, one task I participated in, was escorting the Governor General in his open landau to the Opening of Parliament."

"Fantastic," said my father.

"However, I changed shirts after some years. I left *the Force* and became a member of the Sûreté du Québec. But please come along and meet my family."

We got up and followed Etienne to a booth near the kitchen.

"This is my wife Xiu, and this is our daughter Samantha Ying," he said proudly. Then he pointed with his other hand at us, and said, "This is the Prince of Goodland, Gordon von Aybesford and his daughter Gloria."

We shook hands and then we were seated for the second time. Samantha is a stunning teenager. The shape of her eyes is Asian, but the color of the pupils is a light gray. The color of her hair is dark blond.

Have you ever watched Death in Paradise? There are new episodes on neo-TV every Thursday evening now. Samantha thought that the name of the television series fitted the name of the restaurant. She had a CD with the melody you hear at the start of every episode.

"I have a pen friend in Shanghai. Her name is Ying, too," I remarked, "Xu Ying".

"Ying stands for *gifted, wise*," said Xiu, "it's a common name for girls in China."

"The meaning of Xiu is *elegant, beautiful*," said Ying amusedly.

"Today we are celebrating Samantha's thirteenth birthday," Etienne explained. "This is the reason for my outfit. I like to make her laugh. For today, Samantha has permission to play her fancy music in the restaurant.

Xiu put plates, cutlery and chopsticks on the table and a waitress brought a bowl with steaming jiaozi, a sort of Chinese stuffed dumplings.

"Help yourselves, please," said Xiu.

"What would you like to drink? Wine? Beer? Brandy?" asked Etienne.

My father opted for a Guinness and I tried a Chinese beer.

Conversationally we learned how Etienne did fare in his first years in Québec and that he later moved to the capital, Québec City. Fourteen years ago Etienne got married to Xiu, whom he met in the Chinese restaurant that was owned and run by her parents.

"Are you the lord of Edelweiss Castle," Etienne asked my father.

"Yes, that's right. I follow a compulsory curriculum, you know. I thought I had to accept the responsibility. So I shouldered the burdensome legacy. How about you? Are you the landlord of The Paradise? Did you give up police work in Canada?"

"Actually I quit the Sûreté du Québec and started my own investigation team fourteen years ago already. My paragon has always been Allan Pinkerton. It had been on my mind for a long time, to become more independent, to work as a private investigator. As much as I like police work as such; I have an aversion against paperwork and command structures. I dislike waiting for official channels to react. In short: I don't like to be the slave of bureaucracy. I like to be a free agent."

"But you are only forty-four now, isn't it? You must be ten years my junior, I think."

"That's right! But I have been very lucky. I came to an agreement with the Sûreté du Québec to work as an independent consultant. So the start was easy enough. And then I found a wonderful wife. She does not constantly worry when I'm on duty. I have an irregular job. Luckily she has herself a challenging job that demands a good deal of her day."

"I see," said my father. "So you started your own business in Québec City. How did you come to London; was that through your wife?"

"My wife's grandparents had this building here and the Restaurant Paradise. When they retired and went to China so as to enjoy their sunset years in their native country, my wife's parents inherited the restaurant along with the real estate. They did not waver to go to London.

All of a sudden we too were face-to-face with the question, shall we move to London? The longer we thought about it, the more we got used to the idea. Samantha Yin was also not averse to going. All of a sudden the three of us were keen on turning over a new leaf and starting life anew in a fresh place."

We nodded astounded.

"I can work in London as well as I can work in Québec. That's also one of the benefits of working independently. We came seven years ago. It's Xiu's business now. Her parents still play an active part. We get on well with one another. We live in the apartment on the top floor of the building. The home office is on the third floor."

"The Home Office? This sounds like the Ministry of the Interior to me," I said.

"It's my joke, of course. The buildings name is The Home; and the office is my office in The Home and at home at the same time. But it's not to be confused with the Home Department," said Etienne laughingly.

"Do you still entertain relations with Canada?"

"I still work for the Sûreté du Québec now and then. I'm sort of a liaison officer for Europe."

"Fabulous! I'm deeply impressed. Are you concerned with the English police, too?"

"Oh yes. One day the Metropolitan Police wanted my assistance in a case that bore reference to Canada. When the cooperation went successfully, they gave me even a contract. Meanwhile I have also a good rapport with the Secret

Intelligence Service."

"The MI6?"

"That's right. But tell me one thing; how could you tell so quickly who I was?"

"I don't rightly know. It was a bit of many things. The color of your eyes, a tuft of lighter hair peeking out under your black plait; but certainly also the way you move and the sound of your voice, unconsciousness perhaps, you know. Well and the fact that you knew who I was. Of course I could see from far off, that you are not a Chinaman. But anyone can see that."

"You would have become a good policeman."

"You mean like the one in The Mousetrap? We have been to the show tonight."

"Oh, have you? Amazing, isn't it. Over sixty years running now without a break … tell me, how is your father? Has he married again? I hope he is still in good shape?"

"No, he never married again. But yes, thank you, he is in fine fettle, not only for his age. He was eighty-nine in August. He is still engaged in sustainable development and farming. He has even some project going with the Prince of Wales. Last summer he spent on the Orkney Islands. There is research being done there, they are concerned in utilizing Marine energy."

"Marine energy? What's that supposed to mean?"

"It concerns different forms of thermal, mechanical and physicochemical properties of ocean water. The whole thing is still in its infancy but very promising."

If my father will find someone, to whom he can explain natural or technical phenomena, you can hardly stop him. So I had to take immediate action, and I said, "Dad remember; we must be up early tomorrow!"

"Yes, we must go to Newport," said father, facing Etienne.

"Newport Place, Newport Court, Newport Street, you name it! Everything's just round the corner," said Etienne.

"No, I mean the real thing, Newport in South Wales. Sorry, we must really crawl out of bed early tomorrow morning. But we must find an opportunity to get together one of these days."

Thereupon we thanked them for treating us. We bade each other good night and good bye. The two men promised one another to keep in touch by e-mail, and to meet soon, so as to talk about old times. My father said that they must visit us soon; that they are welcome to Edelweiss Castle at any time. Samantha was delighted.

"What is his family name, I mean Etienne's," I asked on the way to our hotel.

"I once tried to find him in the internet, but without result," my father answered. "In Canada he has probably assumed another second name too. His name will have been too long for any input mask of a computer system. It was Oberhimmelfreundlicher," father said, smiling. "Supposedly he took on a French last name as well, or an English one. The e-mail address he gave me bears no reference to his second name, because it reads: Etienne, then some number of three digits, and then @gmx.co.uk – where is it … ah," he got out a piece of paper, "look here." I read: etienne915@gmx.co.uk.

§4

The Stable Window

Hundreds of years ago, Edelweiss Castle was built close to a steep rock face – a cliff that dropped down to the River Holly. The rear wing of the building ran parallel to the Holly which flows in a roughly north-southerly direction in this part of the country. The other means of protection for the building had been man-made walls and moats. During the Siege of Edelweiss in 1529, the people of the small village had found refuge within the castle's walls.

Historically, and explainable on grounds of the topography, the land beyond the river had emotionally always been considered enemy territory, so that the provinces Goodland and Cyclamen – the land beyond the river Holly – never got around to spanning the river with a bridge. But there was a means of traversing. Behind the castle a narrow path of stairs had been hewn out in the blue rock, down to the river, where a ferry allowed crossing over to the farmlands and vineyards.

Above the flood mark was a little house, called the ferryman's house. It was partly hewn into the cliff and partly built of stone. The farmlands and vineyards within a semicircle around the ferryman's house on Cyclamen soil provided a splendid vista of the imposing white structure on top of the fabulous blue wall of rock.

Since the mid-fifties of the twentieth century, Edelweiss has grown from a quiet village to a quiet small town in its own right.

In the year 2014, Edelweiss was still interspersed with farmhouses, meadows, fields and forests. There were only small business enterprises. Edelweiss had a high attractiveness to lovers of nature and to recreational athletes. Many of the people who had settled down and built themselves homes were such who had found work in the aspiring industrial town Cowford, the capital city of Goodland province. The city boundary of Cowford was up the river — a bare thirty minutes' drive away.

On entering Cowford coming from Edelweiss, you caught sight of the newly constructed Aybesford House. The building housed the headquarters of the Aybesford Corporation. The central departments were accommodated here as well as the staff departments. There was no executive suite, only the president's office. Here, every Monday morning at seven o'clock punctually, the directors of the different plants and factories, most of them resident in Cowford, met with the president Gordon Aybesford for a breakfast discussion. On the other working days, they conferred via the internet.

On Monday 19 May 2014 the meeting had lasted quite unusually long already, nearly an hour and a half, when Mrs. Achmadi, Aybesford's secretary opened the door of the conference room a tiny crack and made an urgent sign to her employer. The main topic of the discussion today had not concerned the corporation directly, anyway. They had talked about the previous day's election. Early indications in the late afternoon had already pointed to a clear outcome.

"OK, ladies and gentlemen, there is no immediate action required right now. Let's address ourselves to the events of the day."

The directors got up and shook hands as was their custom, and began to spread themselves towards their respective corporation divisions. Aybesford went into his office, Mrs. Achmadi at his heels.

"The trainees from South Africa and Australia have been waiting for half an hour, sir. And the district attorney wants to meet you urgently," she said. "Shall I make you a connection right away?"

Why am I not surprised, he thought to himself. To the secretary he said absentmindedly, "What's on the agenda for this morning?"

"Well, after the welcoming of the trainees you are to deliver your lecture at ten o'clock! It's Monday; even if it's an unusual Monday."

"It will certainly be a Monday to remember. OK, try to reach her right now." Aybesford sat down at his desk and looked at the front page of the Cowford Daily News that was still spread out as he had left it when he went into the meeting. 'Goodland has voted!' ran the caption. '91% participation, of these 66% blanks!'

"She's on the line!"

"Thank you!"

"Good morning, Melitta! What can I do for you?" Silly question, he thought to himself immediately. Why was he so apprehensive?

"Listen, Gordon, could you spare an hour so that we could meet today … a delicate matter. I think we should talk as soon as possible. You probably know what I have in mind."

He looked at the rightmost column of the papers front page. There was a small item, which would have made the leading article on another day. The caption ran 'TV Presenter Xanda van Aanstryk, 49, died in her sleep!' He was not so sure what Melitta meant exactly, but he did not inquire further.

"If there is no imminent danger, could it wait until afternoon?"

"Afternoon is what I had in mind. What time do you suggest?"

"How about having lunch together in the dining hall at the University of Applied Sciences? I give a lecture there from ten to twelve. I wouldn't like to let my students down. If you could manage it would be perfect?"

"Good idea, Gordon, it's not so official there. The weather is divine today. So I can wait for you on one of the benches near the fountain in the park, in case you are arrested by one of your students."

"Thank you for being so understanding!"

Gordon succeeded in phasing out his lecture a few minutes before twelve, and put quizzers off until next time, so as not to make the district attorney wait. One hand in his trouser pocket, he sauntered alongside the artificially created lake. In his other hand he held his slim ostrich feather briefcase which he used exclusively for his much-thumbed scripts.

"What a beautiful day," said Melitta Stern, approaching him from sideways behind. She was wearing big sunglasses, her magnificent head of hair shining honey-colored in the sun.

He had not noticed her. He had been looking towards the

fountain where all benches seemed taken. Furthermore he had expected one woman, not two.

"Mrs. Kalanda, may I introduce Mr. Gordon Aybesford to you. This is Mrs. Dalia Kalanda, Detective Chief Inspector of the Cyclamen City Police Department. She is on a visit to the District Court in Cowford and I wanted to seize the opportunity to introduce you to one another."

Aybesford and Kalanda shook hands, the former being in the dark. He wondered what the significance was, but he said nothing.

"Mrs. Kalanda and I don't much care for lunch," said Stern in a questioning voice.

"I can do without, too. We could find ourselves a bench further afar, where we have our peace," he suggested.

While they strode along the pond and through the trees, Melitta Stern asked, "On what subject are you reading at the University, may I ask?"

"Thermodynamics and fluid mechanics," said Gordon Aybesford, recovering his composure. But he was still wondering what this was all about.

"Dear me! This sounds dangerous! What is it exactly?"

"The subsets we are doing are about the thermal and flow behavior of gases and fluids. They are prerequisites for designing turbines, compressors, car engines and so on."

"Are you doing research too?"

"No, research is a full time job. It occupies you day and night. No, I only incorporate new findings into my scripts as they emerge. There is no research being done in these fields in Cowford. We only offer instruction for our engineering students."

"I'm surprised that you can spare the time even for teaching. One would think that you had enough on your plate?"

"My job is a matter of *letting the horses pull the cart*. I got into the habit of only holding the reins in my hands."

"And the stick?" laughed Melitta Stern.

"No, only the carrot!" replied Aybesford. After a short silence he continued, "I think thermodynamics and fluid mechanics are the only subjects I could pass nowadays at an examination. This is so because I have been teaching these subjects for the last twenty-five years, since we installed the University of Applied Sciences in Cowford. At times I'm overcome by a feeling, that thermodynamics and fluid mechanics is all that is left of my academic training as an engineer. Does it ever strike you, that we work hard to earn a degree or some other qualification, and as time passes, we forget everything again? Only knowledge that we teach or use otherwise regularly, will not fade, but grow."

"The important thing is to know, where you can look things up," said Mrs. Stern, laconically.

"According to a popular saying," said Mrs. Kalanda, "Education is what is left, after we have forgotten all the facts."

They all agreed laughingly upon this wise saying.

When they had found a quiet spot and were seated, Stern began, "It is actually Mrs. Kalanda who has something to say to you, Gordon; but she is complying with a wish of mine. I wanted to acquaint you with her, because you and I we know each other from childhood on and there are some thousand people in the employ of your corporation. Let alone the reputation of your family."

Whereupon the strongly-built DCI pushed her thick

glasses with the clipped on sun shields up her short brunette bob, and spoke, "What we are talking here is unofficial and understood to be absolutely confidential."

Aybesford nodded his approval.

Kalanda went on, "Mrs. van Aanstryk lived and died in Cyclamen City so it's a case for the Cyclamen police." She looked from one to the other of her dialog partners. "According to the results of yesterday's general election, it is not unlikely that Goodland province will become independent while Cyclamen will remain with Austria. Our investigations must therefore start in Edelweiss with full efforts before it may be too late." She looked Gordon straight into his eyes. She displayed a cocksure behavior.

When Gordon's look did not betray unease but showed curiosity she continued, "Her demise is due to a poisoning, so it was either suicide or murder. As soon as murder should be ascertained, police investigations will move into gear."

"For what reason should my family or anybody else in Edelweiss have a desire to kill a woman in Cyclamen who has no connections to Edelweiss?"

"Well, at first sight Mrs. van Aanstryk had no enemies. On the other hand there was this interview the day before yesterday. Rumors have started within the force, that somebody could have ministered her some poison, so as to hinder her from doing the interview. If she had conducted the interview, the outcome of the election might have been a very different one."

"Are you going to assume that somebody in Edelweiss poisoned Mrs. van Aanstryk when she was miles away?"

"I assume nothing but I must consider everything. I must take into consideration every possibility and follow up all leads.

One possibility being, that the instigator was in Edelweiss while an accomplice in Cyclamen put the deed into action."

"Outrageous!"

"The intention need not have been deliberate murder. But somebody who had an interest to hinder her from doing the interview might have administered an overdose unintentionally. What I mean is that the police will have to come and ask questions. Mrs. Stern and I want you to be prepared. You yourself can speak with the people involved beforehand. And you are free to employ a lawyer or get otherwise legal advice."

"But what about her colleagues in the Cyclamen City TV studio? And her private social environment? The murderer is often to be found in the own family. Why should members of my family and my staff come under suspicion?"

"Very simple! As I said before: the interview may lead to a secession of Goodland from Austria! Therefore, we have no time to spare. But you need not worry. We will investigate every other possibility."

"But this is absolutely ridiculous! We at Edelweiss Castle are not planning a coup d'état. All we want is more democracy!"

"I'm not accusing you of anything; nor am I accusing any other person in Edelweiss. I just wanted to tell you in confidence as matters stand. You are welcome to contact me at any time, if something bothers you, I mean the police perhaps undue … actually I'm doing this only out of kindness."

Gordon looked at the district attorney Melitta Stern who nodded her approval.

"Yes, I know. I'm sorry; I was never before in such a situation. This is alright. I thank you very much, indeed. But when it comes to an investigation, I'm a suspect as well. I put also in my two cents, at the beginning of my speech."

"I'm very glad you get the point," said the Detective Chief Inspector of the Cyclamen City Police Department, smilingly.

As the dark fell, Gordon Aybesford sat alone at the big table in the kitchen-diner in Edelweiss Castle. For more than four decades this had been the main day room for the family. It had been their heaven of home. Here they had had their meals and their talks; here the children had done their preparatory school works and had played about when the weather was miserable outside.

In the evenings they had read books to one another. To Gordon's mind, the success of the room had been due to the fact, that there had never been a television in this room nor any other electronic gadget. Regrettably, two or three years ago when the twins Melis and Nicholas had begun to spread their wings, this convention had come to an end. It was roughly at the time when Gordon suffered from his severe illness. How critical it really was, he had never disclosed to anybody, not even to his spouse. But he had changed his hazardous way of living to a calmer one.

The room was now Gordon's refuge. In its peacefulness he could think best. This room was a replica of the kitchen living room in the Andalusia farmhouse, including the big window which looked into a stable.

These days the castle stable was the habitat of twelve sheep, white ones, black ones and spotted ones. They were free to leave the stable into the meadows at their own will during daytime, in summer as in winter.

The other windows looked out in the castle yard, but he had drawn the curtains nevertheless; he felt more cosy and unobserved this way. From the old castle moat he heard music. He drew the curtains of the stable window for the night, but not quite. To look at the sheep, even when they were asleep, was a spirit-soothing meditation for him. He wallowed in reminiscences.

He has often listened to the story and he has often retold it; the narrative of how his father Joseph had the south portal broken out and the moat partly filled up in order to have a driveway from the castle yard to the lot to the south of the castle. Then he had the Andalusian style farmhouse built farther off. He, Gordon, was then still a baby. Father had a dream about living on an Andalusian farm and he made the dream come true.

He had set his mind on producing Andalusian style goat cheese and selling it in Germany, Denmark and Austria. Because he loved his farm animals, he wanted them near to him. Therefore he left an opening between the living room and the stable.

When the family used the room sporadically at first, they thought there were always too many flies pestering them. Consequently, after a year, mother had insisted on closing the breach with a window pane, and the living room was converted into an eat-in kitchen in which the young and the old loved to be.

He remembered lively, when he was about six, the family was unanimous in the decision to have an identical room built in the castle, so as not to have to migrate perpetually. Instead of goats they would keep sheep. A large section of the coach house was emptied. He had watched the building workers battering walls down and constructing new ones. First the brick shell for the stable was brought to completion.

Thereafter by hanging a lower ceiling from the original one, a similar living room began to materialize. They all decided that also the windows in size and number must be broken out and finished exactly so that the wish room would become identical to the model. A sleeping person brought into one of the rooms should, on being woken up, not be able to decide was this the eat-in kitchen in the farmhouse or the one in the castle, provided all curtains were drawn, also those of the stable window.

After concealed installation of plumbing and wiring was completed, when the windows and door frames were fastened in their places, the walls plastered and painted and the floor laid, the Aybesford family were as happy as the sheep next room.

When the joiner had put in the doors and a cabinetmaker had installed the custom-made furniture, and when eventually the curtains and lamps were affixed, they sat together and celebrated. Now their home was their castle – or their castle their home?

Gordon Aybesford sighed. His father has lived his dream. He still occupies himself with farming, sustainable development and alternative energy sources. He is a child of nature and lives in close touch with nature whenever possible. He sometimes sleeps in one of the stables on a bed of straw, feeling well on hearing the occasional noises of the horses and the goats. On warm summer nights he even sleeps sometimes in the open. Perhaps this is what he means when he voices one of his sayings: "He who loses his childhood dies."

He, Gordon, had loved jet engines from the day he set

eyes on one on a testing bench in a refit factory. His dream had been a career with either Rolls Royce in the United Kingdom or Pratt & Whitney in the United States. After finishing his studies at Vienna Institute of Technology, he had submitted his application to both of them and had got two positive answers.

When suddenly his father, then sixty, seemed on the brink of death, he let himself be pushed by his family to show responsibility and to concern himself with the family property. In a sort of existential fear, his first rash action had been to appoint Walter Nadler, father's right-hand man for many years, as an administrator of the estate. He even had a villa built for him, on the other side of the castle square.

But soon he realized that more than mere administration was called for. Blessedly father recovered by and by and helped here and there, but actually he rather tended to see more about his private interests. Three years later, after Gordon had got married, his father in law had entrusted him with the management of a weakening engineering works.

Gordon was successful and it had given him the idea, to address himself fully to the task of buying engineering companies which were meandering along and then streamlining them according to his ideas. In doing so, he kept an eye on establishing and making us of synergy effects.

His train of thoughts was stopped when the door was opened gently. "Here you are, Gordon! What has come over you?" It was his wife Eleanor.

"Nothing, I'm listening to Mozart from the moat. It's rather faint tonight, due to the south-west wind."

"Shall I switch the lights on? Why are you sitting in the dark?"

"I sat down, and it became darker and darker."

They laughed at that and Eleanor lighted two candles. Then she fetched a decanter and two glasses for red wine and put them on the table.

"Can one get a snack here?"

She ran her fingers through his thick, gray hair. "Certainly sir! What do you want? We have cheese, bread, crackers, cheese crackers, ... "

Gordon sighed.

"What is it that exercises your mind, Gordon?"

"Father reaches the age of ninety. Why does he not come out? Why is Jacquy not adamant that the truth comes out? I have a good mind, to hire a private investigator to have the matter cleared up eventually. Now this interview and the poisoned woman into the bargain; I have a hunch these matters are interrelated."

§5

The Council of Philosophers

At this point the door opened again – more forcefully this time. It was Melis, their fair-haired teenage daughter. Are you smooching in the dark?" she asked.

"Gently does it! Turn on the light, silly," said her mother.

"Rupert has come to visit. He said he couldn't find anybody."

Not long thereafter, Gloria's dark mane appeared in the doorframe with Rupert's round face looming behind her. Scarcely had they entered, when Melis' twin brother Nicholas made an appearance too. "Here you all are," he said.

Rupert was welcomed by his parents; Eleanor urged them all to be seated.

"It is just over a year since all of us were here united," said Gloria beaming. "I'm starving. What about an impromptu dinner? Is everybody hungry?"

Nobody answered in the negative, so Gloria said enthusiastically, "Let's have a look in the pantry what we have got."

Rupert, Gloria and Melis embarked on a food hunt, while Nicholas stayed behind to get the cooking started.

When his siblings returned from their hunt, Nicholas said proudly, "I've already switched on the big stove top and put on the giant pan. I've found edible oil in the sideboard; it's already boiling."

"Very good," praised him Gloria.

Rupert opened some cans of mushrooms and a can of peas.

Eleanor and Gordon watched amused and with delight, as their children cut ginger, onions, tomatoes and garlic.

"Gloria has such a cheerful habit of mind," said Eleanor in a low voice to her husband.

"Yes, hasn't she. She does everything with contagious enthusiasm," replied Gordon. "I think she has outgrown her love-sickness eventually. She has settled down very nicely in the corporation, too."

By now, the cooks put everything into the big pan along with water and rice. Eventually they added salt, pepper and curry.

"We can eat in twenty minutes!" announced Gloria.

"Will somebody go and ask grandpa and Aunt Agnes, if they want to join in," said Eleanor excitedly. "This is really an unexpected coincidence; a chance to get all together."

"I'll go," said Gordon.

"Let the children do it," replied his spouse. "Perhaps somebody can find Jacquy too."

"I stay behind then and add some more ingredients. Who knows who else may be coming," said Gloria.

Rupert, Melis and Nicholas started on their way. They had not to look far for Aunt Agnes. She was right outside in the hall way. She was Gordon's aunt really, the sister of his late mother. Her parents together with their two young girls had found a place to stay in the castle in 1945, after the war. They were from the Sudetenland, from where they had been expelled by the Czechs.

Agnes had then been eleven and her sister nine years old. As time had gone by, both of the girls had begun dreaming of Joseph in a harmless way. When they grew up, Joseph fell a little in love with both of them. Eventually, in 1959 Joseph married Barbara, the younger one. A year later, Barbara gave birth to Gordon.

When her sister died, Agnes secretly had cherished the hope that Joseph would marry her after a year or so of mourning. But Joseph had made no move to marry again at all. When she had been almost fifty, Joseph chanced upon an opportunity to help her in having a heartfelt wish fulfilled. She adopted a three year old boy child from the Netherlands.

The woman who parted with the child had got the diagnosis to be fatally ill. Her last will had been that the boy should retain his name, which had also been the name of her late husband, namely Jacob de Jong. Jacquy, as the boy was called from the beginning in his new environment, has been a family member under the protection of Joseph Aybesford ever since.

When the children returned at length, they had not only Joseph Aybesford in tow, but also Walter Nadler Sen., Naran Dasgupta and Claas Mabutu. Nobody had found Jacquy.

"Here comes the complete council of philosophers! Good evening gentlemen!" exclaimed Gordon.

"The young ones said we must all come; I don't know if it is alright?" asked Joseph. "Every Monday evening, Claas, Naran and Walter come to the farm for our being together. You know — our philosophical talks."

They had come over from the Andalusia farmhouse where Joseph still resided, although he had also rooms in the castle.

Walter Nadler Sen. was nearing seventy-nine and lived

in the household of his son in the castle administrator's villa. Some years ago he had lost his eyesight. To compensate for his deficiency he invented most curious tasks for his diversion. The latest was cutting his hair himself, with the aid of a pair of scissors only. He announced that there wasn't any law which stipulated you to trim your hair in a conventional way. He blamed his limited mobility for his putting on flesh around the waistline, which circumstance in turn increased his sluggishness.

Claas Mabutu was sixty-six. Joseph had facilitated his immigration from South Africa when Claas was twenty-two. When he had met him, Claas was serving tea in Union Building, the parliament in Pretoria, and he was totally without kin. His mother had been a Xhosa woman who had become pregnant by her white employer.

Joseph and Claas have always been like father and son. But Claas always observed some distance and respect, as he did with everyone. His skin was dark but his hair had gone white; white was also his mustache as well as his rudimentary beard which grew underneath his lower lip. With his intellectual spectacles he looked the most intellectual of the four seniors.

Naran Dasgupta was a former government spokesman from India. He had a spare figure and a quiet tongue-in-cheek kind of humor. Born not into the right cast, he had made his way gradually into the Sansad Bhavan in New Delhi nevertheless. Being unattached, he embarked on a journey to Europe upon retirement. He loved horseback riding. In Austria he heard of Cyclamen Province and its peculiar palatial farmhouses. On rides across the country he photographed and made sketches at his leisure. On one of those rides on horseback he came across Edelweiss Castle, which looked like an overly large version of the farmsteads, with towers added at its four corners. The remarkable sight of the white castle on the blue level rock took his breath away and cast a spell on him.

He slowly rode down to the river. Beyond the stream was a dwelling in the crag. A steel cable that traversed the water allowed a boat to hang from it, so that it was not carried away by the flowing water. He dismounted and looked on as a woman, by holding the rudder in the right angle, could cause the boat to glide along the cable, from the opposite bank over here, only under the power of the flowing water. A sign informed him, that he had no right of way.

When the woman had disembarked and come near enough, he inquired about the castle and the ferry. He was told that the ferry provided the only means of crossing the river for twenty kilometers up or downstream. It was only for the people that worked on the Cyclamen side of the river but had their homes in Edelweiss. Using the stairs in the rock was not without danger.

In former days a ferryman had operated the boat. But the present lord of the castle had upgraded it in such a way, that it could be called from or sent to the other side by means of a remote control device. The ferryman's house, partly built into the crag, was unoccupied in these days.

On the next day Naran Dasgupta paid a visit to Edelweiss by bus. Wandering around in the publicly accessible park in the grounds north to the castle, he had deliberately overlooked an *Off limits!* sign. In this way he discovered the crooked path that led down to the River Holly. He could not refrain from exploring it. He found the rarely used ferryman's house that he had seen the day before and was fascinated by it and its surroundings.

Back up on the plateau he made inquiries in the castle and was fortunate to encounter the friendly face of Claas Mabutu who made a meeting with Gordon Aybesford possible. Eventually he got Gordon's permission to live in the small house. It was exactly what he had dreamt of. Almost only such people who lived in Edelweiss and pursued their daily work beyond the Holly used the ferry mornings and evenings.

Naran Dasgupta got also permission to build a stable for a horse on the other shore, from where he could undertake his trips on horseback. Soon, the small-boned dark man with his flawless set of white teeth got the byname ferryman. He had settled down some years ago and was now seventy-three. He made no move to ever move on. In Joseph, Class and Walter he had found friends whom he liked to talk to about anything and everything.

"It would seem that tonight we witness one of the finest hours of Edelweiss Castle," said Eleanor. "Such an illustrious table the kitchen diner has never seen before. You are just in time for a simple dinner."

"Not much for me," said Walter warily, when they had taken their seats after a lengthy palaver, and Gloria served him with a portion of the newly created rice dish. Then she took his right hand and put a spoon into it. He preferred it to a fork.

"The air smells of spring. I think the concert must soon be over," mused Walter.

"Grandfather, are you aware that you might write history?" asked Rupert after they had been eating for some time.

"Is my television appearance the reason for your coming in the dead of night from Dafins?" asked Joseph.

"To be honest, yes! I feared to find Edelweiss in turmoil! You know, everybody asks me: 'what's going on in Goodland?' But I'm glad to see, everything is as calm as usual."

"Appearances are deceiving you," said Gordon. "It bubbles below the surface! Now that more than half of the citizens of voting age indirectly are for autonomy, the enactment of the declaration of independence is only a question of days and many people are working hard for it. Next Sunday, on the twenty-fifth of May, we are summoned to take a vote on the independence of Goodland explicitly. This is the day of the European election, as you know. So it will be killing two birds with one stone!"

"Will Goodland be big enough to exist on its own?"

"Don't fall for this fright spectre. This is the lie of all Eurocrats, that without the EU all European countries are lost beyond recovery. But too many counterexamples refute this nonsensical assertion."

"It's the curse of politicians; they are doomed to be story-tellers," said the ferryman.

"Are you serious about that, Mr. Dasgupta?" asked Nicholas.

"But of course. I give you a simple example. When a Western statesman meets an Eastern high politician, he has to bring up human rights. When the TV announcer mentions this incident, most people think that the westerner acted in brave and noble manner. In reality, the staffs of the politicians have agreed upon beforehand about what is being said."

"Europe and The European Union are two pairs of shoes," said Joseph. "Europe is this lump of the earth that has the largest number of cultures and languages. This is the Europe we love. But this variety of different species is endangered by the transnational companies, because they want all people on this globe to be alike, like ants, but only one species of ants, *The Blind Consumer Ants.*

The European Union, on the other hand is the means by which the transnational companies want us to domesticate. We are allowed to vote people who nobody knows into the European parliament, but the power in the EU lies with the commission and the council which lie at the feet of the transnational companies."

"After the referendum everything will go very fast," said Gordon. The new independent state's name shall then be Sustaining or Sustainland or something like that."

"Only the Crimeans where faster," said Melis. "We beat the Catalans, the Scots, and the Basques. Nearly all teachers spoke today of how the European Union has degenerated from a community of shared values to a community of lobbyists."

"Grandfather, father, are you members of The Sustainers? Because you sound so informed and involved!" enquired Rupert.

"No, no!" came the answers, quick like two shots.

"With our family history it would not have been appropriate for any one of us to engage in politics in Austria," said Gordon. "But I don't quite know about you, father. Why were you carried away like this on Saturday morning? And why did you want to give an interview, in the first place?"

"Well, it's no secret that Franz Haversack has asked me repeatedly to join them. I always told him that there was no way, because of their separatist ambitions. On the other hand, most of their ideas have been my ideas long before their time.

After my recovery from the pulmonary embolisms, when I was fifty-nine, I became a corresponding member of the

Brundtland Commission. Two weeks ago, I called Xanda van
Aanstryk and said that if she would give me the chance to talk a
bit about sustainable development, I will agree to do an interview. Nobody knew she was doomed to die, dear soul. I was
smitten with surprise, when I heard of her passing this morning."

"Granddad, what exactly does sustainable development
mean," asked Nicholas.

"Well, my grandson, as a grandfather of four, I'm glad the
other three are also present to hear your question. Sustainable
development would not have become an issue if human beings,
like other beings, were contented with satisfying their neces-
sities of life. For the humankind, food and shelter and clothing
apparently do not suffice. It is not the deficiency that breeds
the greed of the humans but the abundance.

Last summer I visited an ethnic group in the south of
Venezuela. They live in huts covered with foliage. They wear
loincloths, and live on wild plants and the fruits of such. And
they go hunting and live happily and contently. Admittedly,
this is an extreme example. But to be heard, one must cite
extreme examples.

Let me give you an example of the contrary extreme: the
Austrian politicians have much too high salaries as compared
to the incomes of working people. But one of the first things
the new government will enforce will be higher remunera-
tions for themselves and higher taxes for the workers. You can
count on that.

The higher the standard of living is the higher is the greed.
And the advertising industry arouses new needs continuously.
Our planet is being exploited to such a degree, that the end of
the human race is in sight.

In the Brundtland Report the term *sustainable development* is defined as *development that meets the needs of the present without compromising the ability of future generations to meet their own needs*. It's of course a worldwide concern, not just an Austrian one. Louise Chevrolet assured me that she was in the picture. When she began to ask me silly questions I became annoyed."

"You shouldn't have said the bit about the slip of the tongue, granddad!" interfered Melis.

"You are right, Melis. I don't feel good about it. But I didn't even know that she had earned the nickname Miss Pardon by then. And when you are being interviewed on TV you have not the time to grope for the right words. This is my only excuse for the unwise saying; that it came automatically, like my whole outburst.

Also my prompting the audience to cast invalid votes happened by itself. But for this I have an explanation. I have often wondered why people abstain from voting in protest against candidates or political parties. The politicians blame this on the citizens; call it voter fatigue or immaturity.

If you go and tell them *I don't want you*, they cannot fabricate excuses. I must say, I do not regret what I said with regard to voting. It obviously helped the folks to get back some of their dignity. The people of Goodland sniff the historic opportunity they have opened up for themselves and they will jump at it.

"You have opened it up," said Nicholas.

"Is some rice dish left?" asked Walter, and Eleanor gave him some.

"Louise Chevrolet may slip now and then, but I think she is such a nice person," insisted Melis.

"I think a slip of the tongue can happen to the most experienced speaker, and when they go ahead with a smile, it
is as if nothing had happened. But when an announcer pauses
and says *pardon* beamingly, she makes herself the centre of
attention, and takes the focus off the message that is being
conveyed, interrupting thereby the flow of information,"
said the ferryman.

"As I said before, I did not mean it. One must learn how to
live as long as one lives. I will never repeat this mistake, I will
probably make others," said Joseph and laughed.

"I worry about what the world is coming to," said Aunt
Agnes.

"Have you heard? Another one slumped to the ground,
also last Saturday. Not in Goodland but in the early evening in
Zandenburg Today. A church tax collector collapsed when asked
how he feels threatening people with the bailiff when they
are in arrears with their church tax, but the pope preaches
Christian love. So it's not only the interviewers who are in
danger of collapsing but also the interviewees," said Eleanor.

"I happened to see it too," said Rupert. "When *Province
Today* is on, I switch around between Provinces. By the way,
yesterday the Swiss voted about minimum wages of eight-teen
Swiss francs per hour. It was turned down. What about you,
father? Are you for or against minimum wages?"

"Minimum wages may spell the end for small businesses.
I am against minimum wages, but in favour of a maximum
wage," replied Gordon. "Only a few months ago, it was also
the Swiss that turned down a maxim wage of, I think, eleven
times the wage of a worker, or something like that. I would
suggest that no person can earn more than five or six times the

wages of a skilled worker. It is not good when there are too wide differences."

At that they plunged into an excited discussion, which was still under way, when Aunt Agnes confided in them that she was tired. Thereupon Eleanor accompanied Agnes to her room. When Eleanor returned she said, "Now the concert is over. Have you found the solution to the problem of just remuneration?"

"We are discussing another problem now," said Joseph. "I think, like in Switzerland, the people should make the important decisions, not the representatives of the people in parliament or government."

"It will be an interesting experiment, to navigate the course of a country by means of administrators rather than of a government; administrators that implement the will of the populace."

When this aspect had also been examined and talked over in detail, Gordon cleared his throat. "I'm going to tell you something now," he began, "under the pledge of secrecy. Do you understand me, you two youngsters?"

The twelve years old twins, Melis and Nicholas gave their word of honour.

"Xanda van Aanstryk's departure from life was not a natural death; it was suicide or even murder. Should they find that it was murder, we must reckon with the police's coming to the castle and asking questions."

"Let them come, we have nothing to hide," said Melis courageously.

All of them had a good laugh at that.

"If it was murder, and if the murderer is not found out, there will remain a flaw on our family name; this is what worries me," said Gordon. "The political revolution that lies ahead will be remembered as having been triggered by what grandfather and I said the day before yesterday. Malicious tongues will go on to guess that Xanda van Aanstryk was given poison by one of us. Not with the intention to kill, but so that the interview should go out of control.

"The motive being, that grandfather should have an inexperienced interviewer to deal with?" asked Eleanor.

"Exactly," said Gordon.

"But it was exactly the other way round," said Joseph. "I was anxious to have Xanda van Aanstryk as an interviewer."

"Do not worry, Gordon! Wait for the events to take their course. The police will find out what really happened," said Eleanor soothingly.

"The question is, if they are willing to find out the truth. In times of political shift, you cannot know who is friend and who is foe."

"You can always employ private investigators, if the worst comes to the worst," said Eleanor.

"This is exactly what I had in mind. But there again, whom can you trust? I would not trust an Austrian in this situation."

"Perhaps this Etienne in London could be helpful in some way or other!" suggested Gloria.

"Yes, exactly! I was thinking of him," said her father. "I could get hold of him this afternoon."

"Has he changed his name as you expected him to? Or has he still this longish one?" inquired Gloria.

"When he came to Canada, he made concessions to both language groups. He began to use the French version of his first name, and he adopted the family name *Friendly*, sort of an

English extract of his original name.

"Why not invite him to come and investigate the circumstances that led to Mrs. van Aanstryk's death?"

"He would rather not come and make enquiries because he might not be unbiased, he says."

§6

Sovereignty for Goodland

In the late afternoon of Sunday May 18, when the results of the general election became evident, occasional scenes of jubilation took place in the Province of Goodland. However, the key players as well as the supporters of the Sustainable Development Party wasted no time in wallowing in the flush of victory. On the contrary, they kept cool heads and acted without delay in organizing a plebiscite for next Sunday.

On the coming Sunday, 25 May 2014, the people living in the European Union were called upon to go to the polls. When attending this EU election, the men and women in Goodland should first vote for or against the independence of their province.

In the week between the general election and the Goodland referendum it seemed that all people of Goodland were thinking and talking politics and nothing else. That Goodland should ever become an independent state had in recent years been talked about; but only in subjunctive, as a faint nearly impossible hypothesis. And now all of a sudden every elector was called upon to say *yes* or *no*.

The Sustainers had posters printed overnight, and

members and supporters posted them everywhere. But opponents of the idea of defection were also not idle. They stuck their own posters, sometimes on top of the adversaries' ones.

In parks and on street corners people delivered sermons and spoke their minds, sometimes with the aid of electric megaphones. Fights occurred once in a while. All things considered, excitement was everywhere but people remained prudent enough. Schools remained closed.

In this same week Joseph Aybesford increasingly had felt the need for being on his own. In terrific speed old structures were tumbling and transforming. And he should be the cause of it all? He went about like a ghost, a ghost in a dream. On Sunday evening he went into a rarely used little room in the castle.

There was a television in it and a sofa. He wanted to see the results of the EU election and of the Goodland referendum not in company but on his own. He switched on the TV and lay down on the sofa. However he was so exhausted that he instantaneously fell into a deep sleep.

All of a sudden he was awakened by fortissimo piano tones. Looking at the screen he saw Chatia Buniatischwili playing fiercely and making a dramatic mien which changed by degrees to buffoonish with the change of the tune. Had he overslept? He switched to videotext. EU election: sensation in France – protest voters came off first. Goodland referendum: all districts had a majority for independence.

Also a majority had voted for the name Goodland to remain. It should become the name of the new state, in case the province should gain independence. He rubbed his eyes. Was this now a dream or reality?

On the next morning, Walter Nadler Jr. wrote the following lines in his blog: 'When on Saturday a week ago, Peter Dorset spoke about a possible outbreak of a Third World War, and Jacquy anticipated serious consequences to be triggered by Joseph Aybesford's interview, I joined in; I made fun of writing a book about the historical event. Since last night the consequences are on the table and visible. Goodland is an independent state.

Jacquy had feared that the appeals of the two Aybesfords would have severe consequences for the owners of Edelweiss Castle. He knew only too well, that the nobility are forbidden to be active in politics in Austria. Archduke Otto von Habsburg, who was the last Crown Prince of Austria-Hungary until its dissolution in 1918, lived not in Austria. He fled during the Nazi period to the United States with a visa issued by Aristides de Sousa Mendes. He was politically active on an international level.

When last night it became clear that the majority of the Goodlanders had voted for secession, reporters stormed Goodland's state parliament in Cowford. The SDP had given currency to the rumor that the Declaration of Independence would be celebrated there.

The Sustainers however wanted to avoid possible clashes with the Federal Austrian Police. Only two TV teams had been given confidential tips. Equipped with light gear, they had lain in wait in the wood near The Fox and Hare in Edelweiss. In front of these and a few insiders, myself and some carefully selected reporters for gazettes included, Franz Haversack read the Declaration of Independence on behalf of the people of Goodland.'

On Wednesday May 28, three days after the plebiscite, Franz Haversack, the chairman of the SDP, the Sustainable Development Party, was hosted in the Golden Egg, the cafeteria of Edelweiss Castle; he had asked for a meeting with Joseph and Gordon Aybesford. Also present were the ferryman, Claas and Walter Nadler Sen.

"Thank you for taking the time to see me," said Franz Haversack, his blue eyes beaming.

"You look as if everything is plain sailing now?" said Joseph.

"Signed, sealed and delivered," said Haversack. "Everything had been prepared beforehand. The mayors, the law courts, the police, everything went smoothly. A few public servants defected to Austria for fear of forfeiting their pension claims; which is nonsense of course. Some migration to and from Austria in the next weeks is to be expected.

"This is a sign that the world has resigned itself to the new state Goodland."

"Absolutely! Very little fuss is made in the European press. It's as if they wanted to hush it up. As if they were ashamed that it could happen." After a moment's pause Haversack carried on, "A lot remains to be done, of course. The most pressing problem is to establish an election system over the internet."

"But in the age of internet banking this is no big problem, is it?" said Walter.

"It's not a big technological problem, if that is what you mean. But we have many ideas to be implemented for the new state. We want the people to vote by ballot on all issues. The problem will be to mobilize as many citizens as possible. Especially those who were against autonomy must be motivated to give all they have; to avail themselves of the opportunity of building a real democratic state."

"I didn't even know that your ideas were that forward-pressing. You seem to envisage a new democratic system," said Joseph.

"If the people agree and join in, we will advance direct democracy much farther than we know it from Switzerland. We have now the chance to take over tried and tested paradigms and improve on them. Especially the internet which is now established in nearly every household offers new forms of democratic societies. But also those who do not want to be on the internet must have the opportunity to vote; be it via snail mail or by dropping a sealed envelope in the town hall, for example."

"But all those men and women who are now in power, who were so determined to hold on to power, will feel cheated."

"This is part of the human evolution. Power was necessary throughout the course of history. It still is necessary in less advanced societies. But scattered isolated cells of advanced human thinking, like Goodland, will eventually take the human kind a step higher."

"But all your soaring thoughts do not consider the hostile conflicts that flare up when no power structures exist."

"The bludgeon-brandishing human will be history one day in the future. Our revolution will be cited as one little mosaic piece in the pattern of human evolution."

"You are so enthusiastic and full of energy, where do you draw this peppiness from?" said Gordon.

"My barber said the other day that I am an idealist. I had never looked at it this way. All I want is to bring about the materialization of a democratic state. It started in childhood.

I liked to listen to fairy tales. In these tales there was always a king that owned and ruled the country. This was seldom the point of the tale but it merely showed the circumstances in which people lived in."

"That's how it used to be," said Walter.

"Then one day I read about a society in which the men decided all issues. Two-and-a-half-thousand years ago they had developed a sovereignty of the people, in Attica. I was spellbound. You will understand," said Haversack, looking at Joseph, "you yourself have served your ideals all your life."

"Maybe I did in a way. But I often think it was only words I produced and that I lived a selfish life, passing on my responsibility to my son Gordon."

"You have no cause to speak in this way of yourself, sir. If it were not for you, everything would be as ever."

"This is the ridiculous part of it. I don't feel as if I had planned something that worked out. I wanted to talk about sustainable development, nothing else. When the interview didn't go as I had hoped for, I fell into a rash splutter. In hindsight I consider the outcome a great success for democracy but not one I deserve credit for. For the last few days I exist like in a dream. I just cannot align my foolish behavior with Goodland achieving statehood a week later."

"Wittingly or unwittingly; what you said was at the back of your mind and in the minds of most men and women in this country. The stubborn will and the courage were there. They had to be aroused, though. Your spark leapt over to the people, you electrified the audience. This is the stuff that decisive moments in history are made of."

Claas, the man of the first hour in The Golden Egg, frowned

questioningly at Joseph. Although he was retired, Claas still liked to make himself useful wherever possible, especially in the Golden Egg. The Golden Egg was still his province.

"Fetch a bottle of Champagne Claas, will you? And glasses! I think we have something to celebrate. I'm glad you came round Mr. Haversack. You have cheered me up. I think that I slowly begin to see things as they are."

"This is the right spirit, sir! The people need you now as a guiding figure. One of the next steps to be taken is replacing the provisional government by an elected administration. Also we need an improved version of the constitution; and we need a president, don't you think? We wanted to ask you sir," his friendly blue eyes looked in the clement brown eyes of Joseph, "would you be prepared to run for the presidency? We're sure you would be elected the first president of Goodland."

"God forbid!"

"My comrades and I are of the opinion, that with your advocating sustainable development for decades you are an example for mankind; comparable with Nelson Mandela, if only in another field. Added to this the secession which you triggered and your dedication to environment, you will be remembered for ever. But you seem not to be very thrilled with what I say. What makes you look so reflectively?"

"Sorry, Franz. But you are talking nonsense, when you mention me in the same breath as Nelson Mandela."

"Let me rephrase my words: show me the citizen of Goodland who is more suited than you are to be president."

"I'm afraid I'm not worthy of such an honor. The president should be an exemplary person. There was an episode many years ago, that people will not approve of, once it is brought into the light of day."

"Why should it come to light?"

"Because people should know who is up for election, for one thing."

"Yes, this is honorable. And what is the other thing?"

"The other thing is that it might be dragged into the open anyway."

"Why do you think so?"

"It might come out in the course of the investigations of Xanda van Aanstryk's demise."

"Oh, what a mental leap!"

"*You* would be the appropriate president, I think. *You* have worked hard for so many years and should now have the benefit of your striving."

"No, no. For me it is far too early, maybe in a few years time. At the moment there is still much work to be done. What about you, Gordon?"

"No, thank you! People would think I've been working behind the scene and helped clandestinely all along. I'm glad about how things have developed, but I was not a driving force. In addition to it, there is no successor in sight who will look after the family property."

For a while none of the six spoke. Then Joseph Aybesford said: "I was just thinking that other regions might follow our example. I wish that such processes will lead to more and more states that are able to manage themselves without politicians. Like a disease, democracy may spread out gradually. Warmongers and other destroyers of morals are then condemned to extinction."

"There will be no need in the future for politicians as we

know them today. We will have officials that minister to the people; administrators that fulfill the peoples will. Also political parties will be of use only in the shaping of the public opinion," said Haversack.

"I hope that your dreams come true. I think that actions of the sort you pulled through will bring about real democracy for Europe. I hope that at the end of the road we find the United States of Europe where the people are in charge and the ministers are the servants as it should be," said the ferryman.

"As regards the accusations of our antagonists, we must always keep in mind, that we didn't steal a country or something but gave one to the people to whom it belongs," said Haversack.

"If it was not for you, my spark would not have found the people prepared as they were," said Joseph Aybesford, slapping Franz Haversack on the shoulder.

In the meantime Claas had filled the glasses and the six men raised them and drank to the health of Goodland and its people.

§7

Pierre de Fermat's Arrival

When on Saturday 14 June 2014 early in the morning Jacquy de Jong entered the Golden Egg for breakfast, Class was already there, not on duty but as a guest. It crossed Jacquy's mind that it had never happened before that Claas, as a guest, had been that early.

The Golden Egg was for all people who lived or worked in the castle and was much-frequented from morning till evening for meals and refreshment. In bygone days the room was a tap room for the knights. After having served many years as a storage room it was renovated and modernized by Gordon. Together with a fitness room next-door it was meant to foster a community spirit in the Edelweiss team.

You paid with your Edelweiss Card here; no cash was used. No walk-in customers were served. There was no entrance from outside, anyway. This had been stipulated in the beginning – also out of consideration for the proprietors of The Castle Inn. In here people mixed and talked sociably.

"Goeiemôre Jacquy!"

Between themselves, Class and Jacquy took pleasure in speaking in Afrikaans and Dutch respectively, every once in a while.

"Goedemorgen, Claas! Hoe gaat het met jou?"

Class ignored the question which was a mere formality anyway, itching after posing his own question, "Have you watched Spain versus the Netherlands?"

"Of course I watched! Unbelievable, I'm still thrilled. To beat the reigning world champion five to one on the second day of the games is a good omen. If they keep on going like this Holland can make it to the finals."

"Yes, and in the final perhaps facing Brazil, because they played also superbly the day before."

"Exactly, they too are at their best. Beat Croatia three to one, not bad."

"Yes, and Brazil scored all four goals! Ha-ha!"

"It makes one already look forward to Rio de Janeiro in four weeks." Although Jacquy was talking soccer World Cup his mind was on something else. He was rummaging in the periodicals. "Have you ever heard of the name Pierre de Fermat?"

"Can't remember, who's that supposed to be?"

"I hadn't heard the name until a few days ago when I read something in here about a kidnapping case, that I merely skimmed over then. But I'm sure he is an investigator who helped Interpol to solve some case."

"What exactly are you looking for?"

"I'm looking for a copy of the French weekly L'Express."

Claas got up. "Wait a minute. There must be some back issues in the container." When he reappeared he put two copies on the table before Jacquy. "The last and the last but one, you're lucky, they fetch the waste paper next Monday."

"Thanks! Let me see. Now I must find out what it actually was ... oh here, yes this is what I had in mind. Last evening,

Gordon told me that he wants the death of Xanda van Aanstryk investigated by a prestigious international investigator; because the police are getting nowhere and keep on asking questions. He wants me to employ some investigation agency with a good reputation but with no ties to either Austria or Goodland. He mentioned this Fermat."

"The penny is beginning to drop. I too have glanced over this article," said Claas, "but I think it was an advertisement."

"Can you read French?"

"Laboriously only. Occasionally I browse over headlines or advertisements. I like to read the comics, like Charlie Hebdo."

"Do you think this is good style?"

"It's easy reading. Don't you think it's funny?"

"I think people who poke fun at themselves are more like-able. Let me see what it says here … has become very famous after his uncoverings in the Gatti-Loumann affair … a French citizen of Italian descent … blah blah blah … look here, even an e-mail address is given … imbecile that I am … here in very small print and rotated by ninety degrees it says *annonce*! You are right Claas, it's an advertisement! Laboriously indeed! It looks as if they want to appeal to a financially strong clientele."

"You can always obtain an offer."

"I'm going to e-mail them right away to establish contact and I give them my mobile number as well," said Jacquy and got down to action. "For the time being this is confidential Claas, agreed?" he said, while punching in the e-mail address of the Pierre de Fermat agency.

They were still eating when Jacquy's mobile rang. He got up and went outside, so as not to disturb the other guests. When he returned he sat down and sipped from his coffee mug.

"This was Monsieur Pierre de Fermat himself," he cackled.

"What did he say? Don't worry; I won't breathe a word to anybody."

"He says that he has been following the news about Goodland achieving statehood very closely. He even asked me if the Edelweiss Music Festival was still going on. I told him that it went its normal way unaffected by political circumstances, that it's over for this year since two weeks and that the future of it rests with the castle only insofar as it provides the location free of charge. He is very intrigued by the idea of coming himself to investigate the case, although his German is very limited. Besides French he speaks English, of course."

"What about a quotation? Does he want to do it free of charge out of enthusiasm for Goodland?"

"Not quite, but his offer is reasonable. He asks for a daily allowance. The collaboration can be terminated by any party at any time. Only in the case that he solves the case unequivocally does he want a success fee."

"Are you going to hire him then?"

"Yes, I'm going to my office now in order to arrange terms in detail, then I'll give him green light right away. I don't want to put off the matter. Gordon is very anxious about it; and it's exactly the agency which he has in mind."

Entry in Jacquy de Jong's note-book: Thursday, June 26 2014. Pierre de Fermat and I had arranged his arrival for today. On my way to the car I allowed myself plenty of time. When I had reached it, I gave it a polish here and there, and dawdled about otherwise. Fermat's airplane was due at a few minutes past one o'clock in the afternoon. Now it was only a quarter past ten; too soon to leave for Kyll Airport in order to pick him up.

I didn't know why it was that I was so keyed up. I made up my mind to go back to my apartment. Scarcely had I put the key into the lock of my door, when my mobile phone went. It was Monsieur de Fermat telling me that he had arrived last night already and has taken a room at Halfway House. He would be ready to be picked up in about an hour. I said that I would come and that we could have lunch right there.

Halfway House is about four miles from the castle. It was laid out before World War One and called thus because it was the stop halfway between Syget and Cyclamen City for the Edelweiss coach service. Incidentally it's situated also midway between Edelweiss Castle and the centre of Cowford.

I didn't enter my rooms but went to the Golden Egg. I had a cup of coffee and told Claas that the foreign investigator had stepped onto Goodland's soil already.

"Why are you so excited, young man," said Claas.

"He came yesterday and put up for the night in Halfway House. Is it not strange? By the way: why don't *you* pick him up?"

"I speak French only the way they speak in comics. You are the diplomat of Edelweiss castle! And I am retired."

On my way to the car for the second time, I was again stalling for time. Slowly I hit the road for Halfway House. On the street I went well below the speed limit and incurred angry reactions from other drivers. And in the end I reached my destination half an hour before the right time.

It was for this reason that I did not drive right into the parking lot in front of the building. Instead I decided to explore the back of the Hotel which had been renovated and added to recently. The lot in the back looked still like a building site with a pile of debris and dismantled scaffoldings heaped together.

I halted the car in a corner of the yard. There was a lorry in the unloading bay but nobody was to be seen. Through a wire mesh fence I saw grazing goats wander the meadow. Suddenly, out of the corner of my eye I discerned a movement. I beheld a man in a tracksuit coming deftly down the fire escape of the hotel.

I looked up higher, puzzling over where he might have come from. In a flash I saw the face of Heidi Forster disappear behind a window. When I wanted my eyes to follow the man again, he had vanished too. I was thunderstruck! In my eyes Heidi is a proud elegant lady that I have not dared to ask out for dinner as yet.

Being ten years older and perhaps appearing a bit stiff at times I'm afraid to get the brush-off. It's not as if I had only a crush on her. It goes much deeper. I can imagine her to be my perfect spouse one day. What nourishes my hopes is the fact that I'm the only bachelor in Edelweiss who is distinctly taller than she is. So I've always been waiting for the right moment.

This very same Heidi was in a Hotel with a stranger in highly mysterious circumstances? And with a guy who was older and smaller than me. Had I deceived myself? Suppose the man was M. de Fermat? Nonsense! I knew that I wasn't thinking clearly, so I started the engine and drove away.

After a while I noticed that I was driving back to the castle automatically. Just as well. I decided to fetch another car. Whatever was going on or not going on, it would not hurt to give the impression that I was just arriving and had not been already there half an hour earlier.

When I came back to Halfway House a man of medium height with mirrored sunglasses, black shining hair and a big black moustache was pacing back and forth in front of the building. His age was not easily to guess … his late thirties, his early forties? His build was not unlike the build of the fire ladder man, but of this one I had only seen his back. Stop it! Stop suffering from hallucinations, I told myself.

It was a sunny day but it was cool for the time of year. This man wore shorts and a short-sleeved polo shirt and he seemed to feel cold. Could this be my man? I got out of the car and casually made for the entrance. The stranger approached me and said, "I'm pleased to meet you, Monsieur de Jong! I'm Pierre de Fermat." He took off his dark glasses and offered his hand.

"Pleasure," I said. "Welcome to Goodland! It's good you could come."

"I would *not* have managed *not* to come! I'm so impressed by what you people pulled off!"

"Why were you so sure it was me right now?"

"Le tissue mondial, the world wide web, social networks, photos, et cetera," said de Fermat, his green eyes shining with delight.

"I also tried to find a photo of you in the net. But all I found were some pictures of the mathematician of the seventeenth century. I didn't succeed in finding your agency."

"Bien; au fond nous sommes une agance secret. It is not important that people know how Pierre de Fermat looks like. I only rove about in social networks under an assumed name and only to find out about others. Many are so pleased with themselves that they announce things that they should better keep to themselves."

"I'm not one of these I hope?"

"Well, with facebook, twitter etc. the yield was small. I only found your photo, a fake age statement and a hint at your important position … and that you are a fan of Antonia!"

Naturally I was more than embarrassed. "I don't take these things serious. Not many do I think. It's just fun. I hope that's all?"

"C'est tout, as far as virtual communities are concerned, yes."

"My God! What else?"

"You want a sample of the deduction skills of your detective? Well, you are thirty-three years old, a bachelor and heterosexual. You have never known your real parents but you think that your mother is still alive. You adore a wonderful girl who is twenty-three but as yet you haven't worked up the courage to tell her. You have legal training but haven't taken your degree … as yet."

"But …"

"Le Voilà! It is not the social media alone!"

"What else?" I managed to utter.

"You leave traces in the net even when you are made to believe that you don't. Par exemple prize competitions, price enquiries … all sorts of enquiries you make … in a nutshell, wherever you disclose something by filling in a form online you can never be sure that it won't be abused. There are people out there which collect everything and sell assorted data. It's a lucrative business!"

"Yes, I have been naïve. I don't even remember where I gave away all this. I thank you for the lesson Monsieur de

Fermat. But we are standing around in front of the hotel …
you must be cold. Have you checked out already? If not, I think
you should do so before we have lunch inside. I take it that you
stay in the castle?"

"Oui, oui, tout est prêt et réglé. I need only fetch my cof-
fers on wheels."

We went inside. In the reception area there were two large
trolley cases and one small one. They were quite heavy too.
We took them outside and put them into my car. For a moment I was thinking of going right back to Edelweiss so that de
Fermat could dress appropriately. We could then have lunch in
the Golden Egg or in one of the other eating places. But then
I thought better of it.

To conduct the first talks on more neutral grounds was perhaps preferable to Edelweiss. It was less likely here in Halfway
House that anybody else could break in on our conversation. I
told de Fermat what I thought and he agreed. He took a jersey
out of his small bag and a pair of light long trousers.

"I quickly put these on in les toilettes. I had been thinking
it was much warmer."

He spoke with a French accent and used French words
occasionally but I was agreeably surprised; he was not trying
to force French on me. And it pleased me how debonair he
was. If he was the one from the fire escape he was covering up
Oscar-worthy.

When we sat opposite one another in the public room, de
Fermat skimmed the menu unpretentiously and opted for a
small goulash with a roll. I was glad because in this way I was
also not tempted to eat too much. I took the same.

"So Goodland was not renamed after becoming

independent?" asked de Fermat.

"That's right. When the state was founded we had to opt under what name it should go. Goodland got the majority. Goodland was good enough for us. The name says it all, you see."

"You have to vote by ballot a lot now, yes?"

"Exactly, but that's the price of real democracy. Of course it will abate in the course of time. But right now a vast number of decisions have to be made."

"Are there changes to perceive already in everyday live?"

"Goodland as a state is only four and a half weeks old. The impact becomes only slowly noticeable. Our new currency is the Good. One Good corresponds to ten Euro. New banknotes and coins are already printed and coined. But you don't encounter them frequently. I think the European money will keep on circulating as long as the Euro lasts. For most Europeans we are only a transit or vacation country. They don't like to exchange."

"I paid my bill in Euro. I think they didn't even mention the Good. What else is new?"

"Well, the *luxury* tax when you buy a new car, which they only charge in Austria, nowhere else in the world, is off the table in Goodland. The people also decided that from January 2015 on tax on electrically powered cars will be halved and tax on conventional cars will be doubled. Plastic and aluminum wrappings for food have been strongly diminished already. School uniforms got a majority. Advertising space bookers must re-train since these big advertising surfaces are no longer allowed. We in Goodland don't fall for advertising anyway; and these giant placards only spoil the beautiful landscape of Sustainable. As from yesterday, logos on cigarette packets are no longer allowed. Everything will turn from crazy to normal now that mature consumers make the decisions. Political leaders almost inevitably pander to big business, why so, I wonder sometimes."

"Did you say Sustainable, tout à l'heure?"

"Did I? Sorry, this was a slip of the tongue; it's because Sustainable was one of the possible options. It was my favorite but Goodland won the race."

"This is what I had expected. Most people here are conservative, not only in their habits and values. I take it that you were a supporter of the idea of independence from the start, oui?"

"The answer is yes if by start you mean the day before the general election in Austria. This was five and a half weeks ago. Before this day, before Joseph Aybesford gave this interview, it just didn't seem to be a possible option. He asked the question: 'Shall we again vote for stupendous tax hikes?' Indeed, in Austria they are already discussing new taxes again. *Land of Taxes* it should say in the tiring Austrian national anthem instead of *Land of Mountains*. There are not mountains everywhere but taxes are. Only breathing is tax-free as yet."

"The taxes must be. The state needs money."

"There is a word like thrift. No individual can live beyond his or her means. The politicians display the grandiloquent demeanor like their predecessors in the monarchy one hundred years ago. To them, *thrift* is a foreign word; but *a new round of tax increases* is familiar vocabulary for these squanderers of national wealth. Politicians are already crying for a raise of their expense allowances. Among them are people who have never done decent work in their lives."

I paused. "I shouldn't get exited like this. Sorry for letting myself get carried away. That's not my problem anymore; anyway."

"Five and a half weeks ago Mrs. Xanda van Aanstryk died."

"Yes. Let's come down to business. My duties in the palace reach from the right insurance policy for every Aybesford family member to recruiting staff for the cafeteria. In short, I'm the factotum of the castle. Your client is the palace in the form of Gordon Aybesford. He wants to meet you at least once a day in order to stay current and discuss the case with you. You will get to know the Aybesford family this evening."

"Très bon."

"I'm also both the liaison officer and the provision officer, so to speak. You can approach me regarding all matters. Most people in the palace are sufficient fluent in English. If you want to interview folk outside it would be advantageous to take somebody native with you for the first contact, so that they come to trust you. I'm not going to impose my company on you. But if you want somebody to escort you, please tell me. If you need a car or a toothpick, please tell me."

"Très bien! Now that we talk shop perhaps you could just as well tell me of what nature your relationship to the deceased woman was?"

Although I had been expecting the question sooner or later I sat thunderstruck. I had not yet digested the event with Heidi and the fire escape. I decided to let out nothing for the moment. De Fermat did not seem to notice anything however. He looked as if he were interested in what a couple at a neighboring table was ordering. Or was he trying to lull me into a false sense of security? "There was no relation whatsoever. I only knew her from the screen, the way you get to know a television presenter."

"Did you ever talk to her?"

"No, never."

"Did you ever happen to see her in the street by chance?"

"I don't remember ever having seen her by chance." I knew it sounded not true and I felt how my opponent scrutinized my face and my body language.

"Do you know of anybody who could have wished her harm?"

"I haven't got a clue."

"Do you have any idea at all who might have poisoned her?"

"Not at all, monsieur."

"Do you know somebody who was acquainted with her?"

"No, I know of nobody."

"Are you also descended from aristocracy? Your name is it not a nom à particule? The *de* in your name is it not also a prédicat nobiliaire like in France."

Now I was certain that he was taking me for a ride. I tried to carry it off well and said, "De Jong is a Dutch name and it simply means the young one."

The waitress took the plates away and asked if we liked some mehlspeise. "We have freshly baked apfelstrudel, it's still warm," she said. "Pastry, pâtisserie, gâteau aux pommes" she added by way of explanation, smiling at de Fermat who had mumbled something in French. I ordered two apple strudels at the risk of de Fermat not liking it and two verlängerte. I expected M. de Fermat to ask what a verlängerter was but he seemingly had not grasped much. The waitress brought the pie and the coffee.

I was relieved when de Fermat spoke up again. "How far are the police?"

"As far as I know they are not even working seriously on the case. It's no business of the Goodland police because the woman was poisoned in Cyclamen City, which remained with Austria. The police there are making no progress as far as I know."

In the evening I introduced de Fermat to Gordon and his whole family, including Joseph and Aunt Agnes. In their private dining room we had dinner at the big dinner table and afterwards the chief, his wife Eleanor, their daughter Gloria, de Fermat and I sat together.

Gordon Aybesford said, "I'm glad matters are going to move now. On the very same day that suspicion was raised that Xanda van Aanstryk could have been murdered, rumors have surfaced that the palace might be involved. The police came and asked awkwardly around. We had to alibi one another, which is not satisfactory. Since the revolution, Goodland's papers let the question rest but this isn't satisfactory either. The fact that the calls for monarchy in Goodland are growing ever louder is a disservice. It gives Austrian newspapers reason to fuel the rumors."

"With your permission I would like to talk tête-à-tête to each member of your family and thereafter with the rest of all people who have business in the château," said de Fermat.

"You do just as you like. Today is Thursday. For next Monday, June 30, I've made an appointment with the Chief Detective Inspector of the Cyclamen City police, who is in charge of the case. At ten o'clock you'll meet her. Her name is Dalia Kalanda. I offered cooperation. I wonder what will come of it."

§8

The Forensic Doctor

Mrs. Dalia Kalanda had been pacing up and down her office for a while. Then she walked over to the balcony door, opened it and stepped outside. On the balcony she made deep breaths. Her bosom undulated in time with the breathing. The Detective Chief Inspector was in a dilemma.

She heaved a last deep sigh and betook herself back into her compartment. Should she accept Gordon Aybesford's offer to help with the van Aanstryk case? His intention is cooperation rather than help. And cooperation meant help from the police. She didn't want this sly French sleuth to get too nosy. If she let him scrutinize the file, he is sure to feel entitled to snoop about in the police station and in the whole building. They are like crab lice.

If the Aybesford's had something to do with the poisoning, why should they employ a private investigator? Are they trying to blur traces? Or was some member of the castle involved, and Gordon was so naïve not to assume it? When she had first met him, six weeks ago to the day it was, he had appeared to her like a romantic artist rather than a hard-nosed realist.

She could not hinder this French investigator from snooping

around. But to disclose the police file? Well, he needs not get everything! And it might be good to know what the snooper is up to! The pendulum swung in favor of Cooperation.

Looking up from her desk, she saw through the glass partition how Aybesford and his attendant were led in by the reception secretary. The female was about to usher them into a conference room. Not quite sure if this was right she cast a glance towards the DCI, who waved vigorously to bring them into her room. Kalanda welcomed Aybesford and the latter introduced Pierre de Fermat to her.

The name Fermat sounded familiar to her. This man was probably an investigator of some reputation. But she would not admit anything to the effect; she made no mention of it, anyhow. Also she did not want to admit right away that she had made up her mind to play along. When they had taken their seats she said therefore without much ado, "The case comes to nothing. We have followed up all leads but ended up in dead ends only. It doesn't make sense to carry on looking where there is nothing. If it was murder, after six weeks all traces are cold. We have no evidence that it was murder and there are no suspects left."

"As long as I do not read in the Austrian press that the case is cleared up, I cannot be satisfied. They want my father to run for President of Goodland. The state of Goodland cannot be satisfied as long as there is any uncertainty," said Gordon. "Consider this: if Monsieur de Fermat finds out the truth on his own, all the credit goes to him. But if you opt for cooperation, you can always claim that you did everything in order to solve the case."

Kalanda did not like Aybesford's talking about the truth

and credit. The pendulum swung against cooperation. She said, "I did everything in order to solve the case! Mrs. van Aanstryk died six weeks ago. A week after her demise, the detachment of Goodland came about. From this day on, Edelweiss was out of reach for the Austrian police. In this single week that we had at our disposal, we talked to everybody in the castle and to all possible friends and neighbors."

"Yes, you really did."

"The suspicions against the initial suspects could not be substantiated. We have nothing that would back up a request to Goodland for legal assistance. There remains a self-denunciation as a last resort for you."

"No need to get sarcastic, chief. On the other hand, it might be worth a consideration!"

"Those initial suspects who live on Austrian territory are also all cleared. We had five more weeks to question these. As I said before, we have run out of suspects."

"Or is it possible that there are people in Austria who are not really interested in shedding light upon the case?" said Gordon Aybesford.

That's enough! She thought; and aloud she said, "I'm sorry gentlemen. But I cannot make out the meaning of starting from scratch. And I do not have the manpower. We lost our best staff members to Goodland. Now if you'll kindly excuse me!"

But she had not reckoned with Fermat's suavity. His strong points besides his shrewd and observant intelligence were his sense of minute details, his presence of mind, his obstinacy and his sweet manners, if need be. He said, "One more minute, please, Madame Kalanda. Look here, your lack of manpower is the best reason for me to investigate on my own. I promise

I'm not going to pester your staff. I shall not take up a single minute of your precious time or anybody else's."

"So what do you want?"

"All that I would ask you for is the statements of the initial suspects. As is best-known to you, guilty people sometimes change their statements after a while or when asked by somebody else."

"There is something in what you say. And it is not only the guilty people who are prone to varying their testimonies." she said somewhat mollified. "OK, you can have the statements."

Turning towards Aybesford she said, "But Monsieur Fermat will not get a contract; that is to say, there will be no remuneration from our side. This is just an informal agreement under six eyes.

Nothing of the sort had been put into play, so Fermat and Aybesford looked at one another.

"What do you think about that?" the DCI said, fixing her gaze through her lenses on the two men, one after the other.

"Just as well," said Aybesford who hadn't expected more. "Monsieur Fermat is in my employ. All we want is the statements and perhaps the odd information now and then."

Dalia Kalanda pushed a button, and said "Dunstig!" and lifted her head and looked out into the cube farm.

She was about to press the button a second time when a man in her viewing direction was starting the process of getting up. When he stood eventually, lean and tall with curly blond hair and bespectacled, he looked as if he had swallowed a broomstick, so bolt-upright he appeared.

When he came slowly nearer and also later when he was inside the DCI's office and when they shook hands, he never turned his head. His nose looked at all times in the direction his trouser buttons looked. He was above thirty and had a big wart in the middle of his neck.

"Mr. Aybesford wants to make his own investigations concerning the van Aanstryk case," said Mrs. Kalanda. "Monsieur de Fermat here is conducting these private inquiries. We will hand over all statements made in the interviews. Nothing else! Have I made myself clear?"

"You did make yourself quite clear, ma'am, absolutely!" said Special Constable Dunstig. Turning to Fermat he asked "Are you Belgian?"

Aybesford and de Fermat laughed at the remark. The DCI looked embarrassed. As if she wanted to save Fermat an answer, she said quickly to Dunstig, "You will arrange a password-protected account for M. Fermat so that he has access to the statements online – all the statements of the initial suspects and other witnesses. Initiate it right away so that it is available as from tomorrow at the latest."

Facing Gordon Aybesford she said, "Nothing, but absolutely nothing that you find in the file must be disclosed to other parties. I hold you responsible. If Monsieur Fermat makes new findings he has to share them with us. Failure of doing so is abstraction of evidence. Also potential findings can be made public only upon consultation."

"Right!" said Aybesford, "I'm glad we came to an agreement, Chief Inspector."

"If you have any questions, do not hesitate to contact Special Constable Dunstig. Should he for once not be available you contact me, OK? You contact no other officers!"

When Aybesford pushed the Down button for the lift,

Pierre Fermat said, "I go down the stairs. I'm going to scout around a little more in the building; and I shall spend this afternoon in Cyclamen City."

"Good! As from tomorrow you must take a car from the car pool in Cowford. You can take my old Mazda Xedos that you so admired, if you like. She needs to be moved, anyway."

"Oh yes, that would be splendid, thank you. See you tonight!"

Pierre de Fermat roamed the building, scanning nameplates of departments and the people who worked in them. This was part of his endeavor to get into tune with the official building and its people. This was part of the way to put him in the mood for hunting. It was an irrational process; but it contained also the chance to encounter something interesting that might have a relation to the matter at hand.

In his young days he had lived, in an old castle. He had then taken pleasure in roaming it at night with a little pocket lamp and a couple of self-made false keys. There were many rooms which were full of old furniture, paintings and picture frames.

He rummaged, but he took nothing away except a book now and then. These were the only books at his disposal at the time, because his mother didn't own the castle, but was a tenant only. When he borrowed a book, he memorized the exact spot where he had found it. As soon as he had finished reading, he would return the book to its original, forsaken place.

The tingling sensation he conceived now in getting the scent of this new environment, brought back memories of his adventures in those bygone days.

He had now reached the basement. There was only artificial light. People bustled around. Nobody asked him what he was looking for. Should he be asked he would adopt his most foreign demeanor and announce in his French tinted English that he could not find the way out.

"… Frau Doktor …" he involuntarily overheard somebody say. He had not heard the rest, but Frau Doktor could be a physician.

He followed the woman in a haphazard way, keeping a few paces behind. Her brunette hair was rather short; a bob you could call it. She had on a white blouse and black jeans. Thirtyish, he thought. She was now entering a cafeteria or canteen. Quickly he was at her heels at the end of a short queue.

"Excusez-moi chèr Madame!" he said politely, touching her arm slightly.

"Ja, bitte?" she said with surprise, as she turned.

"Please tell me, must one buy a luncheon voucher first, or can you pay afterwards. I've never been here before."

When her astonishment had settled she became quite helpful: "I would give you a meal ticket but have only this one on me. For the set meals you can buy tickets in bulk at a reduced price. But you can buy what you take at the cashier after the serving counter."

"Thank you very much indeed!"

"You are welcome!"

Quickly Fermat fetched a tray, cutlery and a napkin, thereby loosing contact to his prey. But when he had paid for his meal he was pleased to see that she aimed for an unoccupied table. It seemed to him that she had even delayed her stride a little so that he could follow. "Do you mind?" he said, when he reached the table at which she now sat.

"Please take your seat!"

"May I introduce myself? My name is Fermat. Pierre de

Fermat. Ô; un moment, s'il vous plait! Mon porte-monnaie! I think I put my wallet on the counter," said Fermat very fast and sprang to his feet. He was all in a fluster.

When he had recovered his purse and sat down again, she said, "My name is Elisabeth Forster. I'm a forensic doctor. Aren't you the French gentleman whom the Aybesfords have employed? You are investigating the van Aanstryk case, aren't you?"

Flabbergasted, Pierre de Fermat said, "Gossip runs very fast within this building, vraiment."

The doctor guffawed, and then said, "I too live in Edelweiss; we are neighbors!"

"I see – Forster! yes of course. Are you Peter's spouse?"

"That's right."

"Enchanté. I'm pleased to meet you. You are one of those médecins intelligents one can see every afternoon on television de nos jours. There is no crime movie without a laid out corpse nowadays; and there is no corpse without a forensic doctor explaining in detail the cause of death."

"I'm not quite sure if you say this mockingly. But howsoever; many people think indeed that physicians are a cleverer sort of people. My husband is a mathematician. These are members of a really intelligent species. You should know – with your name! They work with abstract entities and concepts. And out of thin air they make definitions, assumptions and proofs. But the general public thinks they are mere masters of calculation."

"I don't share your opinion. No one in his right mind will cast doubt on the fact that there is no profession for which more brain power is required. But I think the man in the street cannot have any idea about what the everyday work of a mathematician is. Everybody who ever dipped into a lecture will know that it is not about calculations. We mere humans know no more about the work mathematicians do, then a frog at the stream bank knows about the universe."

"You must tell this to my mother's chiropodist. The other day she asked me, if my husband can find work in his profession, when computers do all the calculating. Stupid fool; it is the mathematicians who build the algorithms on which our world hinges; our part of the world, at least.

"Where is your husband employed?"

"He is an associate professor at the university here in Cyclamen."

"Both of you have jobs abroad now."

"Indeed. Who would have thought it! But the trip to work has not changed so far. However, at the beginning of next year, my husband will take up a professorship of Theoretical Physics in Cowford."

"He must be very capable," said Fermat, nodding appreciatively.

"Let me come back to my profession: when in a movie a forensic doctor opens a thorax or puts an organ onto a weighing device, this is deemed to be impressively awe-inspiring."

"But it requires a certain aptitude, isn't it?"

"Yes, indeed; but this aptitude was tested with the beginning students in Cowford. We had to hold and inspect dehydrated organs that were placed in the open abdominal cavity of dehydrated bodies. You also had to watch operations. And you were watched as you were watching. Those who did not pass these tests were singled out."

"There are people who cannot see blood or meat, not even

of les animaux, the animals."

"That's right. But even among the ones who don't mind handling raw meat of animals are many who faint, when seeing human blood."

"C'est ça; c'est irrationell, la race humaine."

"One could write a book, on the subject of irrationality of the humans. A striking example is ... no, we are eating."

"Don't let me disturb you. I'm not irrational. My mind can differentiate between my meal and the topic of conversation."

"But what I'm going to say is delicate!"

"Feu vert! Shoot!"

"Well, it's fitting the situation. We eat food that may be the cream of the crop. But when it has passed our clean, healthy, noble body, we find it disgusting."

Pierre de Fermat burst with laughter. "Totally irrational," he said.

"You are an exception; because only the mention of the topic causes nausea with most people."

"For me, a single-cell organism like a cotton thread is a marvel; not to mention a human body."

"It is overwhelming to hold a human heart in your hands. I often think if everybody would have to do this – once a year say – a lot more people would be aware what violence they do to their organs when they light their first cigarette in the morning or when they drink alcohol regularly."

"But it is not easy to get a place to study medicine at university, n'est-ce pas? You have to do difficult theoretical admission exams and must pass with high grades?"

"Yes, this is because training places for doctors at university are expensive and therefore limited. With admission examinations one tries to prevent self-important imbeciles from taking talented students the place to study. Training places in mathematics are far less expensive. But only the most gifted ones make a start; and still only a few attain the end of the road. I know what I am talking about. I gave it a try myself. This was how I met my husband Peter."

The longer he talked to her the more he was impressed by her way of speaking. She was very precise in her way to express herself. She made no attempt at fishing for applause for her achievements.

"May I ask how it is that you tend to deal with dead people rather than with living ones?"

"I have been and still am fascinated by the chemical and physical processes in the human body. You can't study these in a living person. And there is a cynical side to it as well. I despise a big subset of humanity, the greedy and the stupid. The two often go hand in hand. My husband would express it mathematically, 'The stupid are not necessarily greedy but the greedy are always stupid.' We belong to a circle that is concerned with the growth of greed in the world."

"Greed and stupidity are part of my métier. I've been a policeman earlier and am a private investigator now. Greed is often one of the motives for a crime; another one being passion. And most criminals are stupid because they do not consider the consequences of their deeds. Almost all get caught in the end, when they think themselves clever and save."

"I admire you for your campaigning for justice."

Pierre de Fermat had his counterpart now in the fitting mood, he thought. He raised his forefinger slightly, hinting at discretion. "I come from a visit to the Detective Chief

Inspector Kalanda. I'm not supposed to talk about it. But she told me everything, and I've got access to the file."

"Everything? The two poisons?"

Fermat gambled. "Yes. Prussic acid wasn't it and ... I forget. I must look in the file."

"The nicotine before noon was not lethal; only the Hydrogen cyanide in the evening." Dr. Elisabeth Forster contributed helpfully. "But I mustn't talk shop either."

"If somebody asks me, I'll deny point-blank that we were talking a single word about the case," said Fermat.

"OK, I too will admit nothing," she said and distorted her full lips in a grimace. "Oh, the bloody fool is coming," she uttered almost inaudibly.

Instinctively Fermat asked: "Dunstig?"

"Yes! How can you possibly guess? But he hasn't seen us yet!" said Elisabeth Forster, who sat facing the entrance of the canteen.

"I better go now. Au revoir! Better he does not see us together. You have been very friendly; and interesting to talk to." He left, having eaten only a little. But he hadn't been hungry, anyway.

§9
The Sailor at the Edge of Town

Pierre de Fermat stepped out of the official building and halted. He looked about, left and right, in search of a bookshop or a news dealer where he could buy a map of Cyclamen City. Seeing nothing of the sort he decided to walk towards the central station. He knew the direction but could not think how far it was.

He always took pleasure in exploring a town by making use of public means of transport. As he walked he became aware that his brain was in the process of multitasking, or rather in the act of whirling about impressions and ideas haphazardly. This state of mind, he thought, was appropriate when you hit the pillow; In your sleep the brain would sort your thoughts and bring about ideas, fresh thoughts and sometimes solutions. In the daytime you have to make an effort to concentrate on a single item at a time.

Well, in the first place, why was the Detective Chief Inspector cooperating only unwillingly and not fully? Whom was she shielding or thought she was shielding? These questions would make it necessary to look fully into her life. This could be quite a task in itself, although he did not think that she had much of a private life. Or had she? I can always investigate her living environment later, should everything else fail, he thought.

Secondly, this was a piece of good luck – the encounter with the forensic doctor. Two different poisons; this was the first time he had heard about it. And he had read a lot about the case in different newspapers. Also in the discussions with the people in Edelweiss, nobody had mentioned this fact.

Was it a fact at all? Had Doctor Forster been probing him? She is a smart one, that's for sure. But why should she play a game with him? Or was it really something that the Detective Chief Inspector was trying to hush up at all cost? I must leave this to the gray matter to elaborate on it in my sleep. The subconscious perceives more than the conscious. Thus were Fermat's reflections.

After walking for about ten minutes he spotted a newspaper kiosk on the other side of the road. He went over and bought a city map. He spread it on a free table of a sidewalk café nearby. He fished for his small notepad and consulted it for the addresses of Xanda van Aanstryk and her parents.

To his utter astonishment he saw on the map that they had lived at close range to one another; a few blocks distant only, at the southern edge of town. It was too far off for walking, he decided. On the other hand, he registered that he was no longer far from the central station. There was also a bus depot next to it. He would take a city bus.

Two waitresses were chatting inside the café but they hadn't spotted him yet. Just as well. He folded his map and walked on. When he had come to the bus terminal he studied the timetables and consulted the map again and decided to take the tramway number sixteen. Its final stop was quite near the van Aanstryks' house.

After about half an hour's drive the loudspeaker announced, "Solar Pasture Center! This is the last stop but one." It's the station next to Xanda's flat, Pierre Fermat thought. Everybody got out. He was the only passenger left.

The streetcar moved on again and immediately the loudspeaker informed: "Wood Road! last stop; all out!" Fermat got off and watched the tram disappear into the woods. Was there a turnaround loop? Indeed! The tram reappeared in a short space of time. This filled him with a childish pleasure.

He turned around and started to walk into Wood Road. The first villa on the left was Number 1, the van Aanstryks' home. A house after the fashion he had seen so many in Holland, only bigger. He would pay a visit to the house later. Maybe not until tomorrow; it was probably a better idea, to visit them in the company of an interpreter.

For the moment he wanted to reconnoiter the surroundings. There was a row of about ten single-family homes built along the edge of the wood on the left. You could tell from afar by the shrubbery in the front gardens that they have been inhabited for quite some time. On the right, when he walked on, was a town house complex. The homes seemed freshly occupied; before the front doors were still gravel paths.

Behind the line of houses was a huge area with buildings under construction, the whole lot blocks of flats. When he came to the end of the row of town houses, Solar Pasture Street entered on the right. He turned into this access road. It led into the city. On his left as he went was a large maize field and subsequently were four apartment buildings, arranged in a square. The arrangement of the four blocks was called The Avril Court.

On the right, just opposite Avril Court was a shopping mall, named Solar Pasture Center. Behind the center was the streetcar stop at which all passengers had got out except him. The first block after the maize field was Avril 2, the address of Xanda's freehold flat. Avril 2, together with the three other blocks arranged in a quadrangle, shaped a sort of inner courtyard, although the buildings were not interconnected.

With the exception of Avril 3, all frontdoors gave onto the inner square. There were access-roads and parking lots. The kernel of the square was a park with a lawn, footpaths, birches, a children's playground. There were also benches, distributed at irregular intervals. Fermat wandered alongside the blocks. He found the nameplate which said *van Aanstryk* on one of the upper doorbells of Avril 2.

There was not much coming and going. He stood for a minute before the front door, which was locked. Thereafter he continued his round. In the playground were some ten children. On one of the benches sat three women in conversation with one another. On a bench near the playground sat an older man with a white beard, glasses and a sailor's cap. He held his right arm protectively over a big bulking plastic bag which was stuck between the armrest of the bench and the man's hip. On top of the bag was an umbrella.

Having finished his round, Pierre de Fermat approached the bench with the man on it. So as not to alarm the occupant, he sat down close to the left-hand armrest but not before asking the man's permission with a friendly gesticulation. The man seemed to be an odd fellow and Fermat didn't want to blurt right away. But it was the man who started to talk, "Nev'r see yar before round heere."

"I'm a stranger here," Fermat said in English.

"Where do you come from?" asked the other; to Fermat's surprise also in English.

Fermat's surprise must have shown because the other felt compelled to explain, "All my working life I was a sailor. I grew up in our farm house that was exactly over there." He pointed with his umbrella towards one of the apartment blocks. "Only one of us brothers could get the farm. Since childhood I had felt the urge to go to sea. So one day I bought a one way ticket to Rotterdam and shipped on board a freighter."

"You spent your whole working life at sea?" asked Fermat, and genuine astonishment showed in his face.

"Aye! When on leave I visited regularly here. And when retirement age came, I somehow was drawn back to my roots as I had been drawn to the sea in my younger days. People think that I've seen the world, when in reality I have only seen a lot of water." He chuckled.

Fermat nodded approvingly.

"Well, I've also seen many a seaport town of course but not too many sailors' pubs. I have a flat in the very same block that stands on our erstwhile grounds." Again he pointed with his umbrella towards the block. "This block and neighboring Avril 2 were the first two to be erected. The block parallel to the road and the one nearest to the city were built two years later."

"You are lucky; you have this park so near your abode."

"Aye! I need the open air. It is my elixir of life. Four hours a day I act as a voluntary Children's playground attendant; two hours in midmorning, two hours in the afternoon. Have you come on account of Xanda van Aanstryk's demise?"

I have been closely monitored, Fermat thought. He decided that the other was not as odd a fellow as he had meant him to be. And luckily he was rather talkative. His umbrella possibly served him as a walking aid. He owed him two answers now already.

He decided on letting the cat out of the bag: "My name's Fermat. I'm a French investigator. I'm commissioned by the Aybesford family. They want to elucidate the mystery surrounding the death of Mrs. van Aanstryk."

"Ah, I thought as much! Xanda! I knew her from an early age. Her parents, Laurens and Marike van Aanstryk immigrated from the Netherlands because Laurens had developed a phobia to live in the polder below sea level. When they arrived I had been a Jack Tar for some years and I knew already a few scraps of Dutch. When on leave I went to see them every time."

"Did they bring Xanda with them?"

"No, no. She was born here. When they came, Sheep Pasture was quite a secluded hamlet. The city did begin to encroach only twenty years later. Eventually Sheep Pasture was incorporated and is now an urban district of Cyclamen City. They renamed Sheep Pasture to Solar Pasture and every roof of every building must be fitted with photovoltaic panels.

Besides my parents' little farmhouse there were three other farmhouses and two cottages. The van Aanstryks bought the farm house at the edge of the forest, over there." He pointed with the umbrella. "They had a try in farming, but soon started a market garden and imported also flowers from Holland.

Xanda was their first child."

"Did they have more children?"

"Yes, they had, but they all died. There was another daughter, and two sons. So much the more they loved and adored Xanda."

"Is Xanda's flat at present unoccupied? Do you know?"

"The son, Titus, still lives at home. But since the incident I've scarcely seen him. He surely stays with his grandparents. He has done so before his mother died; most of the time, anyway. Maybe he will come back later, and make the flat his place of abode; after a while, when he and his grandparents have got over the tragedy a little.

Poor chap. When he was a schoolboy he lost his father in an accident. This has unhinged him a little; that's what people say, anyhow. If there was foul play with his mother's death, I wouldn't preclude putting it down to him, poor fellow." He seized his umbrella and got up quickly.

Unnoticed by Fermat a little black dog had approached the sand pit. One of the little children offered it a portion of sand on a little red plastic shovel. But the attendant pointed his umbrella at the dog and opened and closed the device a few times rapidly. Upon which the dog, terrified, went on the run.

"They have no business in the children's playground," the sailor explained, sitting down again. "They soil the sand and the lawn, if you let them."

"Tell me Mr. ..."

"My name is Max Siegenthaler. Call me Max."

"My name is Pierre. Tell me, Max, what makes you think that the son Titus is capable of poisoning his mother?"

"All I said is that I wouldn't rule him out. Nearly

everybody is capable of everything when driven by circumstances. And for a deranged person circumstances, at times, may look distorted."

"I think you have also met with your share of odd persons in your life. Tell me, turned your seagoing life as romantic as you had imagined it?"

"Oh, it was not a bee that somebody or something had put into my bonnet, if that is what you mean. I never had a sense of romanticism. I was used to working hard on the farm. When I first got to sea, living on a ship was a little like living on a farm, only better; because you had your free time for resting and reading.

Almost everything I know about the world I know not from the sea journeys but from the books I read during these journeys. And you need not care about board and lodging. And if you don't throw your money around at the ports, you can save handsomely." He patted his fat plastic bag and looked impishly at Fermat.

"You can't be serious!"

Max laughed, "These are only old clothes. As soon as Miss Solder comes to take over here, I'll bring these over to the charity collection bin at the street car stop."

"I can take it when I go back!"

"Thank you! But I will go with you. There is a collecting point behind the mall too, by the way. But man needs exercise! My motto."

"Exercise for your body as well as for your brain," agreed Pierre de Fermat. "This Titus, what does he do for a living?" asked Fermat after a while.

"He works in the municipal garden centre. You see, years

ago his grandparents closed their business when they were offered to manage the city owned garden center. They negotiated with the city administration a rededication of their business property into building land.

Then they partitioned it into building lots and sold these. The row of villas over there edging the wood is the result of this lucrative business. They had also pulled down their old ramshackle farmhouse and built themselves a modern comfortable house after the Dutch fashion with clinker facade."

"Ah, and Titus trained as a gardener with his grandparents?"

"Exactly! He is now roughly twenty-seven and it seems that he is very happy and does not aspire after more."

"And Selissa, Xanda's daughter? What does she live on?"

"She is two years younger. She did not seem affected by her father's death; probably because she was younger and not so extremely attached to him like Titus was."

"But what's she doing?"

"She lives in a flat on the other side of town. She trained as a visual merchandiser. But the last I heard was that her grandparents helped her to buy a well-established second-hand shop in the city. As far as I know she is single too."

"Did Mrs. van Aanstryk adopt her maiden name again after her husband's death?"

"No, she was adamant to keep her name after her marriage. On the contrary, her husband assumed the name van Aanstryk. I think she insisted that her children should have her maiden name."

"Isn't that unusual?"

"It is unusual around here; and it was more so, back then."

"Did she wear the breeches?"

"Rather. When they went together in the car, it was always she who steered. She had also the reputation of being a strict teacher, whereas Manfred, her husband, was an indulgent fellow, always friendly and helpful."

"She was a teacher?"

"Yes, she had trained as a teacher; she was very good at languages."

"How is it that she became a television presenter?"

At that moment Miss Solder appeared in order to take over the guard. Obviously she was a student who had a stack of books on her arm. The two men rose and began walking towards the woods.

"There was a casting one day and she attended. Evidently she performed satisfactorily at the audition because she got the job. There were rumors that there were occurrences of some kind at the school which induced her to look for something else to do. But this was long ago. She worked only a few years as a teacher."

Fermat lifted up Max's bag and was carrying it for him. They walked quietly for a while.

"Her husband Manfred came also from one of the farmhouses that are now all dragged," said Max and pointed with his umbrella back at the shopping mall.

"Did he run the farm?"

"They lived on the farm for a few years, I think. Manfred had a try at cultivating the soil besides sheep farming for a short period. But when he found work with the railway as a shunting worker he leased the pasturage as well as the acreage. Working for the railway gave him more security and more time for family life. Tragically this was where he found his death. Xanda inherited the house with the land. When the settlement activity reached the hamlet, she waited with the selling of the farm until she was threatened with expropriation."

"So they grew up adjacent to one another?"

"That's right! They grew up next door to one another, so to speak. Manfred was three years her senior."

"When did you say this Manfred died? Fifteen years ago?"

"Did I say? Don't even remember. But if I had to say a number, I would say twenty years is closer to the truth, because Titus was in his first years of school."

"Have there been no other acquaintances, other men, I mean, since?"

"Well, I can't say if she had affairs, if this is what you want to know; because I've noticed nothing. But there was a man, until about ten years ago. He came almost every day after work and left in the morning. They spent every free weekend together too and they went on holiday together. He had also children, but they were of age, it was gossiped. I never saw them. Everybody said how lucky she was to have found a worthy partner. It went on for a couple of years. But one day it was over."

"Do you happen to know his name?"

"Nope!"

"What license plate was on his car?"

"I can't help you with a license plate number. It is too long ago and it didn't really concern me. One couldn't help noticing, however. Wait! Registered in the Alfalfa region, this comes into my mind now. Yes! He used to live near Alfalfa, in Syget, I'm sure. But her parents will surely know." He pointed with his umbrella at the van Aanstryks' house which they were passing right now. "Xanda and her lover spent a lot of time at this place here, too. I can help you with interpreting. No problem."

"I'm going to see them soon, but not today. Thanks anyhow."

When after a few more strides they had reached the stop, a tram was waiting. Departure in 2 minutes it read on the electronic information board! The 3 had just changed to 2. Fermat shoved Max's plastic bag into the sheet-metal container. Crossing the rails and turning round, he said: "good bye Max! You have been very nice. I've loved talking to you. Thanks for your assistance!"

"No problem, Pierre! You are welcome always. You know where you can find me, if you need further help."

Fermat inserted a ten euro bank note into the ticket machine, pulled a ticket, collected his change and climbed into the tramway.

§10

The Conscience-Stricken One

Pierre de Fermat was on his journey back from the municipal boundary into town. Almost without thinking he got off the tram, when he caught sight of the Cyclamen regional broadcasting studio.

He entered by the portal. Seeing that the front desk was not occupied, he looked for an information board. The uppermost entry was no longer Mr. Wiesel, but Mr. Berraneck. He found also the names Mr. Langer and Miss Chevrolet. Fermat went up the stairs onto the first floor and found Mr. Berraneck's office.

An arrow showed him to enter next door. Unflinchingly he entered the secretary's office. Obviously the woman did not bother to tint her hair. Or she did it very skillfully. At any rate, her coiffure was a piece of art in salt and pepper; and very elegantly styled. The woman was very sure of herself. Fermat was impressed. So much so, that he was forced to consider what to say and how to begin.

He beheld her questioning look and said: "Excusez-moi chère Madame!" Opening thus he knew to score by causing astonishment. "My name is Fermat. I know I should have made an appointment."

The director's door had been half open. It opened now fully and a little bald man holding a big pipe in his left hand appeared in the frame. He offered Fermat his right hand and said: "My name is Berraneck. Pleased to meet you, Monsieur de Fermat. I've heard that you are helping the Aybesfords, who of course are anxious to clear their name.

I'm very glad in fact that you have dropped by. Maybe we could do an interview with you. When everything is settled and cleared up, I mean. You have already met Mrs. Sigmund. Come along please, M. Fermat. No, leave the door open. Mrs. Sigmund does not mind my smoking. But perhaps you do?"

"No, not at all," lied Fermat.

"You may be surprised that Mr. Wiesel had to pack while I, the culprit, have succeeded him. I would have understood had they put me in the repository. Wiesel would have exiled me, had he remained head of the studio. I'm sure you would like to hear what happened on Saturday 17 May 2014, M. Fermat?"

"Oh yes! Your way of looking at the day's happenings, s'il vous plaît, Mr. Berraneck." Fermat was very pleased that Berraneck made no fuss, but on the contrary, seemed eager to help. Mrs. Sigmund served them coffee. Then she came again and put a carafe of water and glasses on the table before them.

"At eight o'clock Mr. Langer left with the technical staff for Edelweiss. Mrs. van Aanstryk and Miss Chevrolet who shared an office were both present at eight. I know because I entered their room at that time and asked Xanda when she would leave and by what means. She said that she would leave at ten by her private car and that with an hour for twenty-two miles she would be on the save side on a Saturday morning;

now with the new tunnel bypassing Cowford. The live interview was to start at eleven."

"Did she seem different when you spoke to her? Did she strike you as being in a certain mood? Was there a departure from conventions in any way?"

"I didn't notice anything unusual at the time and I can't think of anything in retrospect. But half an hour later she came to me and said that not under any circumstance can she go to Edelweiss. I didn't at once conceive the gravity of her condition and tried to persuade her not to let me down at the last moment. I have nobody to replace you quickly, I said. Whereupon she became unusually impatient and snapped that I can do the interview myself."

Fermat answered with a nod.

"Then I saw that she was seriously ill and offered to call a doctor or an ambulance. She would hear nothing of the sort and said that all she did want was to go home and lie down. So I said, wait a minute, I can't let you drive on your own; I'll bring you home. You leave your car here! Then I went quickly to tell Miss Chevrolet to prepare for the interview."

Fermat nodded.

"Thereafter I went back to my office and fetched my keys. When I was ready to take her home, I was too late; she had already left. Her car was nowhere to be seen in the parking lot. This is all I can tell you about the happenings this morning as far as Mrs. van Aanstryk is concerned. I blame myself every day since, for not having done more."

"Je comprends."

"So I turned back and I made for Louise's office. At that moment I saw her come out of *my* room. She was flustered and she told me that she did not want to substitute Xanda van Aanstryk. When I said 'let's talk about it without ruffle and excitement,' she became nearly hysterical and refused point-blank." He looked at his pipe which lay in the tray and had become cold. Then he looked at Fermat.

Fermat nodded his comprehension. He did not want to interrupt the train of thought of his counterpart. An opponent that talkes is every investigator's dream.

"I went into my office to calm down. What is the worst possible case? I thought to myself. I was not thinking about Xanda's sickness by this time. This thought was present at the back of my mind though. The worst case regarding the interview was that it would not take place; cancelled due to sickness. Period.

Obviously Xanda had told nobody about an agreement with Joseph Aybesford. That there was an agreement came out later. That's at least what he said, so as to make plausible that it had been not in his interest that Xanda be replaced by somebody less experienced." He drew a deep breath and looked at his pipe but he withstood.

"So I went into Louise Chevrolet's office and said: 'Okay! You need not do the interview! But listen to me; only think for a minute: what is the worst possible case that could arise if you *did* do the interview?' In the meantime she had also calmed down and she said, 'The worst possible case would be that I don't know what to say, that I make a fool of myself. Why can't *you* do it?'

I said, 'Look, Aybesford is nearly ninety, I'm nearing sixty. Do you think people like to see two old men? No, they like to see a beautiful young lady interviewing a man of reputation.'

I let that first sink in and then I continued: 'If it does not go as smoothly as you wish then it's not so serious at all. On a Saturday morning very few people are watching TV. When on the other hand you perform nicely, you can have another chance next time.'"

Both men drank from their glasses. They looked at one another and then out of the window, engrossed in thought.

"Louise had been over to Edelweiss last summer when we shot scenes in the castle, the parks and other odd places. So in a way she was familiar with the matter. I recapitulated historic dates and other facts with her. Louise made notes on a piece of paper. It was a quarter past ten, when somebody drove her out to Edelweiss. We thought it better that she drives not on her own so that she could concentrate on the task ahead."

Pierre de Fermat nodded his head.

"In the belief that I had improved on the worst case scenario, I went into this office here to tell Wiesel. He was not in however. I learned later that he had seen the broadcast by chance in a department store while shopping. Towards eleven I went to the studio in order to follow the performance. When I saw her fall in a faint, I nearly got a fit myself."

"This is the first time I hear that it was that serious. A sudden feeling of faintness is not unusual under stress. Some people think even that she did it on purpose so as to get out of the predicament. I hope mademoiselle Chevrolet could ride out the crisis. Is she alright now?"

"Even if she did it purposefully, you don't do such a thing at a whim. She was clearly traumatized. But, sadly, she wouldn't hear of seeking medical advice. She insisted even on coming back to the studio. So on the evening of this day I suggested to her to read the news on the radio. I figured that it would help her to overcome the trauma.

I think this is what she felt too, because on the next morning she came in early and was eager to read the news on the radio again. But she back-pedaled when she heard that she had to announce the loss of Xanda van Aanstryk. She could not bring herself to appear on TV since. So eventually I insisted that she gets medical help. In the hospital they have suggested that she visits a special clinic."

"Oh, ok."

"Therefore I have decided to arrange hospitalization in a sanatorium for her. For about two weeks she is now in Dafins for deep-sleep treatment. She is on my conscience, Xanda is on my conscience and the secession of Goodland is on my conscience. Tell me, Monsieur Fermat, why have I got a promotion instead of solitary confinement?"

"You should take your drops, Mister Berraneck," said Mrs. Sigmund, putting a little cup with a clear liquid in his hand.

"You are not to blame for anything, least of all for Mrs. van Aanstryk's death," said Fermat. "The unlucky thing was that she had not told you about the agreement with Aybesford. Has anybody aired any idea how she might have been poisoned? Were there rumors in circulation at the time?"

"On election Sunday when she was found dead in her bed, the coffee cups had long been out of the automatic dishwasher; there are so many every day," said Mrs. Sigmund. "And she had no enemies," she said as an afterthought.

"When the police came on Wednesday, they found no trace of anything suspicious. If the coffee had been tampered with, it could also have been meant for somebody else. For Louise for example," said Mr. Berraneck, "although she has no enemies either. But then, who has had enemies before the events? Now I have many people against me and get threats by phone and by mail."

"There was ill feeling between Louise and Gloria Aybesford last summer," said Mrs. Sigmund. "Gloria had been in an on off relationship with Donald W., the disc jockey and singer. She had pulled the plug finally, but not for the first time. So it was perhaps not so final. In any case when Louise was seen in public whit this Donald, Gloria was said to have affronted Louise, or even threatened her. But these are only rumors I heard at the time.

"I'll never forget what Xanda said on the day Louise did her first live performance," said Mr. Berraneck.

"Oh yah," said Mrs. Sigmund. "She said 'I am not going to live beyond fifty. I'm going to jump off the city tower or the river dam before that.' But then, she was in a bad mood this day because they had spoilt her hairdo or the color of her hair at the hairdresser's."

"It can mean something this," said Fermat. "Did she make such remarks more often? Was she indicative of suicide tendencies on other occasions too?"

Both Mr. Berraneck and Mrs. Sigmund shook their heads.

"Is there somebody in the studio with whom she was close friends?"

"You may think that we are all a big family. But we are not. Actually nobody here in the studio is close friends with anybody of his colleagues," said Mrs. Sigmund. "On certain occasions somebody buys his colleagues a drink and then we sit together and celebrate a little and talk also about private matters."

Fermat nodded.

"As far as I know she never went out in recent years. She lived out of the world but spent a lot of time with her parents. It was different when she had a partner. But about ten years ago there came a day when it was all over abruptly. Malicious tongues say that she was penny-pinching and had nobody to pay the bill after they had separated."

"All things considered she was very cooperative and reliable, and an eloquent speaker," said Mr. Berraneck. "The thought is incredible that somebody wanted to kill her. Then I would rather guess suicide. I think she was sometimes depressed; but she knew how to cover her problems and to pretend festive, merry feelings."

"Now that we talk about her it dawns on me that she might have been jealous of Louise Chevrolet and every other younger colleague that was recruited," said Mrs. Sigmund. "As Mr. Berraneck just said, she was expert in covering up her true emotions."

When Fermat left the broadcasting studio he was exhausted and felt a ravenous appetite. He took a cab to Aybesford House in Cowford.

The caretaker was informed that Fermat would fetch the Mazda Xedos. "She is filled up. Be careful, she's an old lady, not a Ferrari."

"Don't worry! I have in mind to slide along and listen to the music of the six-cylinder engine."

Driving from Aybesford House to Edelweiss, Fermat was looking forward to having a decent dinner. He was waiting in the turn-off lane in order to turn into the grounds of Halfway

House. He noticed at the last moment, that the driver coming in the opposite direction, for which he had been waiting to pass, was Jacquy de Jong.

Next morning at breakfast in the Golden Egg, Fermat waited for Jacquy to comment on the encounter, however Jacquy let not slip out a word; neither did Fermat. "If you are free this morning, would you accompany me to the van Aanstryks? I don't think they know much English," said Fermat.

"Why do you think so?"

"I met a neighbor of theirs yesterday. His name is Max Siegenthaler. He is roughly their age and knows them since they arrived from the Netherlands in their youth. They were quite young and had no higher education. They have been working hard. There will not have been time for studying something else than what was essential for their daily needs. In the beginning they had to struggle with the German language, no doubt, and with all the formalities for public authorities. They bought an old farm and started their own business."

"Why did you not ask this neighbor to help with interpreting?"

"Oh, he nearly urged me to let him help me. But everybody has their secrets that they rather share with a stranger than with a neighbor. I was also not in the mood to interview them right after speaking to Max. I wanted to give myself time to think of the right questions to ask."

"Fine! That's alright with me. It gives me an opportunity to speak Dutch. I came to Edelweiss at the age of three, so I forgot every word of Dutch that I may ever have known before I turned up here. When I was about five, having this Dutch name and coming from the Netherlands, it began to appeale to me to learn the language properly. Joseph Aybesford obtained Dutch children's books and gave them to me, and later school books.

When in primary school we started to learn how to write, I learned every word that we learned in German also in Dutch. It pleased me when I found out, that the relationship of Dutch to German was so very close. Joseph Aybesford started to talk in Dutch to me and so did Claas." He made a movement with his head indicating the latter. "He speaks Afrikaans. This is what Dutch developed to in South Africa since the sixteenth century. It's sort of less sophisticated."

"Hé oui!"

"Infected by my hobby, my mother also started to read Dutch magazines and even books. You know Agnes, my adoptive mother. She is also linguistically gifted. At the age of eleven she got driven out after the war by the Czechs for being Sudeten German."

"What a guilt; were she expelled on her own?"

"No, not even the Czechs are as brutal as that, I hope. No, she got expelled together with her mother ... and her sister Barbara, whom Joseph Aybesford married later on. But they had to leave all their possessions behind. Her father was missing in Russia after the war, they thought. But he had fled to Austria already. With the help of the Austrian Red Cross they found him soon. So they became reunited in Edelweiss Castle."

Fermat was surprised at the enthusiasm and the talkativeness Jacquy displayed. He had expected him to shy away from meeting the van Aanstryks. He had to reconsider his theory, that Jacquy knew more than he admitted. All of a sudden and for the first time Jacquy gave the impression that he too was interested in solving the riddle of Xanda van Aanstryk's death.

He was also amazed at Jacquy's claiming a good command

of Dutch. He had expected him to interpret in German. "Très bien. We can take the Mazda Xedos. Mr. Aybesford placed it at my disposal. The van Aanstryks live on the fringe of Cyclamen City at the final stop of the tramway number sixteen. Xanda's flat is only a few strides away."

"Have you made an appointment?"

"No, I want to avoid making it look too official. To tell you the truth, it is mainly my bad German that prevented me from making an appointment. But you could call them now and explain empathetically what it is about; that the Aybesford family would solicit their cooperation.

I presume this neighbor Max has notified them about my coming visit. Maybe they saw us go by together." Saying this, Fermat pulled a scrap of paper from his breast pocket and gave it to Jacquy with the words, "Here is the number."

According to the unwritten law never to use your mobile in the Golden Egg – but his good manners would have forbidden it anyway to start a phone call in a public place – Jacquy went out nonchalantly. It was Fermat's sixth day in Edelweiss and never before had he encountered Jacquy so relaxed and agreeable.

Jacquy, when he came back, was now even more exuberant; he said hilariously: "I spoke to Mrs. van Aanstryk. She thought at first somebody from Holland was on the phone. We can come anytime. I said we would come in about an hour. So we can leave straight away."

§11

Xanda van Aanstryk's Flat

The Mazda Xedos glided into the driveway of Wood Road Number 1. The impressive clinker brick house formed a contrast to the other whitewashed houses in this middle-class neighborhood. The front door was wide open and so was the backdoor.

So Pierre de Fermat and Jacquy de Jong, when they disembarked, could look right through the hall of the house into the backyard. They could even catch a glimpse of the stone wall at the garden's end and of the forest behind it.

Laurens and Marike van Aanstryk came out at the front door and bade them welcome. When Fermat and Jacquy had expressed their sympathy at the death of the hosts' daughter, Marike led them straightaway along the hallway to the back door. Laurens went to lock the gate of the driveway.

It was a Tuesday. So Fermat had expected Mr. and Mrs. van Aanstryk to look like gardeners or farm workers – in work clothes. But when coming face to face with them, they appeared like pensioned civil servants in their Sunday best. Had they changed clothes for the occasion?

In the backyard they were led to a timber summer house and onto the porch of it. There was a big garden table with comfortable seating accommodation.

They all took their seats and some minutes passed with lively gibberish, Mejnheer en Mevrouw, et cetera.

"Monsieur de Fermat may forgive us," said Marike. "Laurens and I always speak Dutch between ourselves. It's too late to do anything about it. We simply can't bring ourselves to speak German when we are on our own. And we love it to speak to someone with whom we can talk away in the fashion our beaks have grown."

Clearly the van Aanstryks, and even more so Jacquy, were pleased to meet somebody in Cyclamen City with whom they could have a chat in Dutch.

Fermat didn't mind being left out; he looked about. He had imagined the place behind the house, next to the forest edge, to look like a farm place with vegetable beds. But there were only a few little vegetable patches alongside the wall that separated the property from the forest.

A large section of the backyard in front of the patio was occupied by an alpine miniature landscape which served as setting for a model railway layout. A train was climbing a mountain in wide serpentines, passing through tunnels and over viaducts.

When it had reached the maximum altitude of the track layout, it disappeared into a long tunnel and was not to be seen for quite a while. When it emerged eventually, far away from where it had gone in, it got to a train station. In the station it was in wait until an oncoming train arrived.

Seeing that the installation attracted interest, Mr. van Aanstryk said to Fermat proudly, "I activated it before you arrived. It's the mutual work of our grandson Titus and me."

Jacquy had heard what Laurens had said; he translated for Fermat and a little chatter ensued, spiced with astonishment and admiration. While this was going on, Mrs. van Aanstryk went into the house, saying something which Jacquy again interpreted: "They have their cacao every morning. If we want something else, we must say so."

Fermat was pleased with the relaxed atmosphere and did not utter special wishes. By the time the hausfrau had reappeared with a tray, and everybody had filled their mug, the conversation turned to the question of how this disaster could have possibly happened.

Fermat asked no questions but listened compassionately to the grief that soon began to well forth the parents' souls. He had prepared Jacquy beforehand not to interpret continually so as not to hamper their readiness to talk. Better to give the gist of what was said afterwards.

"You must understand. It is only six weeks. Our sorrow is still fresh," said Laurens with shakily voice.

"That can easily be conceived," said Fermat, who had caught the words. "Her whole life she lived with you or near you, n'est-ce pas, is it not so?"

"In the forty-nine years which were given to Xandy on this god's soil, we saw each other every day. Except on the rare occasions when she was on a school excursion in the first years of her marriage; or on a seminar later on," said Marike. "On some days she came two or three times over here. On the evenings when she was not on duty in the broadcasting center she was also with us."

Pierre de Fermat's air gave the impression of eager interest. And he perceived most of what was being said.

"She was born in this place when we still lived in the old little farmhouse. After her wedding they lived for a few years in Manfred's house which was where now the shopping mall is, right over there. While they lived there, Titus and Selissa were born here, in our house. With her husband at work at the shunting yard she preferred not to be on her own all day long."

Fermat nodded understandingly.

"I remember when their daughter Selissa was in nursery school, they moved into one of the new apartment blocks, just opposite. In recent years when her children had become independent, Xandy often ate with us; Titus too, anyway. She didn't have much time for cooking and she was thrifty, of course. This was her only weakness, I think. The legacy is not yet settled, but I think she has left behind a fortune!"

Pierre's eyes expressed amazement.

Marike hunched her shoulders. "Since Manfred was killed while on duty for the railway, she cashed considerable widow's and orphan's pensions. She sold Manfred's farm. The amount she received was considerable. She earned a good salary and we bought them the flat in Avril 2. She had much more than she could ever spend. We can't get over the fact that she should have taken her own life. She was as she always was, when she left here on Friday night."

"Her son Titus, does he still live in her flat?" asked Jacquy.

"That's right, he lived with his mother, and he has also a big room in our house. But he has nothing to do with Xandy's poisoning. They got on well together. He was here, the night she died," said Marike defensively. The poor fellow is sometimes unconventional since the death of his father, but he is not violent.

"I see," said Pierre Fermat and Jacquy nodded.

"Since the day he has found his mother dead, he has avoided going into the flat. He goes only to fetch stuff. When he was seven, he had to suffer the loss of his father and now twenty years later he has to endure the bereavement of his mother; both deaths came like bolts out of the blue."

Fermat bade Jacquy to ask if there was ever another man in Xanda's live after her husband's accident.

Marike had understood without translating what it was that Fermat wanted to know. She said, "There was a man, Mateo is his name, she was madly in love with him, and we liked him all very much; particularly the children went into raptures when he walked into their lives."

Fermat nodded his understanding.

"I can't get the events out of my head: it was early in October 1994 that we carried Manfred to his grave. He had died on the third, a Monday. Thereafter, Xanda was never the person she used to be before his departure. After five years of mourning over his death, she all of a sudden was kissed awake by Mateo Capota. They met on the third of October in 1999, a Sunday. I've put it all down; it was on Sunday the third of October 2004 when she came home late from work in the studio and said 'It's now over for good after exactly five years'.

"There is no meaning to these dates, Marike," said her husband. "After all, she did not die in October. They say that it was presumably shortly before midnight on Saturday the seventeenth of May, that she sighed out her soul."

"Do you think that their love affair was finished for good or did they carry on, possibly in secret for some reason?" asked Fermat.

"This was not simply an affair," said Marike. "And Mateo was no schoolboy! He is eleven years her senior and his wish was to marry her, he did not beat about the bush. I could never ascertain why she shied away from a matrimonial pact. She would never tell. I knew she loved him dearly. I think she did love him until her last day. However, Mateo must have been hurt so deeply by something in her behavior that one day he broke up finally. We never heard from him again. She didn't hear from him again either, as far as we know."

It was at that moment that a young blond man came round the corner. "Hello everybody! The gateway is locked and I forgot the key. I rang the bell for five minutes. At first I thought you are out. Then I beheld a strange car. I had to climb over the wall."

"Why are you not at work? This is Titus. This is Monsieur de Fermat and this is Mejnheer de Jong. The gentlemen want to find out why your mum had to die. They work on behalf of the Aybesford family," said Laurens. "The Aybesford family is connected with foul play consistently by the press."

"This is downright nonsense! Why should the Aybesfords commit murder on account of a silly interview – only to become the first ones to come under suspicion? They have never been politically active."

Titus did not look his twenty-seven years, but he looked like a youngster of twenty. "But murder it was! Mum was sometimes sad at heart, but her job always distracted her. They should bring death penalty back into use. I would like this coward to see hanged!"

"I did not know it was already noon! I have nothing prepared. Go and fetch yourself meat and drink from the fridge

— or the larder," said Marike.

"No problem! I came only to fetch my tennis gear for after work. It isn't noon yet. I must be off, anyway. If the gentlemen have questions, you can give them my mobile number."

"I'll let you out," said Laurens and went away.

Titus said good bye to everybody and followed his grandfather.

"May I note down Titus' phone number lest I forget? And perhaps Selissa's number too, just in case," said Pierre de Fermat.

Marike went into the house. After a while she returned with a slip of paper. "I put the numbers down for you. Selissa has not come to see her mother since Easter; which was four weeks before the incident. Shall I cook you something in the microwave oven? You see, we have lunch later in the afternoon nowadays."

Both Jacquy and Fermat declined with thanks. Fermat expressed the wish to have a look at the flat of the deceased. The wish was granted. With a pleasant look, Marike gave him the keys and Laurens went out with him to open the gateway.

"In former times nobody locked their door," said Laurens.

Pierre tackled the short distance on foot. He left Jacquy back with Xanda's parents, so the three of them could go on chatting to their hearts' content.

The young man looked not as grief-stricken as I had expected, thought Pierre as he went. Titus had a brisk way of speaking but he had a friendly face and a gentle expression. If he has killed his mother, he did it not for profit but for idealistic, perhaps quixotic reasons, he reflected. At Avril 2 he let himself in by the street door and took the lift to the seventh floor. He unlocked the apartment door and went inside.

He heard somebody rummage in one of the rooms. "What an odd coincidence!" said an agreeable female voice.

Fermat was violently terrified for a moment. Thereafter a hefty disturbance set in. At the first moment, when he had heard the noise, he had been sure to have caught an intruder. At second thought – on hearing the voice – he presumed that it was Selissa; he was now thinking desperately of finding a way out, so as not to frighten her.

"I figured you were at the garden center, what's happened?" she asked. "I came to fetch this bowl, if you don't mind. It was buried deep in a cupboard, anyway!" she said, when she came into the hallway and looked up from a colorful fruit bowl of glass, which she held with both hands.

An instant later, the bowl was in the process of shattering on the tile floor into a thousand pieces, accompanied by a loud clattering. Louder than the clattering were the repeated shrieks the woman uttered. She blurted out loud shrieks purposefully so as to alarm the neighborhood.

In a situation like this in his home country, Fermat would have opened the apartment door and said: "Police!" That would have calmed everybody. The lie could always be explained later, if necessary. But at present he would only worsen the situation because no policeman here in Austria speaks with a foreign accent. Also no policeman speaks in a foreign language to local inhabitants.

He raised both hands in a gesture of giving up. In one hand he held the apartment key. He said in English, "I got the key from your grandparents. I'm an investigator." He indicated with a movement of his head the obituary on the wall. Please call your grandparents on the phone to verify."

When she did not replay, he said, "I presume you are Selissa van Aanstryk. Half an hour ago I've also met your brother Titus." When she still said nothing he continued, "My name is Fermat. I work for the Aybesford family. They want me to help them to solve the tragic case of your mother's passing away."

Selissa looked still warily.

"Your grandparents gave me the key so I could have a look at the scene of the crime, if it was one." When loud voices became audible in the staircase, he said, "Please go and tell them that everything is all right."

"We all think that it was murder, because my mother seemed to have had no reason to take her own live," she said eventually. But she said it without conviction like a second class court-appointed legal defender of a suicide delinquent. She then opened the door and appeased the upset block mates. Reassured, the neighbors turned away; but somebody had already called the police.

"May I quickly have a look at the flat? You see this is what I've come for. He had a sketch printed out from the police file last evening. He had also seen photos but he liked to inspect the place of the incident himself. Is this your father? He pointed at a photo on the wall above the sofa."

"Y…es, this is my mother's late husband," said Selissa. "And this is Mateo Capota, my late mother's great love," she continued, indicating a photograph on Xanda's bedside table. My mother had not deserved such a man, and she was aware of it. I did him once good in his half-sleep.

Obviously Xanda had chosen the very best photos of both men, because both pictures looked like clippings out of a film magazine. The first man was long faced with blond thinning hair and a slight moustache; he grinned like Errol Flynn. The other, the great love, with broad cheekbones was dark-haired, and his face wore a mixture of a benevolent and a quizzical expression.

"I'm sorry the glass bowl went to pieces. I'm going to make up for the damage, of course," offered Fermat.

"It was a strange accident, don't bother. Serves me right in a way; I must beware of becoming as greedy as my mother was. Oh yes, I know! Thou shalt not speak ill of the dead, let alone of your dead mother. Boo! Did my grandparents tell you that greed was her only week point? They always do! Did they tell you about Edelweiss Castle? No!"

"After all, this is a piece of luck you are present in the flat. Perhaps you would also volunteer your impressions."

"I'm afraid I have already begun; a reaction after the terror you caused. Or rather after the relief, when I felt certain that is was not a murderer again haunting this flat. But no more of it. Come on, let's get out of here."

Fermat cast a glance at the flinders on the floor and then at Selissa. When she took her handbag and with a movement of her head suggested to go away, he cast a last glance at the obituary on the wall next to the door. In the photograph on it Xanda looked perhaps thirty and resembled her daughter strikingly. Both had strawberry hair cut to length between chin and shoulder. They had both graceful long necks.

On the photos he had seen so far, Xanda had black, pinned-up hair. Within the last minutes he had changed his perception of Xanda's interior substance; but also of her appearance. He glanced at Selissa again and mentioned the resemblance in looks.

Selissa motioned impatiently and they went, leaving behind a complete mess. In the lift Fermat observed that there
was no physical likeness between Selissa and Titus. "I heard
you are self-employed, that you have a second-hand shop in
the city?"

"Is that what my grandparents call my antique shop?"

"Oh, sorry! No, I heard from another source."

She took a business card from her bag and handed it to
Fermat. She said, "My shop is in a back alley but only twenty
steps from the main square. There is a sketch of the layout at
the back of the card. Perhaps you drop in one day and see for
yourself! Then we can talk, if you like."

"Merci! Oui, peut-être! By any chance! Quite another
matter: from my source I also have heard that you trained as
a visual merchandiser. Do you happen to know Heidi Forster?
Were you perhaps in the same school class?"

"Again your information is incorrect. I trained as a shop assistant. But I know the one Heidi Forster from Edelweiss. We
do business now and then.

When they had arrived on the ground floor and came out
of the lift, two police officers, one male and one female, entered by the front door which was wide open and inhibited
from shutting because of the fine weather.

"Where is the commotion?" asked the female officer.

"We don't know of any commotion," said Selissa and,
making big eyes and pointing indeterminately upward, said:
"has the silly woman again seen a mouse in the cellar. But you
should ask the caretaker, flat number one!"

"I must bring back the key to your grandparents. It has
been very nice to meet you, albeit unconventional."

"Yes indeed, it certainly was; both nice and unconventional." Selissa unlocked her car. "Shall I bring you over?"

"I rather walk; thank you all the same. But if you want to say hello to your relatives?"

"Another time! Bye!"

Fermat made for Solar Pasture Street, when Max Siegenthaler approached.

"Hello Pierre! I must tell you something!"

"Hello Max! Nice to see you! What is the matter?"

"This old-timer Mazda in which you arrived. It has been here before. And the guy that came with you, too."

"What exactly have you observed?"

"I've seen this lean fellow with the gold rimmed glasses before. He came in other cars too, but at least once in the Xedos. I saw him when I passed the car. I saw the Xedos several times, but only from my balcony. So I can't say for sure if it was the same guy every time."

"Was he spying on somebody?"

"He pulls in but doesn't get out of the car; just sits. What else should it mean? But I can't say whom he was following or whom he was waiting for. I never saw him get out of the car. And I can't say what made him leave again."

"This might be significant, thanks a lot, Max! I must be going now. The fellow is waiting. Bye!"

"He's having a good time with Laurens and Marike; I've seen them in the garden. Bye!"

Fermat wondered if Max had to climb a tree to have a look into the garden of the van Aanstryks. He also contemplated how far Max was to be trusted. With regard to Selissa he had made mistakes, but petty ones, admittedly.

All of a sudden he beheld Special Constable Dunstig coming stiff and slowly from the shopping mall, waving him nearer.

"Are you responsible for the turmoil in Avril 2? If you can't behave yourself, you better go home to France!"

Fermat put his forefinger to his lips and smiled a mysterious smile. He went over to Dunstig, took him confidentially by the arm and led him back to the mall and behind a corner. "I have to tell you something, between you and me! By the way – do you have handcuffs with you?" Dunstig folded back his jacket and let his handcuffs gleam.

Swiftly Fermat twisted Dunstig's wrists, pushed him to the wall and fettered his hands behind his back. "That will teach you to behave in future, Dunstig." Fermat dodged to avoid Dunstig's kick. "You are lucky I don't attach you to the rain water downpipe. As a bonus I should twist your nose; maybe next time!" After this incident Pierre de Fermat went back to the van Aanstryk's house in Wood Road.

§12

The Retired Judge

"**Bonjour, Monsieur Gordon!** It's the early bird that catches the worm, n'est-ce pas?" said Monsieur Pierre de Fermat; he was sitting at a table in the Golden Egg when he saw Gordon come in.

"To go to bed early with the chickens and to be up with the rooster," said Gordon and sat down so that he was facing the Frenchman. "That's the motto of the people in Goodland. But why are you up so soon, Monsieur de Fermat?"

"I thought that I must have a word with you before you are off," said Fermat in a restrained manner. There were other guests present and a waitress was putting coffee on the table. When the woman was gone, Fermat proceeded: "Yesterday and the day before, I scouted around in Solar Pasture. You know where Xanda's flat is and where also her parents live, not far from the flat, in their own house."

"I see."

"On one of the balconies I discovered a woman spying with binoculars incessantly. She does it very discretely. I wouldn't have discovered her, if I were not on the lookout for such things. There are more than two hundred flats in Avril Court.

There is always somebody likely to watch, mostly elderly, handicapped people."

"Ah! That's interesting."

"I was sitting on a bench and talking to an old age pensioner who is also very inquisitive, when I discovered her for the first time. She was watching us incessantly. I wouldn't have been able to tell that it's a woman at all, because I could only make out her head of hair. But I figured out what number the flat is. On the door bell nameplate it says Larissa Bennent."

"Larissa Bennent!"

"Do you know her?"

"If she is the one I have in mind, she is the former president of the regional high court of Cyclamen. I have a nodding acquaintance with her. But my father knows her better, because she was a friend of my mother. They were of the same age. She must be seventy-eight or something like that."

"If she was on watch on the evening of Xanda van Aanstryk's death she would have come forward if she had a suspicion. But in the police file she is not mentioned as a witness."

"She certainly doesn't spy all day long. Do you want to pay her a visit?"

"Absolutely. Perhaps you could write a few lines for me, for the purpose of introduction. She might be careful and not let me in, foreign as I might appear to her."

"But in the company of Jacquy there should be no problem, I'm sure."

"Now we come to the other point that I wanted to tell you about. At the moment I would rather do without Jacquy's support."

"Are you suspecting him of something?"

"That would be carrying things too far. But it's a precaution. I do not want to explain at the moment; or rather I couldn't explain anything as yet. I have a hunch but nothing more. Some other matter: who besides you goes for a ride in the Xedos occasionally?"

"Well, there is Jacquy. But now and then also my father, my wife Eleanor, Gloria, Rupert, the caretaker, ... they all can take the key. But I think it's only on rare occasions that somebody goes for a joyride. What's on your mind?"

At that moment Gloria entered the Golden Egg. "Good morning, gentlemen!"

"Good morning, Gloria," said both men.

"I didn't know you stayed overnight in the Castle," said her father.

"Because you go to bed with the chickens," said Gloria.

"Yes, we have been talking about the fact only just. Listen, Gloria, would it be possible for you to meet with M. Fermat in Solar Pasture at about ten o'clock? He's going to speak to Larissa Bennent who lives out there, and he wants to be accompanied by a female assistant for a change." He gave Fermat a wink.

"No problem," said Gloria.

"To obtain the judges' confidence you could give her my regards and mention your grandfather. As soon as she is comfortable with Monsieur de Fermat you can absent yourself. What do you think, M. Fermat?"

When both Gloria and Fermat gave their consent, Gordon said, "splendid!" Then he pointed at the paper on the table. "Look at this photograph! Isn't this the chap from the Cyclamen Police? He is the hero of the hour. It says here, ...

yesterday around noon three men were up and about to force open the automatic teller in the Solar Pasture Center when they were hindered by a plain cloth police officer. In order to avoid pursuit, the cheeky gangsters overpowered the police man and handcuffed him. Then they dispersed in different directions.' They give here descriptions of the three criminals. You too were in the vicinity of the Center yesterday, weren't you, M. Fermat?"

"Yes, I was," said Fermat, "and vaguely at the same time too — let me see." Having looked at the newspaper article for a while, he said in an amused sounding way, "Indeed, it's this Special Constable Dunstig. I think he is aiming at obtaining a commendation. But my appearance does not correspond to any of the given suspect profiles."

At that the three of them burst out laughing.

Gloria and Fermat had agreed to meet in Avril Court at ten thirty. Fermat was early and parked his car behind the shopping center. He crossed Solar Pasture Street and made for Avril Court. From afar he saw Max sitting near the children's playground. He went up to him. Max had no pertaining news but talked about the policeman who got handcuffed the previous day.

Fermat also learned that Larissa Bennent was indeed the retired judge as Gordon had presumed. When Gloria's car turned into Avril Court, Fermat went over to where she parked and they made for Avril 3. Because the street door was locked, they chatted until somebody came out, so they could get inside. They did not want to contact the judge via the intercom. When they had got access to the building, they entered the lift and went up to the ninth floor.

While pressing the Nine button, Fermat said, "I have to ask you where you were on Saturday the seventeenth of May in the morning, before the interview, Miss Gloria."

"Why do you ask? Do you think I poisoned Xanda van Aanstryk? I came never near her or the studio."

"Somebody dropped a hint that you were very cross with Louise Chevrolet. The reason seems to have been a young man, a disc jockey and singer. Somebody hinted that the assault might have been meant for Miss Chevrolet and not for Mrs. van Aanstryk."

"I feel a bit sheepish about it. But it is true that I was very furious with her. But that was more than half a year ago. And the disc jockey is finally written off. I say! It's nearly been a year. Friday night I spent in my flat in Cyclamen City. I got up early on the morning in question and went a bit shopping. But I came never near the television studio. They surely have CCTV footage? About ten o'clock I set off for Edelweiss."

They had already left the lift and Fermat said: "Oui, oui. Never mind." But he looked unconvinced, thinking of guises and disguises. Having the knowledge that the poisoning in the television studio was not contrived with the intention to kill, Fermat would not delete Gloria from his mental notepad. And the thought flashed through his mind that Gloria's Brother Rupert was the second member of the Aybesford family who had no alibi. Has he too had a motive?

The door with the nameplate *Bennent* on it had two fish eyes on different heights. Gloria rang the bell. The additional lower peephole was darkened the next moment and a resolute female voice asked, "Who is there?"

Gloria inserted a business card into the mail slot and

explained, "My name is Gloria Aybesford. You know the Aybesfords from Edelweiss. I bring regards from my father Gordon and from my grandfather Joseph. We ..."

The door opened and Larissa Bennent, sitting in a wheel chair, said, "Come in please. I half expected a visit from the gentleman. I saw you talking to Mr. Siegenthaler the day before yesterday and put two and two together. You seem to be investigating the death of the television presenter." She used the English language from the beginning.

While she spoke she propelled her invalid chair into her living room and indicated where they should take their seats – next to one another – and the lady herself maneuvered her vehicle into a position opposite them, so she could look into their faces.

At that moment a nondescript middle aged woman rolled a tea cart into the room. Miss Bennent said, "Here is tea and some cookies; please help yourself!"

Pierre de Fermat looked up and down the judge unobtrusively. She was of slender frame and elegant looking. She had on a flowered dress and her white hair had a light violet shimmer. He said, "My name is Pierre de Fermat and I investigate on behalf of the Aybesford family."

"Very good," said Larissa Bennent. "I'm please to meet you. And I'm very pleased to meet you, Miss Gloria. You probably know that I grew up in Edelweiss and I was friends with your grandparents. Nowadays I'm cut off from society." She said it not sadly but in a matter of fact way, nearly gaily.

Fermat poured himself tea and addressed the host: "Chère Madame, we thought that perhaps you made some observations in the night when Mrs. Xanda van Aanstryk died. Perhaps you saw something that seemed quite innocent in itself, but might be a relevant clue to finding the cause of her demise."

Larissa Bennent sighed deeply. After a moment she said, "You must be of the opinion that I spy all day long. But this is not so. It is true that I bought one of the uppermost flats because I like to have a good vista. When unknown persons hang about I sometimes reach for my binoculars. But weeks may go by without me watching."

She looked as if she were pausing for thought, trying to remember something, to think of grounds of justification. "Last autumn, teenagers were vandalizing in the park and in the children's playground. They destroyed two benches a lantern and a see-saw. People called the police. But when they arrived the hooligans had disappeared."

"Could they not be traced?" asked Gloria.

"They could be identified perfectly on the basis of the shots I took with my video camera."

"Well done!" said Fermat, hoping that perhaps now Miss Bennent would come forward even with shootings of the day when Xanda van Aanstryk died. But she did not continue. Nonsense! She had then had no cause to assume foul play. What should she have filmed? There was no noise as in the case of the vandalism. The police will have asked her anyhow. His confidence subsided. "On Saturday the seventeenth of May, could you make any observations regarding the movements of the woman that was destined to die in the same night? Or could you identify any visitors?"

The retired judge sighed again, then said, "I have notes and records not only of her movements but also of the movements of alien people that came and went on the day in question."

A moment before, Gloria had been about to depart and let Fermat with the woman alone. The contact was made and no translating was needed. But now she became curious and sat back expectantly.

"Why did you not part your observations with the police?" asked Fermat.

"First of all, they didn't ask me."

"This is a grave neglect on the part of the police not to interview the inhabitants of neighboring blocks."

"I'm sure it is. In the early days I was waiting for them to come. But it was as if they had forgotten about my helping them last year. Then I thought to myself that probably the homicide squad knew nothing about the act of vandalism. Had they asked me, I would have fully disclosed my observations.

"Naturellement."

At first I was nearly offended by not being asked. But as time went by I would have been embarrassed if they had come. So I consoled myself with the fact that no one of the people who came to visit her were in her flat when she died."

"But this doesn't imply that nobody administered something to her. She may have died not immediately but maybe hours later," said Fermat.

"I'm aware of the fact, of course. But on the other hand, not one of the possible visitors remained longer in the building than two or three minutes. All four of them I could see only at the front door, not in the flat. Mrs. van Aanstryk probably didn't even open her door when they rang the bell. Except perhaps the first gentleman; he probably came before half past three o'clock in the afternoon. But this one I saw only come out by the front door. I missed his arrival."

Fermat and Gloria nodded their heads.

"It was only days later, that I began to admit the fact to myself that I should have called the police." She paused for thought again. "At first sight the situation seemed clear. She had taken some poison herself. When after some time the police did not exclude murder, I grew troubled but did not dare to give over my observations so late. Most of all, there were people from Edelweiss visiting her or hanging around."

"Where there?"

"Yes, even from the castle. Therefore I was very pleased when I saw you Monsieur talking to Mr. Max Siegenthaler. I deduced properly that the Aybesfords had employed a foreign gentleman to investigate. If you had not come today I would have contacted Joseph Aybesford and told him. I will give you any information I have, Monsieur de Fermat. But I beg you and Miss Aybesford not to tell anybody anything about my observations."

"We promise," said Fermat quick like a shot.

"After all, I could have buttoned my lips and say nothing at all; to nobody. At the risk of harming somebody from Edelweiss I'm going to make a clear breast toward you two now. I wash my hands of it."

"As far as I'm concerned I was about to take my leave now," said Gloria. "But now you are making me curious."

Fermat gave Gloria a wink and said, "You as my assistant are bound to secrecy anyway." Looking at Miss Bennent he continued, "You were not witness to an obvious wrongdoing, otherwise you would have come forward immediately. Am I right or am I right?"

"Yes, of course, M. de Fermat."

"So you need not worry. It is none of your civic duties to make theories and tell them to the police. Only if in the course of my investigations I come to the conclusion that we need your testimony about the presence of a certain person at a certain time that I might have to name you as a witness. We will then say that I paid you a visit and that in the course of our conversation we discovered the connection. Do you understand what I mean?"

"Yes, yes, perfectly!"

"Miss Bennent, if you would rather that I leave, you need not bother to say so. The two of you do not need me as an interpreter; you converse perfectly in English," said Gloria.

"Oh no, no, Miss Aybesford. I would rather you stayed on. I'm sorry I'm so muddleheaded." She rolled over to a sideboard and fetched a laptop computer. On her way back she touched Gloria's arm and said: "I'm sure you are not going to blow the whistle on me." She looked for a moment into Gloria's eyes. "You're a great deal like your grandmother, I must say. You have her green eyes. Barbara was also so beautiful. Do you know what? I'm going to sit at this one corner of the table, you remain where you are and M. Fermat will be so kind as to sit on my other side."

Gloria shifted her teacup more to the left. Miss Bennent positioned her laptop and switched it on while Fermat took his cup and saucer and went over and sat down on a chair at Miss Bennent's right elbow.

While the computer booted, Miss Bennent began her account of what she observed on Saturday 17 May 2014. "We all here in Avril Court were a little proud of having Xanda van Aanstryk as a neighbor. She was a celebrity but she behaved very unassuming. But you seldom encountered her. I think she ran her errands in the city, because I never saw her in the Solar Pasture Center."

The listeners nodded.

"But I saw her incessantly walking over to her parents or coming back from them. I always thought that it was her way of keeping herself in good shape. Occasionally I could see her on her balcony or even in her flat. On some evenings she forgot to draw the curtains or did not care. So I could not help looking directly into her flat. Her flat is also on the top floor, vis-à-vis. But while my block has nine storeys, Avril 2 has only seven. Come and have a look from my balcony."

They went out onto the balcony and Miss Bennent explained to Gloria and Fermat the local situation. As they went back to resume their seats, Miss Bennent resumed also her narration. "On the ominous day I was looking forward to the television coverage of Edelweiss taken last summer and the subsequent opening of the festival. In the days before the occurrence TV spots heralded the special event that Joseph Aybesford was going to give a live interview to Xanda van Aanstryk. I was simply shocked when this dolly bird Chevrolet appeared on the screen. She was to interview this man of the world who cherished big ideas. I had a sense of foreboding. I felt chaos to come. But I had no idea about the magnitude the disaster would boil up to."

"When Mrs. van Aanstryk did not show up, had you any theory why this might be so?" asked Fermat.

"My first thought was that she must be ill. I watched the broadcast and recorded simultaneously, so as to miss nothing in case I should be disrupted by somebody. When this blond newsreader appeared I held the playing immediately and looked over to the van Aanstryk flat but I could observe nothing. Casually I looked down and beheld Xanda's Honda near the front door."

"This is very interesting," remarked Gloria.

"It confirmed my thought that something was out of the ordinary. She always parked her car in the underground parking garage. It was then shortly after eleven o'clock and I continued watching the recording. After the interview had ended abruptly, I admired your father for maintaining his countenance so well and carrying on at ease with his speech. He must be very self-confident," said Miss Bennent, turning her head towards Gloria when speaking the last words.

"Oh yes! He is also a model of a patient and serene man," said Gloria.

"What further evidence do you have in your possession, Madame?"

"The designation *model of a patient man* does apparently not apply to you, young man!" said Miss Bennent merrily and patted Fermat's arm. "There was not much evidence as yet, but some is to come in a moment. As soon as Gordon had finished speaking, I switched off the television and took up my position on the balcony. I intended to take photographs of persons who entered or left Avril 2 and seemed suspicious to me. I was downright restive and had a hunch that something was wrong."

"Ah, you did not videotape?" asked Fermat.

"No, I didn't," said Miss Bennent, and with a keystroke she awakened the screen of her laptop which had gone to sleep a while ago. Straightaway she opened a directory and clicked on the first photo file, named 15-35. It showed, when it opened, Claas in the act of leaving Avril 2 by the front door. "Unfortunately I did not see him enter. I had left the balcony for about ten minutes. The time he left was 3:35 p.m. I think this is Claas from Edelweiss Castle, isn't it him? Your grandmother was still alive, when your Grandfather brought him into the country."

Gloria and Fermat were amazed. "Yes, it's Claas. My grandfather helped him to leave South Africa and then employed him in the castle. It must have been ages ago. Have you knowledge of earlier visits?"

"I've never heard or seen anything that would give rise to this assumption. There is also the possibility that he paid a visit to somebody else in Avril 2.

Here we have a series of pictures of a man who somehow seemed very suspicious to me. He enters with a plastic bag at about 5:55 p.m. and comes out three minutes later empty-handed. He then drives away in a dark car, of which the registration plate is not visible."

"No, it's hidden by another car."

"Somehow he reminds me of a lumberjack that I watched years ago. It happened on a stroll in a forest near Edelweiss. It was before I became dependent on a waking aide or an invalid chair. He and a younger man were felling a tree. He stuck to my memory because of his long gray hair and his green cap. And he had a crooked nose. Even the lumberjack shirt seems to be a similar one. If it is this man, he could be retired these days; the one on the photo looks less corpulent, though. Do you possibly know a man who answers to the description?"

Both Gloria and Fermat answered in the negative.

"Might it be that he works in the woods – or in the sawmill

of Edelweiss Castle?" asked Fermat, and Gloria said, "I really don't know. As I said before, I never noticed the man. But I think I couldn't recognize any of the woodworkers; I know none of them."

A strange silence set in, until Miss Bennent opened the next picture. "This man I have also never seen here around. He came after 7:30 p.m. and left a few minutes later."

Both Gloria and Fermat became fidgety. "Walter Nadler Jr." said both with one voice.

"You mean the son or grandson of the castle administrator? This is interesting. Perhaps you know also the last stranger, a woman. I nearly missed her because it was around 11:00 p.m. – I had already given up – when I went for a last look if the light was still on in the van Aanstryk flat. There I noticed her leaning towards a car. When a regular visitor of the single woman on the third floor came out at the front door, she quickly went inside. After a few minutes she came out again."

Again Gloria and Fermat were completely astonished. "Rita!" they cried unanimously.

"Rita?" asked Miss Bennent.

"Rita Olivero," said Gloria.

"Ah, the Oliveros. Has she taken over The Fox and Hare from her parents?" asked Miss Bennent.

"That's right," said Gloria.

"Could you observe anything at all in the flat of Mrs. van Aanstryk?" asked Fermat.

"The only thing I noticed was that the light in the kitchen was on all evening, all night in fact. The other two rooms of her flat that give in the yard were dark all evening. The one is the living room and the other is the chamber of her son Titus. Lately he stays more with his grandparents. They were worried because she had told them the previous day on the phone that she was not well; and in the morning she did not take their calls. So Titus came over and found her dead. This is all I can tell you."

"The only unknown person is the *lumberjack*," said Fermat. He pulled out a USB flash drive and asked: "Would you be so kind as to copy the pictures for me?"

Miss Bennent inserted the medium into the socket and started the copy process. "I rely on you that the thing is not infested," she said laughingly.

"Do you have in mind the virus infection of the Iranian atomic plants? No fear Madame, my pen drive is not dangerous! By the way, it could come to it that the photo of the *lumberjack* must be made public. I must then have your express permission to do so."

"Then the police will also know?"

"The photo cannot be classified as evidence. So I need not tell them about it. But I think it better to show it to them. If they don't trigger a search, I will. But I'm going to await events, for the time being. Should it come to it, it would pose no problem for you, Madame. It is wise to be wary when obscure people prowl around in your neighborhood. You will say that you simply took the photo because you never saw this man before in Avril Court; or elsewhere, for that matter. You had no reason to tell the police about this visitor, because you did not link him to Xanda van Aanstryk. Basta!"

"And the other three persons?" asked Miss Bennent.

"Basically the same holds true for them as for the *lumberjack*. I assure you, Madame, I will do everything to keep you out of it and not to discredit you."

§13

Titus Eases His Conscience

"The lady seems to have shouldered a burden, which she couldn't bear any longer," said Gloria, when they were going down in the lift.

"Oh yah! The situation had grown above her head by now. But I think we have relieved her of her sore conscience. She did not hold back evidence; the police didn't ask her. She may be a bit lacking in her powers of concentration but she is of sound mind, so she knew quite well that formally she had nothing to fear."

"Had she buttoned up her lips, nobody had known."

"That's all very true, but she was in a conflict. On the one hand she has a sense of justice, and she is a little prone to give herself airs. Both virtues would normally have prompted her to come forward voluntarily as a witness. On the other hand she didn't want to tell the police because of her regard for your family.

This, in essence, is the predicament in which she found herself caught. It encumbered her enormously.

It is manifest that Claas' visit to Avril 2 must have to do with Joseph Aybesford, or at least with the castle. She brooded too long on her own over the things she has watched and taken pictures of."

"What's the meaning of all this? Are Walter, Rita, Claas and my grandfather all of a sudden suspects in a murder case? We felt so certain; we could not imagine anybody of Edelweiss to be involved in the poisoning. Must we assume an Edelweiss conspiracy?"

"Unexpected and strange, isn't it? It is too early though to jump to conclusions. But I think that their offences will turn out to be of lesser severity. To my mind the visit of the *lumberjack* was the hot scent."

"But why a woodcutter of all people?"

"When a woodworker has business in Cyclamen City on a Saturday evening, he dresses like anybody. So I think he was a dummy. But his trace has turned cold. Six and a half weeks have lapsed. Have you noticed that he wore gloves?"

"Do you think that somebody dresses up as a lumberjack to bring a plastic bag full of poison? Why should anybody dress up as a lumberjack only to be more noticeable? And there was no poison found in Xanda van Aanstryk's flat," said Gloria. "None at all."

"Anyway; to me the outfit looks like a disguise; the baseball cap, the long gray hair, the pair of glasses, the gloves."

"If he came masked, somebody might have seen him change his outfit; or perhaps someone could recognize one of the things he used. Shouldn't we make the pictures public? Or do you think it was my father in disguise, for good measure?"

"So as to make the confusion complete? The thought would be screamingly funny if the affair were not so serious."

"Sorry, I'm nearly crazy with concern."

"Your father wouldn't have called me in if he were the culprit. Please don't tell anybody; but for my share, the suspect could also be a woman. The person was reminiscent of Dalia Kalanda, the Detective Chief Inspector of the Cyclamen City Police."

"As long as he or she was not reminiscent of me, I should be at ease."

"Don't let it get to yourself. I must think over the matter in peace and quiet," replied Pierre de Fermat. "The gray matter works best at night, when it's not distracted by everyday tasks."

They had been talking behind Avril 3 and were coming now into the yard. Max was slowly pacing back and forth in the park near the playground. "It is nearly noon; I hope you have not missed important proceedings at your office," said Fermat.

"I would have missed out on stirring events in Avril 3, had I not come with you."

Fermat said goodbye to Gloria but kept her a little waiting as if playing for time. He explained that he must wait for the right moment, so he could disappear. Gloria did not quite understand, what he meant.

But when Max's attention was suddenly diverted by two passers-by and he was sure not to look at them, Fermat swiftly vanished behind Avril 2. So Gloria betook herself to her car with a shake of her head.

Once behind the block, Fermat looked up to the windows of the van Aanstryk flat. On the basis of the sketch in the police file and of his own observations, he determined the locations of the different rooms.

Then he repaired to the adjoining maize field and vanished between head-high plants. He searched systematically row by row and back and forth until he encountered something that satisfied his expectations.

Carefully he lifted the article off the ground. Grunting contentedly, he put it into an evidence bag.

Along the rear of Avril 2, Fermat made for Solar Pasture Street, crossed it and went behind the mall, where he had left his car. He put the evidence into the trunk and then he drove into town.

In the morning he had fed the address of the municipal garden centre into his navigation system. He had also phoned Titus van Aanstryk and made an appointment for noon. They were sufficiently able to converse in English, they had found.

When Fermat arrived at the center, he found Titus taking a rest in the staff room. They went outside for a walk in the grounds of the center.

"How are you getting along with your investigations, M. Fermat?" asked Titus.

"Since we met yesterday, I've made some progress."

"Indeed? Good for you!"

"When I called you this morning, I thought we should speak face to face about your feelings about your mother's death. I knew only what you told to the police. But meanwhile I know more. I must ask you specifically, why you concealed the fact that you found the source of the poison. And why did you cause it to disappear?"

"How did you hit on that?" asked Titus. He looked flabbergasted.

"I've found a new witness. The person had not parted with what she saw because she had not been asked by anybody so far. But she observed how an unknown person brought something into Avril 2 in the afternoon of the day in question. You probably thought that when the maize is harvested in the autumn, four month from now, nobody will become suspicious should the glass be found."

Titus' eyes darted looks in all directions like mad. He thought himself to be surrounded by the police.

"Take it easy, Mr. van Aanstryk. I'm pretty sure you acted on an impulse; did you want to protect somebody?"

"To tell you the truth, when I found my mother in her bed deathly cold and by all appearances lifeless, I called the emergency doctor so as to gain time."

"Stalling for time – to what end?"

"I didn't know myself at the time. I couldn't think clearly. Maybe I thought I'm in for it. It was after seven in the morning and somebody could have observed my coming home. So I thought I had to set off the alarm quickly, so as not to come under suspicion myself. My sister Selissa joked sometimes about killing our mother in order to unburden her of her wealth."

"I see."

"Sometimes I have a dream that we have done her in and must remove all traces in a hurry. Somehow I felt as if I were perhaps in one of these dreams."

"I see. How did you proceed?"

"I went into the kitchen and when I saw the glass of hibiscus honey on the table, I did not think at all. I took it together with the empty cup and the teaspoon and went into the rear spare bedroom. There I threw the things as far as I could out of the window into the maize field."

"Yes."

"I thought it not wise to throw them into the rubbish

chute. After that I put the milk carton into the fridge using a towel. I wanted to avoid fingerprints both on the carton and on the fridge handle. Thereafter I called my grandparents."

"Ah."

"I told grandma on the phone that mother was very ill, although at heart I knew that she was beyond remedy. When my grandma and grandpa arrived, the doctor had already come in and called the police."

"Had the police no suspicion that one of the cups was missing?"

"We have no set, only an assortment of different cups; just as my mother pinched them together; ditto with the teaspoons and other things."

"When you said *hibiscus honey* just now, you said the words as if it was some evil remedy; how come?"

"It's because Selissa always said that we need only put some poisoned hibiscus honey in the larder."

"I see. You thought that perhaps your sister has put the plan into action."

"It was not really a plan of hers. But still, that was in my mind, yes. But I no longer think that Selissa has something to do with it. She was herself totally shaken and denies every accusation vehemently and convincingly too. I know her."

"If I understand you correctly – neither you nor your sister can account for the origin of the glass of hibiscus honey. Nobody can explain, when and by what means the honey came into the flat?"

"That's right."

"Could it not have come from your grandparents?"

"No, it hasn't. Mum must have acquired it in town

sometime recently."

"But you have discussed the matter of the honey with your grandparents?"

"Yes. We had decided to let the matter rest, because it doesn't bring mother back; it may bring about only trouble. But now that you have found out about, you will think it to be a matter for the police?"

"Not necessarily. Not at the moment in any case. First of all, I will have the honey glass analyzed by a friend. If the honey was indeed poisoned, we must find out how it came into her possession; where she could have bought it."

"… or borrowed," said Titus.

"Or if it was given to her; or if it was simply laid at her door by the unknown person who was dressed like a lumber-jack. But why expressly hibiscus – does it bear a meaning, is there some allusion to something special? Has hibiscus honey played a role in the past? Why used your sister to say that all you had to do was to place a glass of poisoned hibiscus honey in the larder?"

"The term *hibiscus honey* was a well-known saying in our family. Phrases like *You should eat more hibiscus honey!* or *Did you eat hibiscus honey on the sly?* and so forth were daily fare."

"So your sister was speaking jokingly?"

"Yes, of course. But she had also had reason to be angry with mum."

"What reasons are there … or were there?"

"You better ask her, not me. She moved out years ago but she has still a key to the flat. She comes here occasionally, to visit or to indulge in reminiscences on her own. Do you know how to contact her?"

"Yes, thanks. I have her mobile number and I know how to find her shop. But this hibiscus honey once again; do you have any remembrance how the jest first cropped up?"

"No, can't remember. This must have been many years ago. But it got a fresh impetus with Mateo's arrival on the scene. I was then about twelve. Have you heard about Mateo Capota?"

"Oh yes, your grandmother told me about him."

"I'm sure I don't know more about the meaning or the origin of the jesting word."

Fermat drove back to the Solar Pasture Center and parked his car. Then he went over to the rear of the block Avril 2 and resumed a rigorous scan of the maize field.

When after a vast amount of time he found the cup unscathed, he put it in an evidence bag. It seemed as if the teaspoon had vanished into the ground. Perhaps it had got stuck in the green of a plant, and had then become overgrown.

Back in his car, Fermat tried to get Dr. Elisabeth Forster on the phone. He was lucky and got connected to her desk phone. He asked her for an urgent meeting in the parking area of the Police Headquarters in about twenty or thirty minutes.

"Tell me your mobile number, digit by digit, I call you back presently," she said.

He could not remember the number of his newly acquired mobile phone and had to look for it. When he had it ready, she keyed it into her mobile as he dictated it. After the last digit she pressed the call button.

When Fermat replied she said: "You have my number now. Call me when you are here. Don't call another number."
Fermat saved her number under *Eliza* and left Solar Pasture in

order to meet her.

When he arrived, Elisabeth was waiting for him. She climbed into the car and sat on the front passenger seat.

"Thank you for coming," said Fermat. "When we first met the other day I got the impression that you could be won over for the Edelweiss position. Regarding the van Aanstryk case I mean."

"What do you mean?"

"The police are not doing their best for whatever reasons; thus compromising the Aybesford family. I felt you are aware of the fact. Am I assuming rightly?"

"I trust you will not unmask me, should something go wrong. What do you want me to do?"

"I think I have found the source of the second poison, and I would like you to verify the assumption. If you have not the means yourself, you surely have a friend in Crime Scene Investigation or better still, in the forensic lab. I cannot bring the police into play, not at the moment. I have proof that they suppressed evidence in the van Aanstryk case. After all, the fact that two poisons were administered I heard only from you."

"That's pretty steep!"

"It's not in the report; at least not in the subset that I have access to. Also it was obviously never mentioned in any newspaper. And there are other things. But a picture begins to show itself now."

"I'll see what I can do."

"Your cooperation could help to bring certainty into the case."

Fermat took the honey glass out of the evidence bag and with a soft tissue extracted a sample of the honey, crumpled the tissue up and gave it to the doctor.

"The fingerprints will be gone, anyway. Even if they were usable, I'm sure they would not bring new insights. The cup could confirm that the poison was drunk out of it, mixed into milk."

"OK, put it into another bag and give it to me. I call you on your mobile tomorrow before noon."

On Thursday morning Fermat was in his room in the castle and studied witness statements on his laptop when his mobile buzzed and vibrated. *Eliza* was calling. He took the call; "Good morning doctor! What have you found out?" he said right away.

She answered brusquely, saying in a hushed tone that she could not talk long. Obviously she had forced the call amid urgent work, perhaps a conference. She confirmed briefly that the second poison was in the sample of the honey. Furthermore it was very likely that the cup had held milk poisoned with the honey and that Xanda van Aanstryk had drunk from the cup.

"That's good news, thank you very much for helping us. Apropos, it would be great if you could manage to be free on the coming Saturday; we are giving a summary of the investigations so far. All of you are welcome to attend; your husband, your mother in law, Heidi, well, all neighbors, in short."

"You mean *you* are giving a summary?"

"Yes; but other things will come into the open. Mrs. Eleanor Aybesford will pay you Forsters a visit and invite you all more formally. She will then say when and where; au revoir, Madame!"

"Good bye!"

Half an hour later Pierre de Fermat left the castle for the Aybesford headquarters in Cowford; he had an appointment with Gordon. Having arrived he was ushered to the president's office by a front desk secretary.

"Bonjour Monsieur de Fermat, Mr. Aybesford is awaiting you," said Mrs. Achmadi, and in the very moment Gordon came out of his room and shook Fermat by the hand.

"Come on, I take you on a quick tour through the building. We can talk while going along. "I take my mobile phone with me – just in case," he said, facing Mrs. Achmadi and a second secretary that was also present. Then the two men went out into the corridor.

"I like to be on the move," said Gordon. "This is better than to sit around sipping coffee. I do this also with other business partners. Furthermore the walls may have ears. Our business is a special one. Did you gain new insights since we talked last night?"

"Oui, c'est ça! My assumptions regarding the poison find have been confirmed."

"So the time has come for a provisional appraisal of the knowledge gathered?"

"Yes, indeed. I have primed Elisabeth Forster a short while ago. I said Saturday, what do you think?"

"Saturday is probably better than Sunday; Saturday evening – with open end. We can't know what discussions might arise. I've been thinking; the best thing would be to invite the two neighbor families over to the castle for an informal meeting with a sandwich bar or light meals."

"C'est super!"

"You tell my wife about all other people concerned that she should invite. Or you yourself invite whoever you deem important."

"Très bien! … An idea strikes me! *All people concerned*, you said just now."

"You seem quite agitated all of a sudden!"

"I *am* excited! The moment you said *all people concerned* my mental kaleidoscope's picture assumed a clear pattern. You know, I think I can do something about the Jacquy case until Saturday."

"Have you found a connection between the two cases? You scare me, you know. What are you planning to do?"

"It's early days yet; but I hope to have cleared up this old case until Saturday."

"You amaze me with your tempo!"

Fermat drove back to Cyclamen City and parked the Xedos in the central underground parking garage. He went up the stairs and got outside on the main square. He found the back alley that harbored Selissa van Aanstryk's antique shop at the first go.

Selissa was in and welcomed him friendly. "This time I'm not going to yell at the sight of you. What's the news?"

"A matter that has nothing to do with your mother's death; but something she was involved in a long time ago."

"But how can I help?"

"I could not fail to see the other day that you do not approve of your grandmother's belittling the weak points of your late mother."

"Was I not sufficiently diplomatic?"

"Your candor is refreshing. I like that trait of you, Madame."

"What is it that you have in mind?"

"If you and I go about skillfully we could ease your grandparents' conscience; and the conscience of some other people as well. If you come with me and do some interpreting, we could even bring them great joy after their grief and loss."

"This sounds like redemption."

"In a way, it will be, yes; and if I'm right in my inferences, then you too will have cause for celebration."

"But you were seeing them only the day before yesterday. Have you got new insights?"

"It was only after I saw them, that I became suspicious unknowingly. The inspection of your mother's flat gave me a first idea. But since it had no relevance with the fatality, I did not think anything of it. The dead certainty came only an hour ago."

"You make me curious; c'est entendu, Monsieur! Let's meet at the house of my grandparents at seven p.m."

"Your French accent is perfect, Madame! Thank you very much. You won't be sorry!"

§14
The Day of the Truth

The Golden Egg had been chosen for the event of the provisional appraisal. It happened once in a while that the castle's cafeteria was reserved for a family celebration, notably when relatives with children where guests in the castle.

Some of the ordinary rectangular tables had been arranged to form a large festive table. The other, bigger rooms of the castle with the old heavy furniture were too intimidating, thought Eleanor Aybesford, the lady of the castle. She had conveyed individual invitations face-to-face. When asked what the occasion was, she let drop only vague remarks as to what the encounter was about.

When pressed by inquiring minds, she had here and there hinted at what sins might come forth. She did this because somebody who had something to hide could refrain from coming or should have the chance of making a confession beforehand. But she admitted also that she herself had to await the events.

At seven o'clock p.m. the situation in the Golden Egg resembled an informal gathering, just according to the hosts' intention. Some had already taken seats, at least preliminary ones. There were no seating arrangements. It had come about by itself that Joseph Aybesford sat with Agnes, Walter Nadler Sen., Claas, the ferryman and the present castle administrator Walter Nadler with his wife Tusnelda.

The center of a second cluster was Magdalena Forster, the landlady of The Castle Inn, whom everybody called Lena. She sat with Rita Olivero, the landlady of The Fox and Hare, Gordon, Pierre de Fermat and Eleanor. The twins Nicholas and Melis were sitting opposite one another, playing at cards.

Gloria, Elisabeth and Heidi stood at the bar. They were in good spirits and enjoyed the opportunity to be together. "Look at Monsieur Fermat," said Elisabeth, "his hair and his mustaches appear to be freshly tinted."

"Now that you mention it," said Gloria, "sometimes I think he wears a wig; and he reminds me of Etienne Friendly in London. You know the man from Edelweiss who migrated to Canada when he was still young. When my father and I met him last summer, he wore a wig with a Chinaman's pigtail; like you see them in old movies."

On hearing this, Heidi burst out laughing loudly and uninhibitedly; she got carried away and simply could not calm herself. This was so contagious, that Gloria and Elisabeth couldn't help joining in; and they got louder and louder.

In a moment Jacquy de Jong, Walter Nadler Jr. and Peter Forster, who were standing a little apart, got also infected and laughed without knowing the reason for Heidi's outburst. Soon they were also screaming with laughter and eventually all twenty-two people present in the Golden Egg – the two waitresses included – exploded with laughter.

You would have thought that the laughing would never

end, when the door opened and Dr. Rupert Aybesford and Miss Louise Chevrolet entered the Golden Egg.

All at once, the hilarious circle lapsed into silence. Everybody looked at them open-mouthed. But not so Fermat; he had been waiting for them to come. He got up and welcomed them to the mystified circle.

Then he availed himself of the situation and addressed the audience: "Messieurs dames, now that we are all here, everybody should find themselves a seat, please. Let's begin in about five minutes, when the two arrivals have made their greeting round."

The focus of interest of course was the appearance of Miss Louise Chevrolet. Everybody knew who she was. However nobody except Fermat had an idea what the reason for her coming was. Rupert took her around and introduced her to those who had not met her before.

Melis and Nicholas were deeply impressed. When she came to Joseph and they shook hands, she said, "I'm very sorry, Mr. Aybesford," whereupon he answered, "I must apologize," but she did not dwell; she moved on, feeling herself in a tight spot.

When Rupert's greeting tour came to an end, Eleanor stood up and said, "Please be seated everybody. I hope you all care for a spoonful of soup. You can choose between meat broth and yellow boletus soup."

As soon as everybody had found themselves a suitable seat, Gordon Aybesford did wait no longer. He got up and spoke, "Friends and neighbors, dear guests! I thank you for coming. As you all know, I have commissioned Monsieur Pierre de Fermat with the investigation of the circumstances that led to the death of Xanda van Aanstryk.

I know that people will cease speaking and newspapers will stop writing as time goes by. But rumors don't die completely. I want the truth to come to light. I'm sure that nobody of the present company is responsible for the death of Mrs. van Aanstryk. Even if it was suicide, I want it to be proved.

But for some reason the Austrian police seem to suppress evidence. In any case they seem to keep up the impression that Edelweiss is involved. Monsieur Fermat will pursue all leads, even if they steer him in the direction of Edelweiss, or the castle, for that matter.

He has easy questions for some of us and we should give him true answers. I hand over now to M. Fermat."

"Thank you M. Aybesford. Messieurs dames, aussi les jeunes. In case you have difficulties in comprehending one or another word I say, please say so immediately. I also suggest that you remain seated, when answering to my questions. Alors! My first question goes to Mr. Walter Nadler Jr."

Everybody seemed amazed. And everybody cast curious glances at the addressed one. Walter was amazed too, and an uncomfortable feeling seized him. "What do you want to know?" he said forcefully.

"Today seven weeks ago, on Saturday May seventeen, at 7:30 p.m., what were you doing in the flat of Xanda van Aanstryk?"

At once, all those present befell an uneasy feeling; were they all figures in a murder hunt now? When posing the question, Fermat had not watched Walter but Joseph Aybesford and Rita Olivero. Both of them featured baffled looks.

"But you were with aunt Mitzi in Alfalfa," came Walter's mother to his rescue.

"Never mind, mum. It's an amazing coincidence that I was in the block of flats on that day. But I was not inside the Aanstryk flat at all. I rang the bell and when a woman asked, 'Who is it?' I said, 'It's Walter Nadler! Is it you, Selissa?' The woman answered, 'Selissa doesn't live here anymore! Since donkey's years!' Consequently I said 'Sorry!' and left.

It was only later in The Castle Inn that I heard of Xanda van Aanstryk's failure to appear for the interview before noon."

"You are acquainted with Selissa but you were not acquainted with her mother, I understand," said Fermat. "But you knew how to find Xanda's flat?"

"I didn't know it was Xanda's flat. But I knew that Xanda was Selissa's mother. I became acquainted with Selissa and her brother Titus some years ago at the youth ball in Cyclamen City. Since then, I never saw them again; neither Selissa nor her brother."

"C'est intéressant!"

"Well, on my way home from Alfalfa on this day, I decided to make a detour and try and find out what has become of Selissa. Her private number is not in the telephone directory, neither is the name of her mother; but her brother's is. So I went to his address. I could always ask him, what has become of his sister, I thought. There was only *van Aanstryk* on the door. The voice behind the door was not encouraging; I felt stupid and took to my heels. This is all there is to it."

"Thank you for your statement Mr. Nadler," said Fermat. "Now Miss Rita Olivero, would you also be so kind as to state what your business was in the flat of Xanda van Aanstryk on the same day but later on, at eleven p.m.? She probably had no more than an hour to live after you had left her."

While these words faded away in the Golden Egg, a dead silence set in.

Confronted with the fact, Rita Olivero didn't know to do otherwise than to admit to having been in Avril 2 at eleven p.m. on that day. The audience waited with bated breath for her explanation.

"First of all, I did not enter the flat. You all know that the Sustainers meet in my Inn regularly. I am myself an ardent admirer of these advocates of independence for Goodland and their guts in pursuing their aim. It was probably silly, but I had given Xanda van Aanstryk money, which I wanted back."

"Where you acquainted with her? Or would you mind being more precise, what the money was for?" asked Fermat.

"We've met years ago. I thought that with her eloquence she could put the right words into Joseph Aybesford's mouth during the interview; words that would support the cause of the SDP. We agreed on an amount. I said half of it now, the rest when I'm satisfied. But she would only do it for the full amount up front.

So when she failed to show up I got angry and phoned her in the afternoon. I said that I had recordings of the handing over and that I would rise hell if she would not give me back the money this evening. So we had an appointment, actually."

"Quite so."

"She said that she was too weak to meet me, but that I could come to her home and fetch the money any time. On this day we had a lot of guests and two helpers were ill. So I said I would come after the closing time of The Fox and Hare."

"This would fit the testimony of the neighbor in the opposite flat," said M. Fermat. "She looked through her spy hole and said to the police that the nightly visitor was a woman. And that she was under the impression that the woman was fetching rather than bringing something."

"Let's have a break," said Eleanor, when Fermat showed a satisfied mien. She urged her guests to take some of this and more of that. She circumnavigated the large table, gave orders to the waitresses unobtrusively and had a friendly word for everybody.

"Walter, I didn't know that you are looking for a wife," said Heidi prankishly. Gloria and Elisabeth beat into the same notch. And also Rita ragged him a little; she was glad that the focus of attention had swerved to somebody else.

Walter Nadler Sen. felt the urge to go to the toilet and Joseph and Claas accompanied him. When they returned from the back of the cafeteria and trod into the limelight of the room, they reminded you a bit of The Three Wise Men of the East, but no one commented on the phenomenon. The whole situation seemed somehow too tense for such a distraction. The question stood in the room if there was a deeper meaning in their leaving the room together; if they had consulted together outside.

Gordon urged Fermat to carry on, and the Frenchman didn't need to be told twice. "We come now to the early afternoon of Saturday the seventeenth of May. More precisely 3:35 p.m. It is my duty now to ask you, Monsieur Claas, what you were doing at the specified time."

"Curiouser and curiouser!" said Agnes.

Because of this unexpected contribution, the tension slackened and the audience changed from utterly amazed to highly amused. Not least so, because Agnes had become more silent with age.

"Claas was there on my behalf," said Joseph Aybesford audibly. "I too had bribed Xanda van Aanstryk. I was anxious to talk about sustainable development. Knowing her, I was sure that with the help of money I could convince her to play along nicely."

"Hé oui!"

"When she didn't show up I called myself a fool. But I contented myself to wait what she was going to do about it. I was even satisfied to let the matter rest, if it came to the worst. But as time went by, I became determined not to let her get away with it."

Pierre de Fermat nodded.

"I called her using Claas' prepaid mobile and told her that I want the money back. If not, I'm going to tell the police, I threatened her. Of course, I wouldn't have done such a foolish thing. Astonishingly enough, she offered that I come to her flat and pick it up straight away.

So I went there and Claas came with me. When we had parked the car, I called her again and said that I was downstairs. Claas would come up and fetch the money. I did not even ask her how she was. The whole episode had brought back old grudges. After a few minutes Claas came back down and we drove off."

"What can you tell us about the encounter with Mrs. van Aanstryk, M. Claas?" asked the investigator.

"She must have been waiting behind the door, because it opened immediately, but only a little, and she gave me the envelope. I think she used to know me by sight. But she hardly looked at me," said Claas.

"What did you bring into the house?" asked Fermat.

"Nothing at all," said Claas, filled with indignation.

"No harm meant!" said Fermat. All people present were rendered speechless, and Fermat looked at everybody around, before he thought it best to continue. "Next I must pose the question: 'Why did you go to Avril Court every now and then, only to sit in the car and watch?' The person concerned will know what I'm talking about."

Everyone looked at each other for quite some time. Eventually Jacquy de Jong coughed slightly. Now all eyes were on him. Everybody looked perplexed and curious when he took off his glasses and polished them with a napkin. Fermat looked at Heidi. She looked concerned. "Could we perhaps discuss this in a smaller circle?" said Jacquy de Jong.

"No, no! Let's have it!" said Joseph. "Today be the day of the truth. Do you want to begin or shall I? It's all the same to me."

Without much ado, Jacquy began to talk: "At the time when I attended school, I often got teased. Schoolmates said that my mother was not Agnes but Xanda van Aanstryk.

I was told at an early stage that I had been adopted from Holland because my parents were dead. So I knew perfectly well that my foster-mother was not my natural mother. I ascribed the teasing about Xanda van Aanstryk to the fact that she had this Dutch name."

Everybody nodded.

"I forgot about the banter as time went by. Even when one day Walter Jr. told me that he had become acquainted with the daughter and son of Xanda van Aanstryk, and that the chap resembled me strikingly, I laughed at it. I had learned how to bear this sort of jokes.

But then, one day not long ago, I found an old piece of writing, which triggered off my suspicions that there might be something in the old teasing. After I had fought with myself for some weeks, I plucked up the courage and asked Uncle Joseph.

He had obviously been waiting for this moment, because he seemed sort of relieved. Then we sat down and he told me everything. Since this day I have sometimes sought an opportunity to catch a glimpse of her."

When faced with awkward silence, Jacquy turned to Fermat and said: "I saw no point in telling this to you when you asked me about her."

Fermat nodded. The Golden Egg had become a very quiet place. Agnes was weeping and Jacquy went to her and comforted her.

But it was Agnes who was the first to find words. She said sobbingly, "Joseph, although I'm crying, I'm bound to say that I feel better, now that you broke the silence. It must have happened in the summer of 1980, when the gardening firm van Aanstryk was commissioned to redesign the garden facilities."

Joseph put his arm about Agnes' back. "You are right. I was fool enough to let myself be seduced by a schoolgirl." After a while he continued. "When I heard she was with child I arranged with her parents that she stays with Jacob de Jong and his wife in Amsterdam.

Jacob and I had been fellow students and had remained friends. She should deliver the baby there. And then Mrs. de Jong would rear the baby. She and her husband were not able to have children of their own. But Jacob died soon and the foster-mother became an invalid.

You leaped for joy when I asked you if you would like to adopt a three year old bouncing baby boy." When saying the last words, Joseph gave Jacquy, who had joined them at the table, a pat on the back. Agnes had stopped crying. The three looked like a family.

The astonishment in the Golden Egg was manifest.

"We should be happy that Monsieur Fermat's criminal investigations led to the uncovering of the truth. And I confess, that this is what I hoped for, when I assigned him to work for me," said Gordon.

Monsieur Fermat made a modest gesture.

"I'm sorry, Gordon, and I apologize also to Agnes, Joseph and Jacquy. But if you want certainty that you are in the possession of the truth, you must first solve another riddle," said Walter Nadler Sen. "On the one hand, I should maybe better keep my mouth shut. But on the other hand, now that the issue has come up, it should perhaps be settled once and for all."

"Whatever are you talking about?" said Gordon.

"Perhaps it is nothing, and it won't change anything; then this will be the day when I have to say to myself, 'you better had remained silent, Walter.' But if I say nothing now, I must go on smitten with remorse and uncertainty."

"By all means, ease your conscience. What is still vague about the matter?" replied Gordon.

Walter Nadler Sen. cleared his throat. "It was mentioned by Agnes before, that in the summer of 1980 the gardening firm van Aanstryk was reshaping the castle grounds. Xanda helped in the firm during part of her vacations. That's what she told me at the time. On the first day she asked me about

Gordon. He was then a student. I told her, that he was on a summer job."

"Yes, I remember. I was twenty at the time and did a practicum this summer. But I did not know her. Why did she ask for me?"

"She didn't say. I said that she looked younger, how did she come to know you. Feigning indignation, she answered, 'I'm eighteen. I met him in a disco', and off she went."

"But I never had seen her in real life until a few years ago, when we met each other at a black-tie function in the town hall of Cyclamen City!"

"Wait a moment! That's not all. They had also instruction to clear out a barn. Later in the day she approached me and said that she didn't know what to do with a certain apparatus, a honey extractor or something. She was not sure if she could dispose of it.

I didn't know what she was talking about. She said I should come and see for myself, she will show it to me. She went up the steep, narrow wooden stair. And I followed her. When I looked up I saw that she had no panties on. Embarrassed, I slowed down a little. When I heard that she stepped on the floor above, I looked up again.

There she squatted, legs apart; invitingly. 'Don't be silly,' I said at first. But she got up and pressed her seducing body against mine and touched me gently until I didn't know what hit me."

"Yes, yes," said Joseph. "In my case it was the circular stair in the north-west tower. She was wise to the fact that I had a collection of telescopes and other physical instruments up there. I asked her how come she knew about the fact, and she retorted that Gordon had told her everything about it."

"The cheeky thing!" said Gordon. "How could she when she didn't know me."

"Of course it happened only once," said Joseph, breaking the ensuing silence.

"With me likewise," said the blind man. "When it was over, she said, 'Your son Gordon couldn't have done better.' I said 'Gordon is Joseph Aybesford's son, not mine.' Whereupon she replied, 'You are *not* Joseph Aybesford? Who are *you* then?' I said, 'I'm Walter Nadler, Aybesford's right-hand man'. After that she looked dumbfounded."

"The brat," said Gordon. "I had never seen her before."

"No wonder, said Joseph. It turned out later, that she was only fifteen years old."

Jacquy looked from Joseph to Walter. Now he was again in the dark. Which of the two was his father?

"You two old donkeys; you were set up for a honey trap and you walked into it," said Agnes. "Now you are in for paternity tests."

An awkward silence was in the room.

Eventually, Monsieur Pierre de Fermat broke it with the words: "With every new truth that comes up, an older truth becomes irrelevant."

All eyes were now on him. He enjoyed this situation for a while. Then he said with gusto, "I can offer a new truth about the descent of Monsieur Jacquy de Jong."

"It seems that we come to no end. I propose a little break; perhaps ten minutes?" said Eleanor.

§15

Etienne Friendly Interferes

The entire time during the pause, Melis and Nicholas were not far from where Louise Chevrolet was sitting or standing. It seemed to them, that Louise had been observing who entered and left the ladies' room.

When she deemed it to be deserted she made for it. She stood in front of the mirror and mended her makeup, when Melis entered the room and looked into Louise's eyes in the mirror. She said, "I haven't seen you on TV for a long time, Miss Chevrolet. I've heard you were sick. I hope you're well again?"

"I'm sure you are Melis, Rupert's younger sister!"

"Yes, I'm sorry Miss Chevrolet. But Rupert hasn't introduced me to you."

"I'm Louise for you, Melis. Thank you, yes, I'm all right again. I was for a while your brother's patient in the clinic. Today I was released and Rupert brought me here."

When at that moment Gloria entered the room, Louise quickly vanished into one of the cubicles. One could hear her locking the door. "Don't be cross with me, Gloria! I didn't go out with him out of spite towards you! He assured me to be through with you. I'm sorry I nearly fell for him. He tried to catch me unawares. I think he is a dazzler and an egotist. But I saw through him after only a week."

Gloria found the scene embarrassing because her sister Melis was present. "Don't be ridiculous Louise," she said. "I feel no grudge against you. Come out again, please. I know myself by now that Donald isn't worth crying over."

Cautiously Louise came out again. "Let's forget it," said Gloria.

The ten minutes interval suggested by Eleanor had stretched to half an hour, when everybody had taken their seats again. Fermat took up the thread. "I'm going to introduce a new truth to you now.

When I was assigned by M. Gordon Aybesford he told me of an older problem that bothered him. He knew of course also the rumors about Jacquy de Jong's stock. But there had never been talked about it in the family. It was a taboo issue.

He was not aware, that Jacquy had meanwhile come into the possession of the truth, or what he thought to be the truth, anyhow. Gordon asked me therefore to apply my attention to this problem alike. We called it the Jacquy case in contrast to the Aanstryk or Xanda case.

The day before yesterday I reported to Monsieur Gordon and told him about what I had found out about the Xanda case, the results regarding the Jacquy case being zero at the time. We decided that we summon you all for a meeting today, in order to get answers to the questions that had arisen in the course of the investigations concerning the Xanda-case.

Up to this point I had not the thinnest idea how to proceed with the Jacquy case. In fact I had already resigned to confronting Monsieur Joseph Aybesford with the problem. But I wanted to wait until after I had successfully solved the Xanda case. Had I not waited with asking him, the wrong truth would have come out and perhaps it would still persist."

When the words had sunk into the listeners, Fermat continued. "So when we were talking about the Xanda case, Mr. Gordon used the phrase *all other people concerned*. I let those who had to make statements pass my mind's eye – some of them have delivered their statement already tonight – and then, all of a sudden, a photo that I saw in Xanda's flat lit up in my mind, and I began to see a connection between the two cases. The solution of the Jacquy case was staring me in the face."

For a few moments, Fermat enjoyed the attention that was granted to him, before he continued.

"When I imagine Jacquy de Jong without his sideburns and the gold rimmed glasses, I find a striking resemblance to Titus, Xanda's son. When I imagine him smiling – which is not so easy – and add a thin moustache, he appears like a double of Manfred, Xanda's late husband. I was determined to learn the whole truth from Xanda's parents.

For this I sought the support of Selissa van Aanstryk, Xanda's daughter. And here she comes! Ladies and gentlemen, let me introduce to you Selissa van Aanstryk."

Selissa had at this moment entered The Golden Egg. Somebody started to applaud and all joined in. She bowed to everybody around, smiling. Heidi came forward to welcome her and took her to where she herself had her seat. Fermat came up to them and Selissa handed him a data medium.

They were talking for a while. Fermat offered Selissa to address the audience herself which she would not hear of. So Fermat continued with his elucidations, after having gone back to his seat.

"Selissa and I phoned during the last intermission, so I knew she was not long to arrive. Last Thursday I let her in on my theory and asked her to help me to speak to her grandparents, Marike and Laurens van Aanstryk.

I had expected resistance from their side but there was none. I had visited them on Tuesday together with Jacquy. They said how after our visit the thought had entered their minds that Jacquy de Jong could be their grandson.

The hunch budded more and more until they were at the point that they wanted to come forward with it. So they had arrived at the same conjecture as I had. Selissa and I had come at the right moment." Here Fermat paused.

"Don't keep us in suspense," said Agnes.

"They recounted the story in their view, as they saw it then and as they see it today. Selissa persuaded them to let her record what they had to say. At first they agreed.

But after a while Marike stopped Selissa with a wave of her hand. But they agreed to record an outline themselves for Joseph Aybesford and Jacquy de Jong. They did the final recording tonight – after many tries, they admit – and her it is." He held up the digital video disk which Selissa had brought.

"With their permission we play it here and now. They did not want to attend because they are in a state, as they put it." He looked at Selissa and she nodded in confirmation of the statement.

Nicholas went to dim the light when Fermat started the playing.

"Mister Aybesford," Marike began, "when at the time Selissa confessed to me that she was expecting she said that you are the only candidate. Only years later she told me in confidence that she had been made pregnant by Manfred; he was the son of our neighbors.

They married six years thereafter when she was pregnant for the second time. It was only then that she confided in me. Manfred did know nothing and she never told him. She spent a year in the Netherlands as an exchange student, staying with relatives. And that was all.

My husband and I decided to keep silent; but now we cannot remain silent any longer. We have not the words to say more at present. But we would be glad if we could see you and Jacquy soon."

When the lights were bright again, everybody looked into thoughtful faces. Only gradually arose a muttering.

The muttering ebbed away when Gordon began to speak. "I want to repeat the words we heard Mrs. van Aanstryk say, just now, 'We have not the words to say more at present'.

'Whereof one cannot speak, thereof one must be silent' goes a quotation of Ludwig Wittgenstein. For some of us, the benefit of having learned the truth will come by and by. Monsieur Fermat has to say another word now."

"Thank you, Mr. Aybesford. I have found out that Mrs. Xanda van Aanstryk swallowed two poisons. The first one was taken in the morning, the second one late in the evening. The second poison was probably laid on her door mat, and she took it later herself. The person who deposited it must have been wise to the fact that she liked to drink a cup of warm milk with honey before going to bed. And that she had a weakness for hibiscus honey which is not easy to come by."

Fermat avoided looking at Elisabeth when he spoke of the

two poisons. He was sure that the police had suppressed evidence, but the reason for this eluded him as yet.

"The first poison, a small dose of nicotine, was probably meant to hinder her from doing the interview in Edelweiss Castle. It was comparatively harmless and Mrs. van Aanstryk had probably been alright again, had she lived to see the next morning.

So I asked myself who would benefit when Mrs. van Aanstryk were not able to conduct the interview? Miss Louise Chevrolet told everybody what horror it was for her to step in. But was this the truth, was she perhaps only acting? I could not exclude her.

In fact, she was the hottest candidate. Her boss, Mr. Berraneck told me that she is in a sanatorium in Dafins. Coincidentally Rupert Aybesford was her doctor in charge. His father Gordon phoned him and I went there, although Rupert had said that Miss Chevrolet must not be questioned in her present state.

He said also, that he cannot make a breach of medical confidentiality. Once there, I told him of the two poisons. I could see that it took a load off his mind. Tonight the doctor and his patient have come and they can tell us now in their own words what they want to tell."

"Miss Chevrolet is no longer my patient, but a good friend," said Rupert.

"Good friend, my foot!" said Agnes faintly.

"Louise was obsessed by the idea that she had killed Xanda van Aanstryk," said Rupert. "She wants me to tell you, that she administered something to her coffee that she knew would make her sick. Something Louise herself had once taken, when she wanted to avoid sitting for an examination.

We have already spoken to Melitta Stern, the district attorney. Louise will be tried in Cowford. Until the trial she stays out of prison.

She will live in the castle and will not leave Goodland. Under no circumstances will she set foot on Austrian soil. Cyclamen is taboo. Now I hand over to Miss Louise Chevrolet. If you please Louise!" He smiled at Louise encouragingly.

Leaning back in her chair, Miss Chevrolet began with making her statement. "From my first day in the television station Xanda treated me in a lofty manner. She tended to disgrace younger women colleagues at large. For a long time I had fostered the desire to play a bad joke on her. Last summer when we took shots in the castle I met Rupert and I thought maybe I would see him again.

But the horror I felt when Berraneck told me to drive out to Edelweiss was not pretended. I can only say that I did it not out of morbid ambition. I very much apologize to all of you for my foolishness and the trouble I have caused." When uttering the last words she looked at Joseph Aybesford.

"I suppose you had also not in mind to spark off a civilian coup," said Aybesford.

This was a redeeming moment and the whole Golden Egg breathed again.

"We come now to the last item of this night of revelations," said Gordon Aybesford. "Another person's parentage will be made known. But in this case the person concerned owns the truth already."

"Let *me* tell," said Lena Forster, the landlady of The Castle Inn. "When my first husband Ian died, I was not even twenty-two years old and my son Peter was barely three. When two years later I carried Heidi, I didn't tell who the father was.

Only in the course of years I confided in my mother; and later in Karl when we contemplated matrimony. He believed me, and not the rumors. I'm sorry that the rumors didn't exclude a single possible candidate in Edelweiss." Involuntarily she looked at Eleanor.

"I was not suspicious, Lena. I believed my husband. But I think we all are very curious what you are going to reveal. We hang on yours every word."

And indeed many listened openmouthed to what Lena recounted.

"And later of course I had to tell Heidi, when she started asking questions. I told her, that her father emigrated overseas. He never came back, because he doesn't know that he has a daughter.

And we cannot invite him to visit us since we don't know where he lives. This is so because he and I became lovers not until the last evening before he left Edelweiss forever.

He used to live with his mother in the servants' quarters in the castle. When his mother died he became an orphan and accepted a call of an aunt in Canada.

The last months before his departure he had a room in the inn. He worked on the farm and helped in the butchery, and in the evenings he helped in the restaurant. He wanted to save up for his journey.

We were often the two last ones to leave the inn. On the last evening we had a little farewell party. When the others had left we got sentimental and then romantic and then amorous. We had agreed that he would not write to me, that we would not keep in contact.

E-mailing was not for domestic use then as it is today. And letters were sure to be noticed and intercepted by my parents. But then it hurt, when he showed no sign of life. I comforted myself with the thought that he was so very young and that he could find his own way in life.

I loved Heidi as much as I loved Peter. I love them still, of course. And Karl adopted them as his own children, not caring what people said behind his back. He always was and is a good father to both of my children."

"How did you find the expatriate?" asked Agnes who knew whom Lena was talking of.

"It won't be long to tell the rest," said Heidi, Lena's daughter. "It's an interesting story in itself. Last year in September a friend was on a trip in England. She e-mailed me and said that she met a man in London who was born and raised in Edelweiss.

He left here more than twenty years ago and never came back on a visit because he has no more relatives in this place. She mentioned also his first name, so I was one hundred percent sure that I had found my biological father. The friend was Gloria by the way."

"But you never said a word about it; that you thought he was your father," said Gloria.

"No, not a single word – to nobody; I acted entirely on my own account. You wrote that his wife owns the Chinese Restaurant Paradise. So it was easy to contact him.

I phoned The Paradise on a Sunday morning shortly before noon and asked to speak to his wife Xiu or his daughter Samantha Ying. You mentioned their names too, in your e-mail." Heidi showed signs of agitation and stopped speaking.

"To make a long story short," Lena stepped in, "she said that she was a friend of Gloria Aybesford in Edelweiss. A day later she had him on the phone and told him the plane truth.

After this they e-mailed and chatted. But she never spoke a word about it to anybody. When he visited in the inn a few weeks ago, she didn't tell either."

It had become late, but everybody was wide awake. Eleanor had made signs to the twins that they should go to bed. But they were too fascinated and thrilled by the unending flow of new disclosures. When she saw that they reacted testily she stopped insisting.

"He was in Edelweiss?"

"Why didn't you tell?"

Those and other questions came from all sides.

"He came only on a slight detour. Actually he was on a business trip in Maria Laah. He said that he would come soon and visit officially and bring his family. He had an invitation to the castle.

He wanted only to find out the lie of the land, as he put it. At first he didn't reveal his identity, because he was afraid that I might react impulsively. He sat in disguise in the public room, pretending to be a reporter from Manchester.

When I went outside he followed me in the ladies room and revealed who he was. But he begged me not to raise the alarm and betray him.

He would visit soon and stay for a week or so. When we were in the hallway I boxed his ears because Walter entered suddenly from outside, and I didn't know what else to do. I was unable to cope with the situation. But he played along marvelously and remedied it, when Walter braced him."

"Peter Dorset!" exclaimed Rita, Walter and Jacquy at the same time.

"The bugger, he played me for a fool! I just can't believe it!" said Walter Jr.

"He's quite an actor," said Rita Olivero. "He could understand everything we talked about. Also your condescending remarks, Jacquy."

"Yes, I'm sure. But somehow he didn't seem real to me. When is he going to come and visit?"

"He is in Edelweiss already, but again on business, unfortunately," said Heidi.

"He is in Edelweiss?"

"Where is he?"

So and otherwise where the questions that buzzed through the cafeteria.

"Il est ici, c'est moi, it is I," said Pierre de Fermat and took off his wig and his moustaches. He had carefully removed his green contact lenses beforehand, while others had been in the focus of attention.

Heidi, Lena and Gordon were the only ones initiated. They were enjoying the moment. All others were struck dumb with astonishment and surprise.

"Thank goodness the masquerading is over now, Etienne," said Gordon.

"Etienne? But his name is Peter Dorset, isn't it?" said Jacquy. The bewildered looks around the table became still more bewildered.

"That's the name he used when he visited here the first time," said Heidi. "Officially he has adopted the name Etienne Friendly in Canada."

"Well done! Laurence Olivier couldn't have played the part better. Welcome back home, Stefan!" said Joseph Aybesford.

"But I engaged Monsieur Pierre de Fermat," said Jacquy. I found his advertisement in L'Express and I contacted him," he exclaimed.

"Yes, after I had pointed him out to you. And I had two copies of L'Express prepared with an extra sheet in our printing shop in Cowford, and Claas had put them aside for you to use," said Gordon.

"When we first met you said that you read every issue of L'Express from cover to cover, remember?" said Etienne Friendly alias Peter Dorset.

"Buggers!" stated Jacquy.

"I'm sorry that I had to lie to you all," said Gordon. "I may as well confess now, that I had assigned Etienne with investigating the Jacquy case before the day of the interview, before Xanda van Aanstryk died. I told nobody. It was my great objective to clear up all doubts. I wished to accomplish lucid conditions. These have been established now; so the older of the two cases is actually solved.

Now the question arises, should we follow up the case Xanda van Aanstryk, or leave it? It seems to me that her second and lethal poisoning cannot have been implemented by a person from Edelweiss, still less so by one from the castle."

Gordon's question was a rhetorical one because he and Etienne Friendly were determined to clear up this case as well. He and Etienne had arranged to observe the reactions of all present. And he awaited protests; and they were not long in coming.

The tension in the Golden Egg had slackened and the whole

crowd was debating. Gradually people rose and stretched their legs. Gordon wanted to make sure also about Selissa's position regarding the solving of her mother's case. When she unreservedly approved, he went to Etienne Friendly and told him. So they sealed the deal on the investigation of the van Aanstryk case for the second time.

Jacquy thought that Friendly had made a perfect fool of him. Red in the face, he screwed up his courage and approached Heidi. "Have you met with your natural father in the Halfway House last week? I imagined to have you seen together there when I picked him up."

Heidi knew that he had been watching. She was glad that everything was cleared up now. She could not refrain from asking coquettishly "Were you jealous?" which heightened the red in Jacquy's face.

So as to ease his shyness she began to speak: "I work at present in the Halfway House. I have made up my mind to take over The Castle Inn in the near future.

So I quit my job and collect experience in other hotels and restaurants for the time being. He was in my room on the morning of the day when you picked him up. When unexpectedly the landlady came to my room, he disappeared via the scaffolding so we avoided explaining."

When Jacquy stammered something that Heidi could not hear properly, she became impatient and said, "Jacquy, you've heard just now that you are not Joseph's son. You will never inherit the castle. What are you waiting for?"

"I never thought of inheriting the castle, Heidi!"

"But since you fell in love with me – I think it must have happened last summer – you behave like a sheep and I cannot talk to you in a normal manner. We are both out of the romantic years. If you are thinking about marrying me as I think you are, we must talk about it."

"I'm such a nothing and much older than you – I didn't know how to speak about it."

I've never heard such nonsense. Much older … ten years were a lot when you were eleven and I was one. I can get killed in an accident tomorrow and you can live to be hundred years old.

And you are not a *nobody*! You know now your descent and you are a cultivated man with good manners and a good character. You neither smoke nor drink, you are good at languages and we like each other; we can make you the perfect landlord of The Castle Inn.

Give up your idea of ever finishing this legal trash. With your shyness you would never be a good lawyer; and you are too honest for this profession.

For becoming a judge or a notary it is much too late. And anyway, Goodland needs not people who have studied fancy garbage. We need people who know how to work. With assiduity an intelligent person can make up for almost any lack of formal education. But an ape remains an ape, even after graduation. Sorry I don't mean you …"

"Yes," said Jacquy.

"What is most important is that we know each other well enough. It is not as if we plunged in at the deep end. I know I sound unromantic. In fact I am a pragmatist."

"Yes."

"My mother had to convince my father Karl too. 'Once you've made up your mind, it's all plain sailing' my mother uses to say. One simply has to make the best of it, one must never waver."

"Yes."

"They say that you have little experience with women. I have not much experience with the other gender either. Don't let yourself be fooled by the pathological ideas about a fulfilled sex life. What counts is a fulfilled life, and that comes with work and doing good things. I'm not saying that I do not want children. I want two. Let's sit down they are all looking at us."

"I suspect that your father Etienne has emboldened you a little?"

"Yes," said Heidi, "because you are an inhibited waverer."

"Yes, I was a coward."

At this moment, Selissa who had gone outside came back into the cafeteria and Gordon said, "Selissa, won't you kiss your brother Jacquy?"

"You should say my half-brother," said Selissa.

"But as from today we know that he is your brother, isn't it? He is Xanda's child and conceived by your father."

"No, he is my half-brother; my mother cheated. Titus and Jacquy are brothers though, unless still other facts appear," said Selissa.

"Are you saying that the father of Jacquy and of your other brother is not *your* father as well?" asked Gordon.

"Precisely," said Selissa. "My biological father is a teacher. He and my mother were colleagues while she worked as a schoolmistress. I am a child of adultery. I have found out long, long ago." And then she and Jacquy kissed each other on the cheeks.

"I hope this was the last secret to come out in the open."

said Gordon; then he indicated to Etienne Friendly to carry on.

"After so many secrets have surfaced and so many mysteries have been solved, all of you seem to be eager to solve the Xanda van Aanstryk case too. Peter Forster is a professor of mathematics, and his wife Elisabeth is in awe of his versatile mind. She says that he defines concepts and devises notions to solve problems or to prove things, of which nobody has heard before.

Peter, perhaps you have an idea how to proceed with the case of Xanda van Aanstryk? I'm not joking. Let yourself your time. Also everybody else is invited to offer their ideas."

"Your business is different from mine," said Peter Forster. "You cannot define a criminal and then prove that he is the culprit. This is a joke, of course.

You have no suspects left, so you must find at least one new one and then prove or disprove his guilt. You must repeat this procedure. After a final number of attempts you will have your man or woman." These words provoked laughter and Peter went on: "Earnestly, I think you should not fish in troubled water. But I don't know what you still have up your sleeve."

"I'll tell you what I have up my sleeve. I think we can work from the hypothesis that Xanda van Aanstryk was well at eleven p.m., after her last visitor, Madame Olivero, had gone.

She prepared for bed and had a nice cup of hot milk with honey. She did not take from the open glass that she had on the sideboard, but had some of the honey that somebody had put on her door mat five hours before. She was in the habit of drinking hot milk with honey before she went to bed."

"Is this all you have?"

"It's good you're asking! This reminds me that I must show you the photos of the suspicious man who presumably put the deadly honey at the door," said Etienne Friendly and projected the pictures of the unknown man onto the wall where they had watched the confession of Xanda's parents before.

"A witness claims, that the man reminds her of a lumberjack whom she watched from a safe distance in the Edelweiss Castle forests some years ago. Two men were felling a tree.

The elder of the two stuck to her memory because of his gray, long hair and his green cap. She feels certain she could still recognize this man, because he had also an unusual skew nose. In her opinion he must be retired today. Unfortunately, in the picture the face is not discernible."

"It could also be a woman," remarked somebody.

"A big woman; yes, could be. The person's appearance is probably a disguise. If he or she is masquerading, maybe somebody recognizes the lumberjack shirt or the yellow cap," said Etienne, looking at the table where Joseph sat. "Does the frame perhaps suggest a specific person?"

"The person looks like a big man, a little plump perhaps," said the ferryman, Mr. Naran Dasgupta.

"The witness says that the *lumberjack* in the picture looks less corpulent than the lumberjack she remembers; if the person in the picture was a lumberjack at all. Has anybody an idea, who this suspicious looking person might be?"

After some minutes watching and guessing Walter Nadler, the administrator of the castle said, "One could think from the physique and the hair that it is Joe Hartig who was one of our woodcutters. But Hartig died some years ago. We couldn't search out any relatives at the time."

"Any other suggestions?" asked Etienne Friendly to everybody around. But nobody had something to offer.

"Like the police in Cyclamen City, you seem to have nothing to go on," said Peter Forster. If I were to find this person, I would study the life of Xanda van Aanstryk. There is only she and her environment left, to be examined carefully. I think it is the only chance to find a decisive clue."

"I congratulate Dr. Elisabeth Forster. She has a very clever husband," said Etienne Friendly.

Into the ensuing merry applause Gordon Aybesford said, "I'm afraid that we have discovered everything that lends itself to be discovered tonight. I hope you have still the stamina to celebrate a little."

§16

Mateo Capota

The official part in The Golden Egg was over. Although it had become late, the crowd lingered – even the children. Etienne Friendly sought the company of Gordon and Gloria. When they sat together, Gloria said, "Aha, listen to this!" and pointed at the piano, where Rupert and Louise were trying to play four-handed a melodic line from Beethoven.

Gordon looked at them and shook his head in disbelief, and then he looked at his wife Eleanor – she was smiling. After a while Gordon asked, "What is your next step to take, Etienne?"

"I need a door opener once more. I must have an extensive conversation with a certain Mateo Capota. Does the name mean anything to you?" When Gordon and his daughter answered in the negative, Friendly carried on, "He was in a longstanding romantic relationship with the poisoned woman. He seems to be the only male who was close to her after she had become a widow. I pin all my hopes on him. He must have known her like nobody else. From what I have heard her mother say, he must have been sick and tired of Xanda. I don't want to take the risk of him shutting the door in my face."

"Like I said, I've never heard the name," said Gordon. "Where does he live?"

"Somebody told me that years ago he used to live in Syget. I looked up the name in the telephone directory. There is actually a Mateo Capota in Syget. I've noted down the address."

"Could he be our man, I mean the poison depositor?" asked Gordon, who had not been listening properly to Friendly's words because he was distracted by Rupert's foolish conduct.

"From all appearances he was never in touch with Xanda van Aanstryk ever since he broke off with her. The break happened about ten years ago already. Why should he take revenge on her and what for? But nothing is certain. Xanda van Aanstryk was a very secretive person."

Gordon nodded his head.

"This Mateo Capota was never questioned by the police, according to the material I have access to. He might be piqued by a private investigator seeking an interview with him. Some people have a way to show their displeasure very impressively."

Gordon nodded again.

"I don't think he is involved in the poison drama. As I said earlier, I think he is in the possession of the key to Xanda van Aanstryk's personality. Maybe he has a clue regarding a suspect he is not aware of himself. I don't want to scare him away by phoning him or walking boldly into his home."

Quite so; I see your point. Tell me where to find him; his address. I'll write a short personal letter tomorrow and let it be delivered by hand promptly. The day after tomorrow is Monday; you can then try to phone him or visit him right away."

"The first time you visit him, I'll accompany you again; with a female visitor he will not be so harsh," said Gloria.

"I think you have found an avid assistant," said Gordon Aybesford to Etienne Friendly.

"Yeah, this line of attack should prove to be successful," said Friendly, displaying a broad smile.

Gloria's account of the visit to Mateo Capota: Monday the seventh of July was a fine day. Mateo Capota had phoned my father in his office early in the morning, when the Monday conference with the board of directors was still on. But Mrs. Achmadi had instructions to put him straight through. It was an act of courtesy, because father did not want to bungle the meeting with Capota.

This gentleman had then not only agreed to a meeting; he had also stated that we are welcome to visit him in his home any time on the same day. He will be waiting for us to come. Mrs. Achmadi phoned Etienne Friendly and he rang me.

The two of us decided that we should not let Capota wait unduly and made for Syget at a quarter past nine, so that we would arrive at his home Hollywood, as his house was called, at about ten o'clock before noon.

"Hello Miss Aybesford, hello Mr. Friendly," thus we were greeted by a schoolgirl with dark eyes and two dark plaits of hair, when we disembarked before the country house. Capota's home was on a piece of land at the edge of town and bordering the River Holly.

The girl stood next to the fence gate and kept it from closing so that we could enter. Then the girl stepped forward and led the way from the garden gate to the house, her plaits dangling as she hopped.

We found the front door ajar. This fact and the behavior of the girl gave us the feeling that we had been expected, although we had not bothered to call and say when exactly we would come.

The girl pushed the door open and said "Mum!", whereupon a black-eyed woman, aged about forty, appeared in the hallway and welcomed us. "You come on account of Mrs. van Aanstryk, I take it. I'm Meta Capota and this is our daughter Vanessa. My husband is catching a fish for lunch. He'll not be long. Please sit in here." When she turned I saw that her black hair was braided in a single waistline-long plait.

We sat in the living-dining room and looked out by the window. The place was terrific with the river perhaps twenty paces away. We saw a man in the act of casting a fishing line out over the water by means of a rod and reel.

Etienne Friendly told me how glad he was that I was with him. And I had been thinking that private investigators are tough guys without feelings. Vanessa brought two tumblers, a bottle of orange juice and a bottle of water. We thanked her and I said, "This must be the first day of your school vacations?"

The girl answered, "It was about time; we were absolutely frying in the classroom – in this heat."

"Nessie is nine years old; she got good grades," said her mother, who entered the room this moment. When she heard the backdoor slam, she said, "Mateo, you have visitors," and for the fun of it she added, "Have you ever known a certain Xanda van Aanstryk?"

"Rings a bell, yeah," said Mateo Capota on entering the living-dining room. "You should know, my wife and I became acquainted with each other in Xanda's flat," he added by way of explanation and laid his arm around Meta's shoulders. "Welcome to Hollywood. We have the River Holly and a copse right at our rear door," he extended his explanations.

When we shook hands, I could feel how Capota's hand was cold and clammy, in spite of the warm weather. A man who calls his home Hollywood must have a delightful sense of humor, I thought to myself. I knew him to be sixty. He was more than medium height and his dark hair was tinged with gray. His broad cheekbones and his knowing brown eyes were capturing all my senses. He radiated serenity and self-assurance.

"Let me quickly wash and change; I've been working in the cellar and then I have angled some trouts. Perhaps you would rather sit on the porch behind the house? There we will be in the open air and still in the shade." When we said that we would love it, Vanessa took the two bottles and carried them outside. We took our glasses and followed. "I'll be with you presently," said Capota and went upstairs.

Once sitting on the porch, Friendly and I congratulated each other on having prepared the land so well. We took in the surroundings. Last Friday's flood had left marks in the shrubbery. There was a metal pole stuck in the ground with the flood water levels of previous years marked on it. The terrain around the house was barely a foot above the highest level ever measured.

"It must be nice to sleep in this house, now in the summertime, with the window open and the rush of the river as a background noise," I said.

"The other side of the river is Cyclamen," said Etienne Friendly.

"The nearest bridge to cross is five miles upriver," said Mateo Capota who was approaching us. He sat down. "You use it when you go to Cyclamen City. You probably came via

Alfalfa?" We affirmed and he said, "It's by far the shorter way."

After a little more small talk Mateo Capota looked at me and said: "Had your father not written in so polite a manner, I think I would not be prepared to talk to you about Xanda and our relationship. He has explained the awkward situation your family is in. I must agree; the uncertainty is not satisfactory.

After a short time of thinking I consented to help. I said to my two girls, 'these are polite people with nobleness of the heart. They will make their visit at ten a.m.' Vanessa believes everything I say, so she lay in wait for you, my wife tells me."

When he seemed to say no more, Friendly began cautiously, "Thank you for your warm reception, Mr. Capota. I had expected you to say that you cannot see how you could help. That's what people usually say."

"Well, Mr. Aybesford wrote in his letter that the case seems to be unsolvable; that as the last choice you want to study Xanda's milieu and personality. There was no implication that I might know something about the case. About the case I know only what was in the papers. Meta and I followed the news closely because we used to know her."

Etienne Friendly and I nodded.

"I think that I knew Xanda as thoroughly as ever you can know another person. In the first months of our togetherness I was sometimes baffled at her behavior. But later I developed a sort of scientific interest in her obsessional personality and studied her downrightly. This did no harm to the spell I was under; she fascinated me increasingly."

"Would it be convenient to you if we meet sometimes in the evening after work, and we talk and you tell me about her?"

"I'm my own master. I freelance as a consultant. I'm a

teleworker, in a manner of speaking. You simply ask me for an appointment when the need arises."

"Do you know this peculiar man?" said Etienne Friendly, spreading photos of the *lumberjack* on the table.

But this one shook his head and said, "Can't say; his face is not recognizable."

"Does the word hibiscus honey ring a bell?"

"Hibiscus honey? In what connection?"

"Titus told me that the word started the four of you laughing, as soon as it was mentioned," said Etienne Friendly.

"Aha! This is what you mean. Why is that of interest to you?"

"I don't know if it's important. But do you remember how this sport arose?"

"I'm sorry, I don't remember."

"Should you ever remember, please tell me."

"If it comes into my mind again, I'll tell you."

"When you heard about Mrs. van Aanstryk's death, did you ever have a hunch about who could have meant her ill?"

"As I said before, I have no hunch. I'm not going to tell you anything about suspicions. I agreed to speak about Xanda's temper and disposition; and even about our time together. And I will do even better than that. I'm ready to give you unpleasant snapshots of our story in writing."

Etienne Friendly and I looked baffled.

"Yes! After our relationship had lasted a year or so I started to note down certain incidents which provided food for thought at the time."

"Ah! And when you had parted you had the time to write about your relation," said Friendly.

"Not quite. The day I parted with Xanda I started off with

Meta. But the breakup was not Meta's fault. We did not part because of Meta and me starting something. Meta worked at the time twice a week in Xanda's flat as a cleaning lady. I had scarcely seen her face before. Every time I looked at her I saw her back. She was either cleaning the floor or dusting a book-shelf. I think she simply avoided looking at me. She also wore a kerchief. She was very discreet at all times.

That I called her to help me clean the flat when I left Avril 2 for the last time was sort of a brain wave.

To be in Meta's company was sudden heaven on earth, after the frustrating years with Xanda. Meta and I married shortly thereafter. It's nearly ten years now."

"Pardon my asking! Was *Selissa* the cause for your separation?"

"In a way, she triggered the decisive moment, yes. You seem to be acquainted with the facts already."

"I'm sure, I'm not."

"No, you can't."

"And you have everything put down in writing?"

"No, I did not write up everything. I did not keep a diary from the start and not continuously. Above all, I did not make notes of the many *happy* hours we spent or when everything was optimal. Xanda's pleasant and charming traits do *not* come across, I'm afraid."

"That doesn't matter for my purposes, I'd think, but it might be good to know. As you said, you began to write incidents down a year after you had parted?"

"It was like this, when Meta and I had settled down and lived in this house for a year and we had our baby, we were completely happy. It was the way I had imagined it with Xanda to be, but which did not materialize. By and by, first without meaning to, I began to analyze this past relationship and looked for reasons of my failure."

"Did you think that it was your fault?" I asked.

"OK! Let's say our failure. But when something doesn't go right for five years and I constitute fifty percent of the team involved I must presume that I made many mistakes. And one must keep in mind that I had her under observation after it had become clear to me that we were caught in a crazy partnership. When the end of our relation was nearing, I sometimes wondered how it will eventually end."

"I'm asking because I myself have been caught in a crazy relationship for a few years. I have overcome the pain of parting eventually. But I could not say what mistake implied the next mistake. I suppress all thoughts that come up."

"I'm not an expert, but I think it's best to let rest the past. I think your reaction is normal and appropriate. Either a man and a woman are made for one another or they are not made for one another."

"I made the mistake to fall in love with an attractive man who has no inner values, only exterior ones."

"We can shake hands, because we were in similar situations, it seems," said Capota.

Etienne Friendly gave me a sympathetic look.

"When I met Xanda van Aanstryk I was not exactly a youngster. I was forty-five. I had two grown up children who were then students and came home only on weekends. She was thirty-four and had also two children, but teenagers. They were ten and twelve. I thought it must be as easy as it was later with Meta. Meta had a ten year old daughter who in the meantime also comes home only sporadically."

"What exactly do you mean when you say *easy?*"

"Meta and I liked each other and we both thought that marriage is the natural marital status. We asked ourselves 'what are we waiting for?' In marriage you must always try to make the best of everything. That's obvious. Meta has housewifely virtues, and I like best being at home. Our common hobby is to live and to reside. We don't need a lot of friends coming and going. There was no official marriage proposal. That's what I mean by *easy*; there were no provisos. We just agreed." When he said these words, his face wore a mixture of a benevolent and a quizzical expression.

"Now you show the physiognomy like on the photo on Mrs. van Aanstryk's night table," said Etienne Friendly.

"She had still a photo in her bedroom?"

"Yes, she had. Well, you said that you like to live your life in unagitatedness; not agitated and disturbed emotionally for the most part. I see what you mean. There are women who nag at you and bring trouble all the time. On the other hand there are the peaceful ones who are trying to keep trouble away from you. My wife is one of the latter sort, she is a very agreeable person," said Etienne Friendly. "She is a Chinese woman, by the way. She is very peaceable."

"Yes," I said. "That's what I thought when I met you both. You surely miss your family."

"I'm thinking of returning home for a few days. I can study the paper about the five years with Xanda van Aanstryk in London. Is it written in the form of a report?"

"Not exactly; it's more a collection of accounts of single events, mostly written on the following day. But every single piece shows at least one aspect of Xanda's character. That is

what you are after, isn't it? However, before you start reading it, you must know something about my background.
Otherwise you will measure me up for a very stupid person."

"Why is that so?"

"Because you will ask yourself, why didn't he pull the
plug earlier?"

"And the answer to this question?"

"The third reason is that I was too optimistic and didn't
want to believe that we could not succeed. I have a tendency
not to give up too soon.

The second reason is that we fell in love from the start and
that the love grew in spite of the occasional trouble we had."

"These two reasons are not alien to me either," I said. "But
what is the first reason?"

"The first reason is more complex. You see, my entire an-
cestry has been diplomats. I was born in Honduras and when
I was four, my family had to leave my birthplace for the first
time. Every few years we changed residence. I attended international schools in four countries but I was nowhere at home.
Again and again I had to leave behind dear friends and embo-
somed places of residence.

These permanent changes of residence fostered in me a
longing for family and stability. My parents died soon and my
first wife left me because she needed to see much company.
When my children became independent and moved out, I got
aware of how lonesome I was. I need not much company, but
I had always the desire to have a family; preferably a big one,
but at least a small one.

So I tried a marriage advertisement. Xanda replied to
it. This is how I met her. She seemed the perfect match. But

although everything seemed perfect, when it came to the point, suddenly she would not hear of marriage."

"I can sympathize with your disappointment," said Etienne Friendly. "The occasional disturbances you've been talking about, were they related to this strange behavior she displayed?"

"This should become revealed to you in the course of reading my records. But essentially it was her immobility altogether. I used to say 'you are the fixed star and I am revolving around you, day and night'. She was not able to change her habits; not in the slightest. But it is not this shattered relationship that you are to analyze, is it?"

"One can never have too many clues," said Friendly mischievously.

"As I said before: when we had been living in this house for a year or so, I began to read my notes, about my crazy years with Xanda van Aanstryk.

It was as if I were reading an old familiar melancholic story. This enticed me to write down single scenes and events and to mull them over after some time. At first I chewed them over with the experience of the actor. Later I looked at it with the eye of the director. I considered in what way a single scene could be improved. Even later I began to see it with the eye of the scriptwriter and it gave me pleasure to relive certain scenes and to rewrite them. In this way I discovered a new hobby and in the end it led to a career as a screenwriter.

But fear not! The set of scenes I leave to you are original ones. They are mundane but true. I never had in mind to use parts of this material as long as Xanda was among the living. The position is different now. I let you the records under the condition that you sign a contract. The copyright remains with me. You have to acknowledge that I will sue you when something gets out. Particularly the delicate issues are private and confidential."

"No problem," said Etienne Friendly.

"The clock says noon," said Meta from the backdoor. "Shall we eat outside? I hope you give us the pleasure and join us on trout meunière?"

"You are cordially invited," affirmed Mateo Capota.

Friendly and I looked at each other. We read in one another's faces that we couldn't say 'no, thank you' at this crucial moment. So we accepted, smiling broadly.

"Splendid," said Mateo Capota. "Yes, Meta; let's have lunch outside. I go and fetch a bottle of light white wine to chink glasses."

We ate the light meal which was delicious. Etienne Friendly and I were allocated such seats as allowed us to relish the scenery. After a while Mateo Capota raised his wine glass and said, "To your health!" When the first sips were taken he raised his glass again and said, "Here's to us! Let's be on first-name basis with one another." All of us said their first names merrily, although they were known to everybody anyway.

After the meal, there was coffee and blueberry cake. Thereafter Mateo brought his laptop and opened a text file with a ready contract which Friendly wanted to be amended. He wanted provisions made for the case that he finds hints at criminal acts in the records. To my astonishment, Mateo faltered a little, before he consented. After the contract was signed, we left the little family. We promised each other to meet again.

"Have you noticed how Mateo hesitated when you brought

up the criminal side?" I asked Friendly when we were on our way back to Edelweiss.

"Yes, I've noticed. I don't think however that he is the one with a skeleton in his closet. But Xanda van Aanstryk was of unheard-of audacity. Not to tell her lover that she is with child and looking for a provider in affluent quarters shows a high degree of criminal energy."

To this I could nothing but agree.

"Maybe Mateo was considering what consequences might arise for Xanda's children ... or even her parents. He had sure-ly reflected on this beforehand and decided not to care. But when I mentioned the aspect and spoke of writing it down, he wavered anew for a moment. But what bothers me is – is he perhaps using the case for promoting his drama that he might release in print now his past lover is no more?"

"He versed himself in scriptwriting while studying his bungled relationship – another unheard-of case; I must think about that in peace and quiet," I said.

§17

Charing Cross Road

Melis and Nicholas were practicing with their unicycles in the asphalted castle yard when Heidi's Peugeot came in through the main portal. Heidi maneuvered her vehicle between a farm tractor and the south portal and got off the car.

At the same time Etienne Friendly, a suitcase in hand, emerged out of a side door.

Seeing this, Melis said to her twin brother, "I think they are going to Kyll. I've heard that Heidi had insisted on seeing her natural father off at the airport. Maybe they let us ride along. Let's ask them."

"Does it not occur to you that maybe they want to be among themselves? You're always so nosy!"

"Hello Heidi, hello Mr. Friendly," said Melis, drawing closer to the car. Are you leaving already, Mr. Friendly? Will you soon be back? It's a long time I've been out to the airport."

Father and daughter returned the greetings. "Would you mind if we take them along?" asked Heidi, facing Etienne Friendly.

"It's fine with me."

"That's great, thank you; it's very good of you both," said Melis.

When they got into the car, Nicholas was no longer in sight. "He is always so shy," said Melis.

"We women are spunkier; but shouldn't you tell your mother you are coming along?" asked Heidi.

"Nicholas knows where I am, that will do; don't worry."

When Heidi pulled away, Etienne Friendly turned his head back to Melis and said, "Tell me, Melis, which grade are you both in?"

"Come on, Mr. Friendly! You know we have just finished our second year in High school. You know everything about us. Why don't you ask me about more serious issues?"

They were now coming out of the portal and entering the public road.

Melis continued, "My main suspect in the Xanda van Aanstryk case is this woman, for example." She was referring to Mrs. Tusnelda Nadler – the wife of the castle administrator – who was crossing the road in front of them.

The remark aroused ringing laughter in the car. Melis too joined in.

When they had calmed themselves down, Friendly asked, facing Melis, "You can't be serious, can you?"

"I am serious," said Melis, stubbornly.

"And what gives you the idea?" asked Friendly.

"I saw her go to the abyss in the afternoon of the day of the interview."

"Is that all?"

"She was carrying a yellow plastic bag."

"Are you sure it was not a red herring?" said Heidi.

The three of them laughed again.

"Where you able to discern what kind of a plastic bag it was?" asked Etienne Friendly.

"One in the fashion you can buy them for twenty cents

in our nearest supermarket. I think she threw it down into the river."

"She probably was feeding the birds; she does it once in a while," said Heidi.

The car was jolting to a halt in front of the airport building. "You take the piece of baggage and I'm looking for a parking space. I join you then in the check in area," said Heidi.

"Luckily you will come back soon, so you have only this one bag," said Melis Aybesford, walking beside Etienne Friendly towards the counters inside the building. She was pushing the trolley with the bag on it. "My granddad usually travels with two heavy cases."

"I'd like to know why they want one to check in two hours before takeoff," said Heidi, who had caught up with Friendly and Melis again. "We aimed at a *one* hour cushion, and you have already completed check in."

"But they have already called the passengers for Munich and London; so I'll rather move off for passport control," said Etienne Friendly who disliked long farewells. He began to bid adieu to his daughter and Melis Aybesford.

"Heidi, can we go to the roof terrace and watch the boarding?" When Heidi consented, Melis said, "Mr. Friendly we'll wave goodbye to you from the visitor's deck. You must look back."

"Alright," said Friendly, who was now already in the queue for the terminal.

The Lufthansa plane was in wait on the airport apron. It shone in the sunshine when Heidi and Melis arrived on the roof. They had to wait for nearly three quarters of an hour, until the shuttle bus joined the airplane and the passengers dismounted and filed for climbing the airstairs of the plane. Before Etienne Friendly disappeared past the stewardess into the black hole, he waved for the last time. He did not know if his daughter Heidi and Melis Aybesford could discern him. Melis had promised to wait at least five minutes after he had entered the aircraft.

When he had found his seat, and when he sat, he looked out by the window. He sat even on the right side; he had a good view at the airport building. However he could not perceive the girls among the many visitors on the observation deck. He was quite sure, that he too was indiscernible for his escorts, but he waved for the last time.

He watched for a while people taking their seats. When the plane was in the air and had climbed to cruising altitude, he took the tablet computer from his hand baggage and tackled the recordings made by Mateo Capota thirteen years ago:

Tuesday April 24, 2001:

My darling Xanda is on duty in the television studio tonight. She won't be home before one o'clock in the morning. Her children, Titus and Selissa, are yonder with their grandparents. That's where they used to spend their time in the past, when Xanda was out − before I had moved in. They have bigger rooms there than in Xanda's flat. I encourage them to continue this practice so as not to antagonize Marike and Laurens van Aanstryk; also I can pursue my office work without ruffle and excitement that way.

Of late I've sensed that our relationship does not go as I think it should. I have made up my mind to review in leisure our time of togetherness. Tonight being on my own, I'm going to set to work looking back upon the last eighteen months. Being an artful person in many ways, I think that I can make out the sequence of events that led to our present situation.

For the first time I begin to understand the benefit that people derive from keeping a daybook. In my childhood I received an ornamented book with the words My Diary on the cover as a gift. Three or four times I wrote into it, before I lost interest in it and disregarded it. When I came across it again years later, I was astonished at the undeveloped handwriting. Amused I put it in the waste paper basket.

As from tomorrow I will note down extraordinary episodes in a journal; maybe sometimes also everyday occurrences. I wonder for how long this resolution is going to last. For a start in any case I begin to put down in writing what comes to my mind when I think back. Maybe I succeed in writing a log from memory which will reveal crucial events? Let's see what I can remember.

Etienne put the tablet aside. Reading from it did not suit his notion. He simply could not bring himself to read longer passages from a screen. He liked better printouts. He unfolded a newspaper.

The scheduled stopover in Munich extended to a stay of unknown length. Somebody was on strike, he heard people conjecture. The passengers were brought to the terminal.

Etienne Friendly took the opportunity to phone the Restaurant Paradise and told his wife Xiu that he would be late, but that everything was okay. Then he called his office. The office manageress Mrs. Sara Lagoons took the call. He informed her about his delayed arrival.

"This minute, Veronica is preparing to drive out to Heathrow so as to pick you up. I must quickly go and stop her."

"You need not meet me at the airport, I can easily take

the train," said Friendly when Sara was back. "I don't know when and where we will arrive. I think there is an air traffic control strike going on. I can also take a taxi when we come to London."

"Is there anything else we can do?"

"A minute ago I dispatched a longish e-mail to you. It contains a report, authored by a certain Mr. Mateo Capota. In the face of his secretiveness I sent it encrypted."

"What key have you used?"

"Omega eleven."

"Must we print the report out?"

"Yes, yes. Reading from the tablet is unsatisfactory; and from the screen in the office too. The notes are very comprehensive. I want you to have them printed out by tomorrow; that is to say, at least roughly the first thirty pages of it. There may be hundreds. But use no small print, so that I can read without my glasses."

"No problem, Etienne!"

"See you then tomorrow!"

Friendly sat in the departure lounge, awaiting the continuation of the journey.

He knew Mrs. Sara Lagoons would delegate the task; probably to Miss Veronica Smith who was the most efficient and versatile employee. But Mrs. Lagoons did not like it when he ignored official channels, how she used to put it. And after all, Mrs. Lagoons was a respectable and conscientious associate who managed all his affairs. As far as secrecy was concerned, he trusted all his staff members.

Etienne Friendly arrived from his visit to Edelweiss in his home in London on the evening of the Tuesday. On Wednesday the ninth of July 2014 he lay on his davenport in the thinking room of his home office in Charing Cross Road in the West End. He had put three cushions under his head in order to be better able to read.

Miss Smith had printed out the notations completely. She had also stapled together sheets of the same date. Then she had punched the bundles and filed them away into ring binders chronologically. The printouts of Mateo Capota's notes were even much more expansive as Etienne Friendly had expected them to be. The filing folder number one lay open on a small table next to the sofa. He took the first sheaf out of the folder and continued to read where he had broken off in the plane:

On the morning of the penultimate Sunday of the month September in the year 1999 I ran my daughter Roxanne to the railway station. Monday was the first day of the induction week of her first year at university. My son Xavier, who was two years ahead of her, had left the week before already. He began his third year and had to sit for a repeat examination. When I went back home a feeling of depression crept over me.

During the whole rest of the Sunday I felt wistful. I did not have lunch. It had come as a shock over me that both my children were now independent. None of them will come home from school every day any longer. This thought span around in my head until I fell asleep.

Fits of melancholy crept up also on Monday; but there were also flares of delight when I considered that my children were now over the worst.

On Tuesday I made up my mind to let a new woman into my life. For six years I had functioned only as father. I decided to turn over a new leaf. I looked for the weekend edition of the Cyclamen City Herald.

I thought newspaper advertisements to be less noncommittal than dating in the internet.

One can imagine that matchmaking agencies are lucrative businesses, but I didn't give them credit for bringing about a marriage between a man and a woman.

Under Marriage I found an advertisement that I decided to answer. A box-number was given, so I wrote a letter and handed it in at the Herald publishing company.

I did not quite trust the thing and had only given my mobile phone number and my first name. If at all, I expected a call on Thursday. But Thursday evening elapsed and nothing happened.

Unexpectedly the hoped-for call came on Friday morning at ten o'clock. 'This is a certain Aleva speaking,' she said. She was a teacher and used the break between classes to call me from the schoolyard. She lived at the fringe of Cyclamen City. We agreed to meet in the evening at the freeway exit ramp that is midway between her dwelling place and my abode.

When I left the freeway I anticipated the worst; I couldn't imagine a woman worth desiring placing a marriage advertisement in the paper. All the more stunned I was when I beheld the woman in the convertible at the bottom end of the ramp.

Later, when we discussed life over a beer, I told her about my thoughts and said how attractive she was. She replied that she too was agreeably surprised. She loved beer and we had a few. When the inn closed, we ended up on the freeway in the rest shop which was open all night. We had a very good time.

Next day I was invited at her home. She had a little son. And there was also a chaperone, Belinda, who was a teacher too. They talked about an investment scheme that a married couple, also teachers, propagated on behalf of the inventor of the scheme. Allegedly, the chaperone had already made a considerable profit.

When she had left, it occurred to me that she had not come as a chaperone but as a promoter of the scheme that obviously was nothing more than a snowball system or pyramid scheme. You had to pay fifty euro and then you had to find ten new participants. And every new participant had again to pay fifty euro and then he or she had to recruit ten new participants.

She had invited me to join the next gathering together with Aleva. The meeting was only for a group of teachers who were friends with each other; and they could bring somebody along.

Soon thereafter Aleva spent an evening with me in Syget. She loved not only beer but also wine. She had brought along her little son. He asked for scribbling paper and crayons so he could occupy himself with drawing and I gave him some. Proudly he showed us that he was able to draw beer and wine. He had drawn two different bottles.

I was in a conflict with myself. She was such a likeable woman but there was her alcohol addiction. I was in jeopardy myself. A few evenings later when I had already retired she phoned and said how lonesome she was. She tried to coax me into going to her place and to be with her. It was too hard to say no, so I went.

Of course she had been drinking; but she was so lovely and irresistible. When she fell asleep, I got up and left. I locked the front door from within. Then I crawled out by a cellar window and went home.

I had made up my mind not to call her again. I did not know how to handle an alcoholic. Next Sunday she phoned me; she asked me if I would accompany her to the meeting of the moneymakers. I did not know how to say no, so I said yes.

Later, when I was on my way to pick her up at her home, I thought to myself, there seem to be so many lonesome schoolmistresses; perhaps I encounter a suitable one at this gathering.

EDELWEISS CASTLE

The meeting was in a side room of The Golden Lion in Cyclamen City. Besides the propagator I was the only male present. Aleva, her son and I took places at the back, farthest from the prophet. Nevertheless, the advertising man referred to me as being able to give testimony for the success of the scheme because I was proficient with computers.

Belinda must have told him that in my work I made use of computers extensively. But what a reckless stupidity and lie! You can't prove with or without a computer that there is a game in the world which only knows winners; not in the long run. But I said nothing. I only grinned. I was not going to spoil the party. All women present were teachers; they will hardly be so silly as to imagine themselves a game with this property.

To Aleva I explained it in this way: 'Today is Sunday. Suppose that you recruit ten players tonight. If every one of these recruits ten new ones tomorrow, then there are one hundred. If every one of these recruits ten new players the day after tomorrow, you have one thousand. If you continue you have ten thousand and then one hundred thousand and on Friday you have a million. That means that after five repetitions you have recruited all inhabitants of the Cyclamen Province. Let's continue this process four more times, then on Monday of the week after next we have recruited one billion people.

The day after the snowball explodes, because you need ten billions of people to be recruited, but there are only seven billions left on this planet. Besides, this sort of game or investment is not legal, it's prosecutable.'

Aleva had not expected the solution to this problem to be so easy. She urged me to tell this to the assembly. But I refrained. You were not supposed to commit yourself this evening, anyway. This evening was only for information. For those interested, next week was to be a meeting with the inventor of the scheme.

But something else transfixed me; a red-headed woman. She sat far

from our corner, next to the wife of the presenter. We had been introduced briefly, concurrently with a lot of others. She had two children
with her. Nearly all of the younger women that were present had one
or two children with them. With the exception of the woman who was
married to the guru, all women were single.

Aleva told me also, that nearly all of them placed marriage advertisements in the newspaper now and then. I watched the read-headed
one all evening and began to contrive a scheme to make a conquest of
her. It became apparent that Aleva had presumed that I knew the red-
head whose name was Xanda van Aanstryk, from watching TV.

They had been fellow students at university. Blatantly Xanda had
retrained and worked now as a television presenter or the like. I had
not known her before however, because I had not been in the habit of
watching Cyclamen TV. She was one of the two widows present in the
side room. All the others were divorcees.

The next day I drafted a marriage advertisement as a decoy for
the red-head woman. I described my wish woman as endowed with all
outer attributes that Xanda had.

I also prepared the right reply for Aleva in my head. When she rang
again I told her that I could not carry on with her. There was not only
her addiction but also her untidiness. And most important, she had not
yet come to a written mutual agreement with her ex-husband.

Xanda replied to my advertisement promptly. She wrote that she
has been a widow and without a suitor since the day when her husband
Manfred died in a work accident in the shunting station. This was five
years ago.

She had a twelve year old boy and a ten year old girl. Their names
were Titus and Selissa. The children were very important to her. She
wrote also that she has been considering remarriage for some time.

When I phoned her she did not take the call, so I left a voice mail.

Two hours later she called me back and we arranged a rendezvous for the evening.

I was ten minutes early. It drizzled and it was getting dark. There were not many people on the town square in Alfalfa. This was where she wanted us to meet. I became aware that a car with Cyclamen license plate approached. Sure enough, the woman who alighted was my heartthrob. Under the edge of my umbrella I could watch her legs nearing me. When we were close enough, I swung back my umbrella and we looked into one another's eyes. "But we know each other," she said. But she said it like under a spell, as if this were a miracle.

"It is a small miracle, isn't it?"

"But you seem not to be so very surprised!"

"The advertisement was fabricated only for your sake."

"But whatever gave you the idea?"

"The moment I saw you, I knew I had to dream up a way of seeing you tête-à-tête. At the gambling meeting we were not even properly introduced. It was not good enough to phone you and ask you out. You probably wouldn't have known what to say in a quick way and for the sake of simplicity you would have declined."

"But what about Aleva? What will she say?"

"This is over. It had never really begun."

"You composed an advertisement specifically for me to read and to walk into your trap? Fantastic?" When Xanda said these words, her voice rang with zest and her green eyes sparkled. "But you surely saw me before on TV?"

"Believe it or not, but I'm sure I saw your face for the first time when we were briefly introduced at this money party. You see, I seldom watch your TV station. I generally try to live without western compulsions anyway. I think one of these compulsions is the habit of watching TV every day."

"*I too don't care much about what other people do or think.*"

"*When Aleva told me that you now work with the television studio in Cyclamen, my first impulse was to wait for you after work. But then it occurred to me, that you might not work regular hours.*"

"*You wouldn't have spotted me. I'm a shy person; I like to be invisible as soon as I'm out of the studio.*"

"*No magic hood could conceal your charisma, Xanda.*"

"*You flatterer!*"

We strolled for a while hand in hand and then entered the Ticino where we stayed until closing time.

Next day Xanda confided in me, that she had explained to her parents that we had met at the information evening about the Ponzi scheme. This was not a lie after all; the children had been present and had witnessed how we met for the first time. But the advertisement remained our secret according to her wish. It was many months later, that Xanda and Aleva met in the street accidentally. Angrily, the latter accused the former of pinching her boyfriend. Xanda told Aleva then the whole truth. But Aleva waived this as a cock and bull story.

The next weekend Selissa's birthday celebration was pending. She had completed her tenth year. They had planned to have lunch at the home of Xanda's parents. It so happened that both my children spent the Sunday at home in Syget. At first they were astounded at my having sought and found a new woman. But they agreed to accompany me to Cyclamen City.

On our way there, the first snow of the new winter began to fall. It was end of October, two days before the Austrian National Day.

Roxanne said something about an arm's-length relationship and Xavier added also something about a long distance for consideration. We'll cross that bridge when we come to it; it's early days yet, I thought to myself.

I think I had not yet realized that I was already head over heels in love with Xanda.

I had met Xanda's parents, Laurens and Marike van Aanstryk, a week before that. I acquainted them as well as Titus and Selissa with my children, Roxanne and Xavier. Then we celebrated together like a big family. When we were eating dessert, the birthday girl proclaimed unexpectedly, "the next occasion we'll be celebrating will be mum's and Mateo's wedding."

My elderly neighbor Mrs. Faderr had soon caught what was going on with me. She had warned me at an early stage not to jump too hastily into my new relationship. She said that I saw things through rose-tinted spectacles and that it was not wise to visit Xanda every day.

But I, like a silly boy, had moved into Xanda's flat shortly after we had met. I did not give up my home however; I went to my house every day. Looking back I am proud of having achieved this, at least. But when Xanda phoned and said that she was off duty, nothing could hold me in Syget any longer. We thought ourselves to be made for each other.

Although we still think ourselves to be made for each other and our attachment has grown since and is still growing, I think sometimes that Mrs. Faderr had been right.

I should have started with more prudence. But she has given up giving advice. She couldn't, even if she wished to, because she quit the boards of this world meanwhile. I wonder where she had got her wisdom from. She had been married for over sixty years to the same man, whom she had met while very young. She outlived Mr. Faderr by several years.

Xanda's family had welcomed me warmly. Her parents are very good to me and the children kissed me on the mouth when I first entered their home. Selissa liked to sit on my lap from the beginning; just for the fun of it, or to watch children's programs. Sometimes I read to her from a book.

On evenings when their mother was in the television studio and the children had not gone over to their grandparents, they loved to lie in their mother's bed next to me. At first, this took a little getting used to. For my taste they seemed too grown for doing such a thing.

Xanda's apartment became my second domicile quite naturally. I was accorded the never used baroque dining room as my office. Xanda has a predilection for baroque furniture. The most remarkable feature in her living room is a hollow marble column. It is situated in the only corner of the room which is not impaired by a door or a window. On it, at little above the height of my head, rests a gold-plated casing that reminds me on the tabernacle in the church in our urban district in Tegucigalpa.

When I was a schoolboy this shrine appealed to me as something mystical with its lockable curved door which revolved when it was opened or closed.

A fitting equivalent to the box was a tabernacle clock in another corner of the room.

One day Xanda opened her safe for me to look inside. She did not show me everything however. Because inside there was one small drawer which she did not open and which she did not comment upon. I did not mention it, because I suspected that this was the hiding place for her most secret belongings.

Of what I saw there was not much to be remembered. There was some money, a pair of wedding rings, a photo in a frame with a black ribbon across one corner. The picture showed a portrait of her deceased husband; it was an equivalent of the picture on the wall above the sofa. This enshrined photo caused me to wonder, how much she had locked away in her heart in commemoration of Manfred, because she avoided talking about him.

I strongly suspect that there is some secret about his death; and perhaps this secret could be lifted by unlocking the secret drawer?

After Xanda had closed and locked up the tabernacle safe again, she retained the golden key in her hand. I let not show my suspicious curiosity but I seemingly shifted my attention to other matters. When she thought I had forgotten about it and was not looking, she let the key disappear under the upholstery of the seat on which she sat.

At the next opportunity, I looked for the key, but it was no longer there. She had managed to deposit it in its secret place of concealment. She had outwitted me.

On evenings when Xanda is not in the television studio we often go out for a meal, and sometimes a little dancing afterwards. Occasionally we go to a cinema or a theater. Every so often we spend an evening at her parents place. In the daytime the four of us — Xanda, the children and I — ride our bicycles and make a stop at an inn for a snack; or an ice-cream in periods of hot weather.

I like those evenings when Xanda is at home and the children are in bed already; or when they are staying with their grandparents. Normally I am the first to have a shower and then I sit in a chair and read in a book. When later Xanda comes out of the shower she likes to sit on my lap.

Selissa has found out about it. When she is at home we can never be sure that she will not come and want to sit with us. Xanda sometimes gets angry; at times she gives the impression to be jealous. Like the other day when I was on the balcony. I was nearly dark. I sat on a chair and looked in the sky.

The evening star shone very brightly. When I got up and went inside, I had to pass the window of Selissa's room which was dark. I thought her to be asleep. But as if she had been waiting for me to pass, *she gave a feigned shriek of horror. Thereupon Xanda got very angry.*

With Xanda having this lucrative job with Cyclamen TV and with her close affiliation with her parents, it had become clear to me very soon, that she will never leave her familiar surroundings.

On the other hand, after the first year I thought that I had had enough of being the lodger. Since it had been also Xanda's intention to marry again and since it seemed we were the perfect match, I wondered what ideas she had about our future. Perhaps she expected a formal proposal of marriage?

So one day I proposed to Xanda. She reacted very amiably but said, that everything was as good as could be. Why change a perfect situation? "Maybe in the years to come, when the children stand on their own feet," she said.

Was there nothing more to talk about? Was there nothing more to explain? Is she off her rocker? Or am I off mine? Is it in the twenty-first century out of date to marry and build a family that sticks together? Mrs. Faderr was no more; she could have told me. It was after this experience that I remembered her and I tried to see the world without rose-colored glasses.

I decided to go back to my house and think things over and await the course of events. I endured to stay away from Xanda for a whole night. I even switched off my phone. The next day Xanda was heartbroken. She came to visit me and I was glad she did. She begged me pleadingly not to do this again. We were in each other's arms for minutes on end. But after this day, everything went on as before.

But I had figured out eventually, that Xanda would forfeit her widow's pension. That was the crux. So, not everything went on as before. I don't brush aside her aggressive remarks as I did before. They make me think now; for example when Xanda says that a little less toothpaste would also do. This is one of those comments that I could laugh about before; but now it gives me food for thought.

What before I had superficially considered being charming weak points of her, I increasingly realize to be signs of pathological miserliness.

Yes, now when I write about it I begin to see. I am the one who drives many miles every day so we can be together. I am the one who pays the bill every time we go out. I'm not a great believer in exchanging expensive presents. I think that being available for one another is the most precious present one can give or receive. But Xanda has brought me to the point, where I let her tell me what gifts I buy for her children and her parents; and to her, needless to say.

Seemingly as a joke she has suspected me once of possibly being a marriage impostor. Suppose she means it deep in her heart! Whatever! One thing is as clear as daylight: I must eventually begin to try to see Xanda and the world without rose-colored glasses. When it comes to money, I have more than I need. Xanda has a good salary, her widow's pension, orphan's pensions and the avails from selling her husband's farm.

She lives nearly for free, because her parents pay back the loan for the purchase of her flat. Considering how she economizes and how penny-wise she even is, she must have accumulated a nice bit of capital.

She will be home soon. I'm glad I took these past hours for considering and to write this down. The sequence of events that led to our present situation is quite obvious now for me. I ignored too often when she rubbed me up the wrong way.

I must learn to flatly contradict her as soon as she makes one of her thoughtless commentaries. I must change my attitude in other ways still. I was going to tell her how the new neighbor looks at me encouragingly when we happen to be alone in the lift. I'm not even quite sure if these encounters with the neighbor in the lift, always happen accidentally. But I'll tell nothing about it.

GERHARD OBERRESSL

Wednesday April 25, 2001:

Last night when Xanda was back, I told her nothing of the woman next door. In spite of this — or because of it — we had a very good time together.

"I wonder," said Etienne Friendly to himself, when he laid the sheets on the table. "At this stage Mateo Capota seemingly knew nothing about the Edelweiss deception. Did he ever find out? I cannot see anything suspicious as yet.

I wonder what he is so particular about regarding discretion. But I have still three and a half years of this relation to read about. There can still arise the one or the other suspicious circumstance. It's likely to get juicy now. In this case jealousy may come into play."

His thoughts were interrupted by the tune to the song which goes *Engeland swings like a pendulum do …'*

"Good morning, Gloria! What's up?"

§18

Yanica Alexandru

"Walter, please! Hurry up! Or you'll be too late and can say good-bye to the job," said my mother. It wasn't for the first time this morning."

However I was thinking about something else entirely. Preoccupied in thoughts, I chewed listlessly and then answered automatically: "I think I phone them and call off the interview."

"Ah, Sir Walter calls the interview off! You were so pleased when they sent you an invitation! Is it again Rita Olivero preventing you from going away? Will you never get loose … she is ten years your senior."

"Nine years!"

"All the same; she is a good many years older than you are. What are you expecting of this … liaison?"

I did not care to answer to that.

"With your degrees in commerce and business administration you have a springboard for right to the top. You could make it to the executive floor. Imagine being chief executive officer of Erdpress Consumer Goods one day; or of some other international corporation."

"Chief executive officer; what a ridiculous job title! Not

even Gordon Aybesford does want to be addressed in this silly way."

"Come on; don't split hairs incessantly over what I say. You are only trying to distract attention away from ..."

"Who says that I'm born a manager? I did my degrees only to please you! It took me long enough."

"You are born a fool! What I want to bring home is that I'm worried about your reluctance to leave the area if only for a few years, because of a woman; and an unsuitable woman at that."

"It has nothing to do with Rita; nor with *not* wanting to leave Goodland. Quite the opposite, I *want* to go to London!"

I enjoyed my mother's sagging jaw for a minute. Then I got up and went to the kitchen window in triumph. When I looked outside, I saw Gloria's new Giulietta next to the gateway of Edelweiss castle. The convertible was open.

Everybody knows that the Aybesfords strictly park their cars in the inner courtyard. So I supposed that she had forgotten something and would come out again soon. I rushed down the stairs and out by the front door, and caught Gloria when she was about to drive off.

"Gloria, mornig! Wait," I shouted.

"Good morning, Walter! Do you want me to give you a lift?"

"No, thanks. This Etienne Friendly, do you think I could assist him?"

"You want to assist him? In what way? By what means? Are you alluding to the van Aanstryk case? But the people around here know now that he is not really a stranger. So he needs no longer a mock interpreter."

"But you accompanied him to Syget only last Monday, in

order to interview Xanda van Aanstryk's ex-boyfriend."

"Quite so! This was not because Etienne needed an interpreter. And it was also not because he needed my crime solving abilities. We thought this to be a delicate matter, and that Capota might not so easily slam the door in the face of a woman. He was under no obligation to cooperate, after all."

"I see. But look, it is more than the Xanda van Aanstryk case. I think that investigating and solving crimes is my real calling. That has become clear to me only through this fatality. What I've been doing in life so far, is comparable to threshing empty straw only. Maybe I could do an apprenticeship, sort of; or at least assist him for a few month so as to get a feel how to get started in the business.

"You seem to be in earnest," said Gloria, her face showing astonishment. "Okay. If you want me to, I give him a call. I'll ask him to get in touch with you and then you both can discuss the matter. On the other hand, you became acquainted with him in memorable circumstances. He knows you well. Don't you think you could as well contact him yourself directly?"

"Still, your word would carry weight with him. That would be very helpful. It's very good of you, Gloria, thanks a lot; have a nice day."

"He will not be up yet. London is two hours behind our time. I call him later in the morning. Bye!" Gloria drove off and I went up again so as to carry on with my breakfast, now with sufficient appetite.

"You are twenty-four and I'm not going to mother you. I don't like it myself. But I can expect that you talk to me like a grown up man. What are you planning to do, all of a sudden?"

"It's this Etienne Friendly; I cannot get him out of my

mind. I asked Gloria to put in a good word for me with him. I would like to assist him in order to find out, if this would be a career for me. It's not just office work but it asks for your versatility. I'm prepared to work a few months even for nothing. In London, feature that!"

"Peculiar. But if you are serious, you should phone Erdpress Consumer Goods and tell them that you have other plans."

"Yes, of course. I make the call right away," I said and went to the living room and switched on the television. But I did not appreciate what I saw. My thoughts circulated around what I should say when Etienne Friendly would call. I was worked up. I should have gone to London without asking Gloria beforehand. Facing Etienne Friendly in his realm he would not send me straight away, I thought. I shall do this as a last resort, in case he turns me down today.

I went outside for a walk. Instinctively I chose the way that would lead me past the Fox and Hare Inn. Realizing it, I took a side path at the next opportunity. After having made a few steps towards the medical center behind which there is the path to the lake, I turned around again and went back to the sidewalk along Castle Avenue.

And then I made a straight line for The Fox and Hare. I'm Walter Nadler Jr., I told myself. I can go wherever I want and I need not hide from anybody in my hometown.

On entering the Inn I heard Rita's voice coming from above. Obviously she was talking to a chambermaid or a manservant. I bent round a corner and looked up the wooden staircase. Through the open door of one of the hotel rooms I caught sight of her fetching new hairstyle. She was demonstrating how to strip the bedding to a person that I could not see. Without her seeing me, I was able to watch her. From afar she looked like a teenager; so delicate and graceful. Has there ever been a more wonderful woman on earth?

It's not the right time, I thought after a while. I was about to slip away when she perceived me.

"Hi Walter; wait a minute. I'm coming down." She pushed a service cart into the lift and started downward. I heard the lift going down to the basement. Moments later, she came up to the ground floor and beckoned me into her office.

Her white work coat was unbuttoned. Under it she had on a turquoise-green blouse. With the amber bead chain around her delicate neck she looked ravishing. We had parted last time in a stalemate position and I didn't know what to say. But she seemed to be in a forthcoming mood. She was about to start talking when my mobile went.

"Sorry! This is important, Etienne Friendly," I said and took the call. "Walter Nadler! … Good morning. Thank you for calling … I was about to call you this moment … sorry I was on my way … I had an accident … I get in touch as soon as I'm back home … Thank you very much indeed … good bye Miss …"

"Alas! This was only Erdpress Consumer Goods. I was to attend an interview this morning, but didn't go. Then I forgot to tell them."

"Why on earth? Are you not well?"

"No, yes; I'm fine. But when I applied for the job two months ago the world was a different one. So much has happened; the independence of Goodland and the death of one of your … friends."

"I say! She hasn't been my friend for years. The same holds for Dalia Kalanda. The two were going together since ages. I was only an interference factor. Apart from this, I cannot see how the demise of Xanda van Aanstryk correlates with your choice of career."

"But I happened to see you with Xanda van Aanstryk in Cyclamen only days before she died."

"This must have been on the occasion when I gave her the money; you know, because of the interview."

"I would only be too pleased to believe you. But you should not lie to me at this point."

"It's the plain truth; please believe me, Walter."

"Then why did you torture me with allusions all these years?"

"I didn't want to distract you from your studies. You had to take your degree by all means. I thought it better to appear gay than to lead the people to believe that I was throwing myself at a younger man.

Your mother once read me the riot act in the supermarket. Sometimes I downright feel branded an outlaw by the local people. That's why I have resorted to catering for day-trippers and business travelers more and more. The Sustainers have become a glimmer of light for me in recent years."

I was incapable of speaking.

"But speaking of career," she went on, "the whole of Edelweiss is talking about Heidi Forster and Jacquy de Jong. It gave me a lot to think about. I think I'm now willing. I don't want to rush anything and you should better wait with a comment and not answer me today. But please think about it. If you can forgive my follies … I mean if you think we could manage in spite of what has happened … I think you would make a good husband and … landlord."

I remained utterly immobile for a while and I felt how my center of gravity sagged to its right position. I could not utter a single word. Then I drew a deep sigh. "Rita!"

"Walter, you are a man now. I can feel it. You are someone to rely on. When I initiated you into manhood after this calamitous party, you were sweet but still very young."

"I was eighteen," I said.

We smiled at one another and I took Rita's face in my hands. She will always be young for me. Let people say what they wish.

"You know," I said, caressing her face. "I think I have made two important decisions this morning.

"What decisions?"

"I decided to become a private investigator. I'm going to ask Etienne Friendly if he is going to teach me the first steps. If he is not interested, I'll find another opportunity. By the way, his wife has also a restaurant.

This leads me to my second decision; if you are in confinement after childbirth I can look to the guests, the books, the staff and the suppliers! So I accept herewith your hand in marriage. But this strengthens only my decision to contact Etienne Friendly as soon as possible. I'm going to take the night flight to London."

"Do as you wish, darling. We have now all the time in the universe." We sealed our agreement with a long, hearty embrace. Somebody knocked at the office door. A cook appeared and asked Rita something about the weekly market. We parted abruptly and I headed for home. I was determined to give my mother a real dressing down.

The twenty minutes walk from The Fox and Hare home I

would have accomplished in ten minutes today, had not Joseph Aybesford crossed my path and stopped my momentum. I had noticed his coming from the mausoleum, and I thought I could make it before we joined up. But he went also at a good pace.

"It's a pleasure to see young people move under their own steam," he said, after we had exchanged words of greeting.

"You are my shining example, mister Aybesford. À propos, Happy Birthday in advance; I wish you all the very best on the occasion of your ninetieth birthday next month."

"Cordial thanks! But isn't it a little, soon? I must first make it. You seem to be so excited; have you found a suitable position?"

"Only just I proposed to Rita Olivero."

"From your good mood I see she has accepted."

"Yes, she has."

"My best wishes to the two of you!"

"Thank you very much. And there is another matter altogether. I've made up my mind to go to London tonight. I want to pay Etienne Friendly a visit. I'm going to ask him if he will take me on as an apprentice. If he is not interested, I will ask his advice how I best go ahead in breaking the first ground in the business of investigating."

"But why? If you are interested in police work why don't you join the Goodland police force? They are in need of personnel. You are fresh from university; they surely would admit you. You are a stately figure on top of everything. There you get free training and wages into the bargain."

"Maybe I will. But for the time being I see it my assignment to contribute to the solution of the Xanda van Aanstryk case."

"I take my hat off to you! A lot of important decisions in one morning, I'm bound to say. This desire to busy yourself in solving a criminal case, is it new to you?"

"That's right, mister Aybesford. Over the last few days I've become transfixed by the psychological aspects of crime, of the criminal mind. I would like to see how he is going about in solving this riddle; and I hope I can contribute my share."

"I see. You want to apprentice with the great master. I have half a mind to come with you; but I'm afraid there is an age limit for apprentices."

"No, there is none. And you know it best."

"You live and learn. Are we walking on together?"

"Only as far as the bank; I must go inside and change money. I need some British Pounds. Do you think that Goodland will be accepted as a member of the Commonwealth of Nations? The changing of money would then be no longer necessary."

"As long as Great Britain is a member of the European Union it will not be so easy. But there are many Eurosceptics in England. Two years ago the British Prime Minister promised an *in or out* referendum on British membership of the European Union in 2017; provided that the conservative party wins an outright majority at the next general election. This is expected next year. If the referendum causes Great Britain to leave the EU, then they will put out their hand for us to join. But I'm not so sure we should take it. The prime minister's attitude towards Austria's rejection of atom energy is inacceptable. But there will be another prime minister. All things must pass."

"True! But I cannot wait that long. Au revoir, Mr. Aybesford! I must be going."

"See you again, Walter. Have a good trip. Give Etienne Friendly my best regards!"

Why did Etienne Friendly not call? Take it easy. From the

bank I went home and checked for e-mails. Only rubbish. No, here, from etienne915@gmx.co.uk; that must be it. Yes, it was. His note said that I am welcome to visit him, preferably straightaway. There is no point in talking the matter over on the phone. Tremendous! He gave his address and all sorts of numbers. That was settled then.

I drove my Fiat out at the castle administrator's garden gate and rode across to Nelson's Garage; I wanted to sell the car on the spot. But Nelson said I could get more if I just leave it there for sale. "I need the money," I said. "I go to London. Perhaps I might not be back for a while. I enter upon a new career. I've been admitted into Etienne Friendly's agency."

"London is not out of the world, buddy. And the agency will surely pay enough to live. If it comes to the worst I can always sell the car and transfer the money to London. You need to show more judicial deliberation, if you want to become a sleuth.

Suddenly I felt stupid. Nelson was right. I must proceed in a more relaxed fashion. "You see, Nelson," I said, "I shall not go on living with my people, when I come back. I'm leaving my family home altogether. My mother had me for too long under her thumb. So if I can leave my car and a few boxes with my things under your custody – that would be great."

"No problem at all."

My friend then agreed to run me to Kyll Airport; but he said that to the best of his knowledge there was no night flight to London. We verified in the web. It turned out that I had to pack my things within two hours in order to catch a flight to Frankfurt.

I had to take this escape out of the country, unless I wanted to wait until tomorrow morning. Connection or no connection in Frankfurt, I couldn't care less. This was not the time for looking for flight connections at my leisure. I was afraid of becoming assailed by doubts if I waited any longer.

This had been a little rash a short while ago, this coming to an understanding with Rita. So many years I have been tortured. She had told me to wait with my answer. I felt like putting some daylight between me and Rita; and between me and Edelweiss.

"I might just as well go for good," I said to my mother who was flustered. I told her how disappointed I was, that she had offended Rita in the supermarket and thus discussed my affairs in public.

Then I made a rush at packing my belongings; one suitcase for the journey, and the rest for storage in Nelson's storeroom.

When I saw Nelson arrive I went quickly downstairs. We put everything into the car. Then we got in and drove off.

At The Fox and Hare we paused for a minute. I had to say good bye to Rita once more. The farewell before had been too hasty. Perhaps everything will fall into place, after all. I told her how I loved her.

At the airport I checked once more. The next direct flight would have been on the following day. I had to move. So I took the envisaged flight to Frankfurt. There would even be a connection to London later that same day.

In Frankfurt I left the arrivals hall and walked around a little. Then I bought myself a snack and a newspaper and sat down in the concourse. When it was about time to board again, I made for the check in area. I was glad that my luggage was in transit so I needed not to queue again for baggage handling. Boarding pass in hand, I went on to the boarding queue and fished out my passport.

Nearing the queuing railing I couldn't help paying attention to a beautiful vestment, a sort of cardigan. But the garment was not knitted, but knotted. It was knotted of colored waxed silk floss. A magnificent head of hair, reminiscent of the Golden Fleece, reached down almost to the waistline of the wearer. Two immaculate, long legs came into view below the hem of the cardigan-like wrap. Two immensely high pink heels formed the foundation of this divine structure.

When I passed I sniffed her perfume. I sneaked a peek at her; and I was not the only who peeked. She had a good face and there was not as much makeup as I had expected.

I slowed down a little. A young lad was seeing her off. She rummaged around in her bag. The boy did not make the impression of a familiar friend or relative or lover.

After a while I scented her perfume again. She had joined the queue and was directly behind me. Before body check we had to put our small belongings into a tray. When I collected my possessions after the check, I dawdled a little. I apologized to the woman and we got talking to one another. I had difficulty in making out every word she said, because she spoke with an eastern accent.

It was then that I saw that besides her cardigan-like wrap she wore also a pink tiny micro-mini skirt, the same color as her shoes. She also had on a dark blue blouse. In her high heels she was my height. Her face was broad. Her blue eyes were wide apart and her eyebrows thin and slightly curved. The inner ends of her brows started exactly above her inner eye corners. She had beautiful lips. Her mouth reminded me of Nadeshda Brennike.

I made way for her and then I went into the departure hall. When I looked again she had disappeared into the crowd. I wondered what flight she took.

While waiting in the lounge, I was thinking alternately of Rita and about Etienne Friendly. I got up with the aim of buying little presents in the duty free shop. At this moment the announcer said: "Ladies and gentlemen, please keep calm. No reason to panic. Because of an abandoned, unidentified item of baggage all departures have to be halted for a little while. Thank you very much." Is it going to be a night flight after all? I thought to myself.

I was already tired of looking around in the shop, when I heard a woman say to another one, "Guarda! Questa indossatrice o piccola diva seminuda!" She was referring to a half naked model or starlet. I looked around and beheld the blond one who was in the direction of the entrance. She was regarding a sculpture. She spotted me too and gave me a smile.

After an hour delay the announcer's voice came as a relief: "Passengers to London Stansted please proceed to gate number seventeen immediately." Excitedly I set off for the gate referred to.

In the shuttle bus I discovered the starlet again. So she too was on her way to London. When she noticed my looking she smiled again.

Same as it ever was. At times when I was unhappy and uncertain about my chances with Rita, nobody liked me. At times when we thought we will manage and I was of good cheer, all women seemed to be well-disposed towards me. I should have let Rita dangle.

I wondered if it was the starlet's doing or if it was sheer

coincidence. But I had barely found my seat when she appeared on the seat next to me. I offered her my window seat. She accepted gracefully. "I'm Yanica Alexandru," she said.

"How do you do? My name is Walter Aybesford." For some reason I wanted to impress her. But she did not seem to be deeply impressed; not at all, in fact. The name seemed to tell nothing to her. We talked then a little about the enforced stay because of the bomb alarm and the delay it would cause.

I was so weary with what had happened today I must have nodded off. I sank into a dream. My new acquaintance was telling me that in her home town all people disguise only their faces but else go about naked. They recognize one another on their lower bodies. I woke up when I felt something touching my lips. Her face was over mine. "I don't care for the drool of your boyfriend," I said, waking up. Then I thought that she had only brushed off some alien element with a handkerchief off my face.

"Are you speaking in your sleep or are you awake?" I thought to hear her asking me.

It was only then that I got really awake. I sat up; I mopped the drool off the corner of my mouth. "I must have gone to sleep. I must apologize," I said.

"No problem."

"You see, I was immensely exhausted," I felt compelled to explain. And then I told her that I was an investigator on an important mission and had had little sleep in the last few days. She displayed a desire to understand and demonstrated sympathy. When I told her that normally I only go by car and this was my very first journey by air, she laughed a cooing laugh.

"But altogether you seem to lead a very exciting live,"

Yanica Alexandru said.

Was she mocking me? "Are you a frequent flier?"

"I'm a kick boxer and get about a good deal. I'm the current champion of both Moldova and Transnistria. You may have heard of Sonja Kikuta. She is a famous Austrian kickboxer."

I was impressed and I let it show. But I had also to admit, that she had just mentioned four or five words that sounded opaque to me. "I know roughly where Moldova is," I said.

"Well, and Transnistria is a renegade province of Moldova. Same as Goodland is a renegade province of Austria."

Was she citing a chance example or did she suspect me to come from Goodland?

"But we are approaching London Stansted Airport. The plane is in its final descent."

"You mean I missed out on the whole flight through oversleeping?"

"Don't bother. I'm glad I had you as my escort, so to speak. In the company of a nice person, I feel more secure; especially now that I know you to be a secret agent."

"Why don't you dress in jeans and sneakers to be less noticeable?"

"Actually this makes no difference. And today it's because of the reception."

Because of her eastern accent I did not apprehend every word se said; and I was at a loss to catch the point of those last remarks.

"Prepare for landing; please fasten your seatbelts," it sounded from a speaker above our heads.

After a smooth landing we climbed into the shuttle bus.

"Can I have your mobile number?" I asked, once we were

in the arrivals hall. After all, she had sought my company; she surely was waiting for me to ask. I fished out my new Smartphone. "Do you have your mobile at hand?"

She took out an outdated mobile phone and switched it on. When she thought that I watched sympathetically, she said that she despised fancy phones; that she preferred desk computers and plain mobile phones.

When my phone was enabled I let her dial her own number with it, so that I could save it."

"I save your number too, is that all right?"

"Certainly," I said. "For how long are you going to stay in London?"

"I don't know yet. Look, I must quickly go to the lady's restroom; it only takes a minute. Please wait at the baggage conveyor belt for me so that we can pass the customs station together."

It occurred to me, that I had no idea for what reason Yanica Alexandru had come to London. Did she want to get something through customs check with my helping unknowingly?

When I saw that she had three pieces of luggage, I fetched a trolley and stacked them onto it. Then I put my suitcase on top and pushed the cart over to the customs facilities.

When Yanica reappeared we went for customs control and passed through without any trouble.

I pushed the cart towards the exit, Yanica Alexandru on my side, holding her pink handbag with both hands under her bosom. When we drew closer to the door, it opened up. Simultaneously, one wing glided to the left and one to the right and at that moment we were exposed to a flurry of camera flashes.

§19

The Home Building

I shall never forget this welcome at London Stansted. Blinded and taken by surprise, I experienced difficulties in collecting my senses. I tried to think. I had cherished secret hopes that somebody had come to meet Yanica at the Airport; and perhaps this somebody would give me a lift into the city. Or at least we could share a taxi. Yanica had mentioned that it was about a thirty-five miles drive. Why hadn't I spoken earlier?

I was in the dark. What was the meaning of this fuss? What am I to do? At this moment Yanica broke away from the reporters who seemed to have become impertinent. She grabbed my arm and indicated to me to move on. "Has somebody come to collect you?" I asked.

"You are being picked up, it seems." With a motion of her head she pointed towards something which seemed to be on my other side. When I turned, I looked into the face of a young woman with light-colored ginger hair and a fair but freckled complexion. She looked at me through spectacles with light-gray eyes. She had a disarming smile.

"You must be Herr Nadler," she said in a matter of fact fashion. "My name is Veronica Smith. I'm coming on behalf of

Etienne Friendly. Welcome to Great Britain."

"If this isn't a surprise! Indeed, my name is Walter Nadler. May I introduce Miss Yanica Alexandru to you?" I said, although I was not sure if Yanica was married or not.

The two women embraced. They seemed to be acquainted.

"Yanica is one of us. She phoned me and said that she thought she has made you out. But you used another name. So she was not sure."

I think I became red in the face. "We only became acquainted with one another at Frankfurt Airport," I said. I hoped it sounded like an explanation. "I guess you have a car, Miss Smith?"

"Call me Veronica. It's over there. A few minutes on foot. I could only get hold of a Mini. It will get cramped, I'm afraid."

"It will work somehow," said Yanica.

The three of us were a good team. We managed to store away three suitcases and a big travelling bag in Veronica's Mini. But it worked out only to the detriment of my seating position in the back seat. The two girls sat in front. It was exactly eight p.m. when we left Stansted Airport for the city of London. "It's about thirty, forty miles to Charing Cross," said Veronica in reply to my question how long it will take us.

"That's what I said," responded Yanica.

Now I knew as much as I knew before asking. The two women then embarked on a discussion of which I heard very little because of the road noise. I think they made also fun about me, because I had introduced myself using a false name and I had pretended to be an investigator. Eventually they talked about kick boxing. Veronica trained also regularly in a club, but only for fun, fitness and for the purposes of self-defense.

I apprehended little; and because of the car noise I gave up taking part in the conversation altogether. The thought of telephoning Rita came to my mind, but I gave it up immediately. With this noise in the background any conversation would have gone unsatisfactory. And then I nodded off.

I woke up when the Mini took a sharp right-hand turn so that the suitcases buried me. I clawed my way out from under the luggage. What was going on? I tried to figure out where we were and I read *Soho Fire Station* on a building. I have read about Soho in fiction. A fire station would have been the last thing for me to associate with this neighborhood.

Then I noticed many shops with Asian signboards. We passed an entrance to Leicester Square Tube Station. Shortly after we had passed Omega Travel, the Chinese Restaurant Paradise emerged. The car turned in at an archway. The name over it read *Home Building*. Veronica passed through and parked the car near the backdoor of the edifice.

"Please pardon my savage way of driving," said Veronica, when we got out of the car. "There seems to be an obstacle at the corner of Litchfield Street. At the last moment I thought it wiser to make the little detour. And I'm not so familiar with the lanes other than the beaten paths."

Only by violent efforts we succeeded in hauling the baggage out of the Mini. After that was accomplished I seized the two biggest items of luggage. Yanica and Veronica took the remaining pieces. We waited for the lift to come down. When it came, an elderly Chinese gentleman got out. Veronica introduced me to him. His name was Cheng Xinde. He was Etienne's father in law. Veronica took us to the fourth floor. She and Yanica had each a room here. There was also a dorm room where I could take up quarters if I liked. Of course I liked it. "Normally guest rooms are very expensive in London," said Yanica.

I feared that I had not looked too good so far on this journey. I did not want to appear a person who is inclined to a lack of self confidence. "Listen, I should like to treat you two to a meal. How about the Angus Steak House, a few steps away? I caught sight of it when we turned into Charing Cross Road.

"Sounds tempting," said Veronica amazed, "but isn't it too late tonight? What do you think, Yanica?"

"Maybe another time, thank you; but how about the Black Sheep? It's also quite near, round the corner in fact. There is informal eating and they have traditional hand pulled beers. But I must change quickly. Give me ten minutes."

We all agreed and went to our respective rooms. I refreshed myself quickly in a bathroom across the hallway. Then I called Rita to tell her that all was well. When I was ready I knocked at Veronica's door.

"Who's there?"

"It is I who am knocking at the door."

"Oh, King's English!"

"I only want to tell you that I'm going downstairs to The Paradise in order to introduce myself. Perhaps, in the meantime, Etienne has come in."

"Wait a minute; I'm going to introduce you to Xiu in case he has not come in yet."

"Meanwhile I start slowly down the stairs."

"You are an impatient agent," said Yanica, who came out of her room. I nearly failed to recognize her. Her hair was now in a ponytail and the fancy clothing was completely gone. She had big glasses on her nose. Jeans and sneakers sat well on her.

She was now much smaller than before. It was funny; but she appeared more feminine now, than before in her starlet gear.

Veronica also appeared and the three of us went downstairs together.

"The whole team uses the steps as a rule. Going every day several times up and down is good exercise," said Veronica. On the third floor she halted and explained that here were the offices of Home Investigatory Services.

"It's for the first time I get to hear this term," I said. Is it not Friendly Investigations?"

"No, officially it is Home Investigatory Services and current is Home Investigations; but Friendly Investigations is not wrong. By the way Etienne occupies the penthouse. It's on the fifth floor. His parents in law, Cheng Xinde and his wife Jianlee also live up there."

"Does Cheng Xinde own the building – or who?"

"Yes. The Home is in the possession of the Cheng family since generations. The firm, Home Investigatory Services, is paying rent as any other firm would have to pay. Well, perhaps less, I don't know."

When we came to the second floor the picture changed. There was no long hallway but a glassed double door. You could look into a gymnasium where a group of old age pensioners were doing gymnastics. "These are our fitness rooms," said Veronica. Yanica trains here regularly; and I too, but not so often. Twice a week, my club has a reservation. The rooms are hired out by the hour. This is where Yanica and I met for the first time."

"Were you on business in Frankfurt?" I asked, facing Yanica.

"Oh yes. Home Investigatory Services has sort of a virtual office there."

On the first floor there was a colorful and gilded gate. It was the entrance to *The Home Theatre*. "The theater is also hired out," explained Yanica.

"Is it a Chinese theatre?" I wanted to know.

"You will have noticed that we are here at the fringe of China Town," said Veronica. "Originally it may have been a Chinese theatre. But nowadays everybody can hire it. We, I mean Yanica, Etienne, myself and others are also members of an amateur dramatics group."

We went now down to the ground floor. Here were two entrances; one to the restaurant kitchen and one to the public room of The Paradise. Both entrances were for the personnel only. We were employees. We entered into the pub and Veronica introduced me to Etienne's wife Xiu, to their daughter Samantha Ying and to Xiu's mother Jianlee. Her father Xinde we had met before. They sat in the family booth.

When we announced our intention of going out for a beer, Xiu laughed and said: "This is quite out of the question. You first must have something to eat! Soon Etienne will be back, too." Obediently we sat down. Samantha Ying is a cute teenage student. She looked athletic in a white bodice with straps.

While we ate, Samantha Ying and her grandparents left the pub. It had become late and the last guests had left The Paradise, when Etienne Friendly came in by the back door. After greetings he changed a few words with Veronica and Yanica. Then the two girls said good night too. Xiu seemed to be in the kitchen from were voices were to be heard. Two girls had begun clearing and cleaning the tables and polishing the furniture.

"You amaze me, Walter," Etienne said, when we were on our own at the table. "How come you want to go into detection so urgently? Gloria said you seem determined to throw away your former ambitions and to delve into crime, so to speak."

"Sales psychology was my favorite subject at university. But its purpose is essentially mean. It furnishes you with cunning and deceitful devices to get the better of others. I think it cheap to juggle with vending tricks. It's as cheap as using mathematics for process optimization. But I think it *not* mean to use psychological methods to catch out a wrongdoer."

"Give me a few particulars. I've talked to the manageress already. She will draw up a provisional contract for three months."

I gave him the information he wanted.

"You must get in touch with Mrs. Sara Lagoons tomorrow. Veronica will introduce you to her. I'll be out again first thing in the morning. Mrs. Lagoons runs the show of the indoor service. I'm not the organizer type. That's why I left the police at that time."

"Neither am I, I'm afraid. I told my mother only this morning. She was the one who urged me to study commerce. And after that I rejoiced her by doing business administration. I have left my home for good this morning. I am determined to delve into the human psychology more deeply."

"If a person has followed successfully a course of study for several years, he or she has proved to have perseverance. Stamina, patience and psychology are basic prerequisites for an investigator. Apart from these it is not so essential what your major subjects were."

"How should I proceed?"

"Mrs. Lagoons shall give you the Capota notes for study."

"Has this to do with the ex-boyfriend of Xanda van

Aanstryk? Has he given you notes?"

"That's right! These notes were made by Mateo Capota; I talked to him last Monday. He made those notations while he was living together with Xanda van Aanstryk. He passed them to me. I want you to study these recordings carefully with respect to a possible motive or other clues. I myself started reading the accounts only this morning. So far I've only covered the first day; the day he decided to start making notes."

I was very excited.

"He compiled a summary about how the relation had started and what his problems were. I can't draw conclusions as yet. I'm occupied with another matter currently. The Aanstryk case is two month old and has been handled by the Cyclamen police. Nothing can outrun us there."

I nodded understandingly.

"There was one thing that struck me when I began reading these notes. Xanda van Aanstryk had a neighbor woman who might mean trouble. These notes are of course strictly secret. This holds for everything else you will see and hear in connection with Home Investigatory Services."

"That goes without saying," I said.

"If after a few months we think that sleuthing is your calling, we must talk again and settle the conditions."

"Very good."

"Within a few days I should be able to pay full attention to our case. As soon as we have come to a conclusion, the two of us go back to Edelweiss. You are not confined to the office. If the weather allows, you can study the notes in one of the London parks, wherever."

"Thank you, Etienne, for giving me this chance."

"Not at all! Would you care for some mutton chops?"

"No, thanks. I have eaten enough. I'm replete. Don't let me keep you. Good night."

"Good night, Walter."

I was the only person to sleep in the dormitory tonight. I had slept in the plane, and then again in the car. I was overwrought by what had happened today. It seemed to me that I couldn't drift off to sleep. Too many pictures and words whirred in my head. I changed my position several times and eventually got up to get myself a second pillow from the neighboring bed. When I snatched the corner of the pillow and pulled, it didn't yield as I had expected, but a terrified cry echoed and reechoed through the nightly hall.

I was not quite dark and I could perceive a person who at that moment switched on a wall lamp. Indignation at first and then amazement and then amusement showed in quick succession in the face of a young Chinese fellow. "Hi," he said. "When did you come in?"

"When I got to bed I was alone in the room. You must have come after I went to sleep."

"Funny, you must have been sleeping like a log. I didn't hear you breathe or snore. I do the dishes in the restaurant after it closes at night. My name is Chen Guo. Good night, then."

"Good night. My name is Walter, by the way."

So I had been sleeping after all. The thought comforted me and I went to sleep again. I slept much better than before this intermezzo.

Next morning I was up and about at seven. My neighbor in the next bed was asleep. Also Rita would still be in the land of Nod, I thought. Twenty-four hours ago I had woken up in Edelweiss.

After the morning wash I moved my belongings into a corner of the dorm room. In my tracksuit I went on a mystery tour of the building. Especially the uppermost floor was of interest to me. But there was nothing of note there except two apartment doors. Probably it was under video surveillance and I might now be recorded for others to see. But I couldn't care less. So I went to the office storey. There was a big conference room. I went into it and sat on a chair. Possibly one day I will here exchange information with other agents.

I sauntered around in the building until I could hear that Veronica and Yanica were up. I heard them rumble about. They appeared in training wear and challenged me to join them in a morning run. I liked the idea and we hopped down the stairs. When we reached Big Ben I had enough and told them to carry on without me. I would go back on my own. I paused for breath on Westminster Bridge, looking over the river Thames, the County Hall and the London eye. Then I went back to the Home Building at a more leisurely pace.

When I went to the bathroom for a shower, the girls were coming back too. When they had washed and dressed, they picked me up and we went down. Yanica opened the restaurant.

"The restaurant opens at eleven," said Veronica. "But we have a key. We are allowed to make breakfast on our own."

"Get the newspapers!" called Yanica from the kitchen.

"Yes, of course; I forgot about it," said Veronica. She went to the entrance door and picked up a bunch of newspapers. She opened one and flipped through it. After a while she said: "Hey! You nearly made the front page."

"Show me," said Yanica, rushing out of the kitchen.

Veronica unfolded the newspaper on a table. There was a photo from our arrival last night, showing Yanica on my side, holding her pink handbag with both hands under her bosom.

"I look so unstylish; the way I'm clinging to my handbag," said Yanica.

Veronica and I protested. I thought she really looked smashing and I said so. There was a short article about Yanica Alexandru, the kick boxing champion of both Moldova and Transnistria. The question was posed if she could possibly become the next Bond girl and the gentleman on her side the new Mr. Bond.

We burst with laughter.

"Alternately we have English breakfast and continental breakfast," said Yanica. "Today we have ham and eggs. Sometimes we have also muesli."

While we ate, Etienne came in. Veronica showed him the newspaper article whereat he got highly amused.

"You are early risers," he said.

"I imagined you were already out," I said.

"No, not *that* early. But I'm having breakfast at half past eight at Trafalgar Square. So I must be going. Veronica you introduce Walter to Sara. And give this to her." He handed her a envelope. "Bye!"

Mrs. Sara Lagoons came in at nine, when the girls and I were coming up from the restaurant. She wore a floral ladies jacket and a gray skirt. Her hair was on the short side of shoulder-length, darkly tinted with blond streaks. She had a longish face with a mouth slightly skew. Veronica introduced me to her in the hallway.

"Pleased to meet you, Mrs. Lagoons," I said.

"Call me Sara. In Home Investigations we are all on first-name terms with one another."

We all went into the open space office. Sara entered a cubicle with glass walls and beckoned me to follow. She closed the door, and went to her desk and put her handbag down. "Have a seat! I understand you have no previous experience, Walter?"

I didn't think this remark was condescending. She was not the stern general that I had thought her to be.

"This is true enough; I'm not experienced at investigating a crime."

"This has never happened before, that somebody applies for the express purpose of helping in solving a specific crime. Are you personally involved in any way?"

"No, no. Not in the least, madam ... Sara."

"It is the first time altogether that somebody wants to learn the trade with us. It's a novelty. The guys we usually work with are freelancers who took their first strides with the police, but who were not able to manage with the discipline. You can see for yourself that our office is quiet. Meetings take place in the conference room. Veronica, Pauline and I hold the fort. Two or three women work half-day. Pauline Buckley has just come in."

She pointed by raising her chin. I turned my head and saw a dark blond young woman. At that moment she looked up at us. Sara waved to her so she would come nearer. When Pauline was inside the cube, Sara acquainted me to her. She had bluish black eyes and black brown eyebrows. She wore a man's shirt and a tie.

"Yanica trains a lot," said Sara when Pauline had left us. "But she does all the odd jobs that arise. She helps in the office and in the restaurant. She does cleaning and field work. She trained as a physician in Moldova."

"She didn't tell me."

"That's just like her. I hear you are fresh from university. You took a degree in business administration. Are you fully aware that you might squander your time if this leads to nothing? We can only give you free board and lodging and a weekly allowance."

"I know my own mind."

"That's a weight off *my* mind, then."

She took some sheets out of a folder. Everything seemed prepared for me to commence. She consulted the message that Veronica had delivered, then she added some data by hand.

"Please sign here. This is a declaration of secrecy. You are fully liable if you part with information about anything that is secret. And secret is everything that you hear or read or see in connection with your contract. Your contract for services you must sign here. Please check all the data first. Please take your time."

I skimmed the contract which seemed to be alright. I signed it and gave it back.

"Here is the USB flash drive with the text files that you are going to study. You can sit and work wherever you want to. And here is a key for the outer office. Hope you enjoy your stay. Good luck, Walter." When she smiled, her eyes became slits, and her face radiated sympathy and warmness.

"Thank you very much, Sara."

I went to a desk computer and started it up. There was no password protection. I inserted the medium and arranged the files in the data explorer window according to date, and double-clicked the first entry.

On reading how Mateo Capota had decided one day to begin with a sort of log book, the years with Rita passed through my mind and suddenly I hit on the idea, to keep a journal myself from now on, starting with yesterday, the day when I had made a good deal of decisions concerning my future life.

Every time I leant back I noticed, that Pauline was making eyes at me.

It was my first day in a job other than vacation work. I was happy. I double-clicked the next file icon.

Friday October 26, 2001:

When last time I wrote in this file I had fallen into euphoria and had imagined to write now every day. It's a pity I couldn't keep it up. Well, I shall eventually accept the fact that I'm not a diary writer by nature. But one thing is certain. To write about my relationship with Xanda half a year ago helped me to change my attitude towards her. It was the reflecting in particular that did the trick. The writing down helps to think honestly and thoroughly. In my work I need to think everything through to the end. In private affairs I tend to decide out of my belly, even on important matters.

Contrary to the entrenched habits, I no longer spend every night in Xanda's flat. And I no longer let her get away with snappish remarks. What helped me was a lucrative contract that I had reeled in and which makes heavy demands on my time. I do most of the work in my home in Syget nowadays. One evening a week, I go for a beer to the Square Pub; it's five minutes' walk from my house. I've made friends with some locals. The idea of marrying Xanda or any other woman is no longer in my head. But there is no reason to abort the situation with Xanda. We are still keen on one another. I think to make the best of my initial idea — to carry on without too much commitment.

One Sunday evening last summer I played at cards with Laurens van Aanstryk in the summer house of his garden. When we had finished and were strolling towards his residence he indicated a spot near the garden stone wall and asked me casually if I were interested in installing a swimming pool there. I declined his offer point-blank. When he seemed amazed, I explained that Xanda is not interested in marriage. He was totally astounded. He and his wife had thought that I was the one who showed no desire for matrimonial devotion.

This conversation must have come to Xanda's ears as the crow flies, because when I returned to the flat she confronted me with the question for what reasons I talked to her folks about our relation. We had had an argument before I went over to visit her parents, and I was out of sorts with her anyway. So I replied what had been on my mind for a long time. I said, "You know, I don't think that Manfred had an accident. I rather think he killed himself in order to escape his living together with Xantippe."

I was nonplussed when she replied quite at ease, "He would never have committed suicide; for the children's sake alone." This was all. No outrage, no indignation. She was not adamant, that their relationship had been a good one. She started no fierce backtalk. This was out of harmony with her usual temper. Since this incident I'm all the more sure there is some secret about Manfred's death and I'm going to find out.

I got up and walked to and fro in the room. I wondered if living side by side always meant trouble, when Veronica came in. She said, "If you want to be more flexible with studying the file, we can make you copies of the printout."

"Gladly, if Mrs. … Sara does not mind?"

"She herself made the suggestion. I'll tell Pauline to run off a set of copies."

When Pauline came with a thick pile of copies she said: "It's not far to St James's Park, if you want to sit on a park bench by the lake. It's very nice there. When you get out by the front door you turn to the right. It's a ten minutes walk only."

"Thanks a lot! Where can I leave the bulk? I'm only taking along a small stack."

"Have you got a key for the office?"

"Yes, for the outer office."

"OK, then we can put the file into this cupboard," said Pauline. Then she helped me to stow away my things. I thanked her once more and I betook myself to my heels.

§20

Broad Sanctuary Toilets

As I walked, I thought how lucky I was. I had a job now and it was left to me where I did my work. When I reached Charing Cross I kept on going along Whitehall until Westminster Abbey came into sight. I turned into Broad Sanctuary and after a while I sat down on a stone base. I looked around, until Mateo Capota's notes got the better of everything and I was compelled to read on.

Sunday November 11, 2001:

Friday night we were guests at a vernissage, a private viewing of a painting exhibition before opening to the public. The local amateur artist who works as a sous-chef in a big hotel had prepared a very nice cold buffet.

When we were back home again and had got rid of our festive garments, I was in for a surprise, when Xanda unpacked her handbag. She had taken home from the buffet as much as she could carry in her bag. For the whole weekend we subsisted on chicken legs and ham sandwiches.

This episode reminds me of one of our cycling tours last summer. We had stopped at an Inn for refreshment. On the way home we were

cycling on a road with car traffic, so we went one behind the other,
Xanda in front. Suddenly I noticed that her bag was so enormously
full that it seemed to bulge. Since I was the last in line, cycling behind
Titus and Selissa, I said nothing and the observation was soon out of
my mind. But back home it became apparent that she had found a
substantial piece of ham in the pantry of the Inn. Maybe I get arrested
one of these days as Xanda's accomplice in crime.

Tuesday November 20, 2001:

"Mateo!"

I had not even noticed that Selissa had occupied her mother's bed.
Xanda had already left for work and I had been dozing, dreaming of
Central America.

"Yes? What's on your mind, Selissa?"

"Why is mom so mean?"

"You shouldn't say such a thing. What gives you such an idea?"

"The other day she said that the bill for electricity is soaring. This
is so because we spend more time in the flat now rather than over at
grandma's. She has marked off a limit on the control knob of my heater
which I must not exceed. She says I can sojourn in your office for doing
my homework."

"Feel free to sit in the office when I'm working. As long as you do
not play noisily you are welcome there."

"I know that she cashes orphan's pensions for both me and Titus."

"Don't bother. I'm going to talk to your mum. I will compensate
her for the increased electricity consumption. It was thoughtless of
me — not to think of it."

"She utilizes you. You pay for so many things."

"But she is also generous. To take a single example, she made me a
present of a shirt and a neck tie only last week."

"She bought you this particular shirt and tie because she liked them. She wanted you to accompany her to this reception. You were supposed to wear a vest and tie. Don't you see that she does this for her benefit alone? Clothes make the man as she uses to say."

Saturday November 24, 2001:

I awoke early this morning. The upcoming holidays already begin to fill me with dread over wading through crowds at the various shopping centres to pick just the right gifts. Today is the first of the four so called shopping Saturdays. On these days the shops have longer opening hours. Even apprentices must show complete commitment and work extra hours in the four weeks before Christmas. I pity the personnel and I am deadly bored. I wish that Christmas were over. Xanda says that I'm bored because I do not think hard enough, that I must devote myself more to the task. I make suggestions but in the end I let her decide what I buy. To me all this seems like a lemming-like behaviour, a compulsive consumerism, a collective hysteria. But then, man is a gregarious animal.

It is of course exactly for this reason that for most people designations like maverick or lone wolf connote negatively. I sometimes wonder how I would be genetically determined by a zoologist. Would I pass as a hybrid creature? Live has made me a self-determined being. When it comes to the point, one is on one's own, anyhow. But I am — or I used to be — definitely a family man.

I think that any person could master a Robinson Crusoe situation. But it's so easy to look out for help. I think that having too many friends is a waste of time. Most men are hollow, anyway. About women in general I'm not so sure. But Xanda is, unfortunately. In my advertisement, besides her outward qualities, I listed some other traits I value in a woman, and of whom I knew that she had them too. I listed

*one trait that I supposed she had it, namely profundity. But at our first
date she wondered what I had meant when listing this trait.*

*Her motto is Fine feathers make fine birds. All show and no sub-
stance is what I usually reply when she cites her favorite saying. I've
given up trying to understand Xanda, but I carry on loving her and
her weak points.*

I startled when somebody touched my shoulder.

"Pauline!" I said when I realised where I was and who had
touched me.

"It was pure coincidence I found you here. I thought you
were sitting on a bench at St James's Park Lake. Instead I find
you here on a stone next to the Broad Sanctuary Toilets."

"I walked on and on; I thought St James's Park was somewhere here. I couldn't find another park then this one."

"But this is no park at all. There are not even benches.
Come with me, I show you."

We strode along Storey's Gate and after a hundred paces
we were entering St James's Park. We went to the lake and
found a bench and sat down.

"I have a few sandwiches for you and a bottle of water; I
must go back, into the office."

"This is very nice of you, Pauline. Thank you!" Her volumi-
nous breasts attracted my looks as if they were magnetic poles.

"No problem. What are you doing over the weekend?"

"I'll read through this whole report. Maybe Etienne and I
are returning to the continent. I can't say."

"If you like, you can come and visit me in my room in St
Martin's Lane. It's only a few paces from the Home Building.
Here is the number of the house; I put it down on the last sheet

of your dossier. Depending on the weather, we can do something together, if you are not busy."

"I think that would be very nice, thank you."

"See you," said Pauline and got away.

I looked after her as she went with her sturdy legs. I didn't know what to think of it. An enormous desire got hold of me.

I began to feed the ducks with chunks of sandwich. When the sandwiches were finished I took a deep breath and then I resumed my reading.

Monday January 7, 2002:

Yesterday was Three Kings Day. In the eyes of Titus and Selissa this holiday was a mock one because it was lost as an extra at-home day. After all it fell on a Sunday. Ungratefully they did not appreciate that Christmas Eve and New Year's Eve had been Mondays and because of that, Christmas Day and New Year's Day had been on Tuesdays.

I'm glad the past four or five weeks have come to an end and a pure new year without Christmas decoration lies before us. I have abhorred this so called Christmas season ever since I began to see through the wheeling and dealing. In the department stores, the constant streams of schmaltzy Christmas carols seem to charm people in a buying mood. I dislike any kind of music that is forced on me, for that matter. I perceive the whole festival as a time of hypocrisy and profiteering. Only in the years when my children believed in Santa I could get out something of Christmas time.

The last two weeks were however not so bad, as regards the running about in shopping centers. There were only some restitutions or replacements of a few mispurchases. And the last week of the year was quite eventful. One or two things have happened which I would never have imagined as being possible.

Xanda was to have leave for two weeks. Her last working day was Sunday December 23. She was supposed to work late that day, but she was determined to be up in time to do some last minute shopping on the Monday morning. Everything seemed perfect. We planned to go skiing for a few days. I hoped that Xavier and Roxanne would join us, but I hadn't asked them by phone. They came home on Sunday and in the evening we had dinner together. I didn't ask them about skiing then either, because they both had announced early that after dinner they wanted to meet with friends.

On top of it, their mother was in the country and a reunion of as yet unknown date and unknown length was lying ahead. She gave up her children to her ex-husband when she moved to Zanzibar City. But when she flicks her fingers they stand at attention. I did not like to meet her, so I did not count on the children either for the Christmas holidays. The ex-husband was peeved. I got in the car and drove to Cyclamen City. Xanda's flat was empty as I had expected. I strolled over to the van Aanstryk's.

Titus and Selissa were alone in Laurens' room where he had a sofa and a spare television. They were watching a show. A piece of advice at the bottom of the screen said 'This program is not appropriate for children'. What nonsense. Would children care? Would it make children all the more curious? That's just tokenism. But then, who is responsible? The legal guardians are.

Xanda gets furious when she catches them out watching unsuitable programs; but that's all she brings about. Sometimes late at night they fall asleep before the spare television while we grownups are in the living room. Xanda is a teacher by training, but she has not much feel for the raising of children. Marike and Laurens don't care either. But I'm not saying another word; not anymore. I've burnt my mouth too often already.

I do not put the case for helicopter parents. But in child-rearing you must set limits and you must be persistent in controlling these limits. These ingredients are as important as the parental love.

I asked the two television viewers if they would like to go for a walk. I expected a rejection. But they accepted enthusiastically. Being at the fringe of the town, we were free to walk into the forest or over the undeveloped area beyond the tramway line. Selissa dreaded the woodland; so we went alongside the forest with the open space on our left hand side, the lights of the city in our backs. The snow blanket was ankle-deep and powdery. The right half of the moon lit us the way. We commented on whether the moon seemed exactly half, when Selissa put a question into the nightly space: "Is it waxing or decreasing?" After a lengthy discussion we arrived at a mutual consent. Titus summarized: "If the visible fringe of the lunar globe is on the right like it is tonight, then the moon is waxing."

We saw a fox in the fields. It seemed as if it was heading for a hamlet that as yet had evaded the grip of the town. We discussed the question what it might find there to eat. Later we reached the spot where the fox had left his tracks in the snow. A little further on, we also found traces of hares. The children were amazed at the difference between the trails of the hares and the foxes.

When we had walked for at least half an hour, we turned around and went back, thereby doubling our tracks in the snow. Since the last snow had fallen yesterday afternoon, no one else had used this path; only wild animals. With the city lights now in front of us, the surroundings seemed less mystical.

Titus and Selissa told me of how their day had been. After this they wanted to hear a Christmas story. I had never cared much about Christmas tales, except the one by Peter Rosegger. I said, "His story is actually an account of how he — while still a child — went to buy

Christmas Joys in the faraway valley below and how he managed to overcome the obstacles that were put in his way when tramping home through the wintery snowy forest in the dead of night.'When I had said as much, they wanted to hear the whole story.

"This must be read, not told,"I said."I'm sure I would fluff it."Then I had to promise to read it to them tomorrow, or as soon as I could get hold of the book. I said that as a last resort I had a copy of Waldheimat in my home in Syget.

Then we brought up the topic that not everywhere in the world Christmas was celebrated like here in Middle Europe. That for example in Mauritius it is summer now and people go for a swim. And when they sing they sing gay songs not solemn ones.

"Mateo, can you remember what you dreamt last night?" asked Selissa.

"We are jumping from one topic to the next, but what makes you think that I dreamt at all?"

"Can you, Mateo?"

"As a matter of fact, I can remember,"I said."But as often happens when you dream, in hindsight the situation seems not real, very out of the ordinary."

"Tell us, please!"said Selissa.

"So be it. I was lying in bed on my left-hand side. I dreamt that all of a sudden I was roused from sleep by a loudspeaker outside who warned of a meteorite which was to hit the earth nearby shortly. At that moment I saw the glowing object come into sight in the upper left corner of a big window at the end of my bed. I sat up. But I was very tired. So as soon as I saw that the celestial body was to come down at a safe distance, far off to the right, I turned onto my left shoulder again and went back to sleep."

"Was there a heavy down-burst? I mean was it deafeningly

loud?" asked Titus?

"If it was, I didn't hear. I lay fast asleep. And besides, do you re-member ever to have heard noises in your sleep?"

"You said yourself you heard a warning over the loudspeaker," said Selissa.

"Maybe I heard a crash but I do not remember."

"Is that all?" asked Selissa.

"If you want, I tell you the rest. But it's as resembling farce as the first part. And it's no real continuation of the first part."

"No matter," said both in unison.

"Okay. In my sleep I felt something crawl onto my right shoulder. It lay there heavily, breathing into my right ear. At that moment I knew in my dream that I was sleeping and that I had to wake up and fend off the monster. With a final effort I succeeded in raising my left hand and feel the big teeth of the specter."

"My teeth are not big," protested Selissa. Both children laughed. They were aware that I had improvised and added a true story that had happened in the past, when Selissa had walked in her sleep.

When we approached the tram terminus near their grandparents' house they started to throw snowballs. The powdery snow was not ex-actly suited for a snowball fight but it was the more fun.

The cheeks of the children glowed when we came into the warm parlor of their grandparents' home. Titus and Selissa promised to go to bed promptly and I knew they would fall asleep soon. I bade good bye to everyone and walked the five minutes that it took me to reach Xanda's flat. Inside the flat I pulled out the key of the door lock. Then I lay on the couch and dropped off fully dressed.

I woke up when outside a jumping cracker went off. Very faintly I heard music from a neighboring flat. I got up and turned on the light. I looked in the bathroom and in the sleeping room. No trace of Xanda.

But it won't be long until she comes home. I decided to pick her up at work. I verified that her car was not in the underground parking garage and made for the television studio.

I spotted Xanda's car in the parking area and went inside the studio building. There was music to be heard and loud laughter and cheerful singing. No doubt about it; a Christmas staff party at an advanced stage was in progress. I nearly overlooked the two women in the dark niche. They were petting; one of them was Xanda.

On impulse I turned around. I think I wanted to go home on my own. But Xanda had discerned me and pursued me to the exit door. She took me by the arm and was adamant that I come in and see her colleagues. I had met most of them on previous occasions. She introduced the other woman to me. Her name was Rita Olivero, she had an inn in Edelweiss and had been responsible for the catering. She was a delicate black beauty.

I boiled with indignation, although I was aware that this had happened some years before Rita had seduced me and I had fallen in love with her. I got up and walked as far as the next vacant bench and sat down, snorting. After a while I read on:

Mr. Wiesel thrust a glass into my hand. Dazed, I raised it and wished a Merry Christmas to everybody. "I did not want to upset the party," I said, because everybody seemed to get ready to leave. "No, no," said Wiesel, "we were about to go, anyway. It's about time!"

Xanda left her car where it was, because she had been drinking. "I went outside to phone you, if you could pick me up, because I have been drinking," she said, when I had turned out onto the road. "It's the only day of the year that I had a drink in the studio. I don't know how it could happen. She is the born temptress. But she is so charming. Maybe we women are all a little les?"

"Maybe," I said. I didn't know what else to say. I was as helpless as a panda with a Stradivari. Under no circumstances did I want to start an argument. I acknowledged to myself that Rita Olivero was an attractive woman whom I could perhaps not resist on an evening when I had hit the bottle. This woman could have her pick of any man all around. But would she care for a man? Tonight I would not kiss Xanda. Not even after she brushed her teeth. What an inverted world!

I was not altogether surprised to find this reference to Rita in this account. I sort of expected something like this, actually. I had known they were companioned in a romantic sort of way. So it was Rita who had started the affair. Or had Xanda simply lied to Mateo? Somehow, this Mateo Capota and I were also in relation now; a relation of men whose women had been entangled in a relation. Crazy world! I read on:

Xanda went to bed. "You won't go to Syget, will you?" she asked.

"I don't think so. In any case I'll be here in the morning for shopping as agreed." Xanda couldn't hide that she was ill at ease. She was glad I didn't say more about the apparent brief encounter that I happened to witness. I too tried to hide my feelings. I was in the mood to go to my house and to return no more; but I knew I would not be able to accomplish it. Tomorrow I would be here again; I will not give up so fast. But go home I will.

When I thought Xanda asleep, I went down. The moment I was about to leave the lift on the ground floor, the woman living in Xanda's neighboring flat rushed in. We both tried not hard to avoid a collision; but it was absorbed partly by her heavy breasts. Still, the impact brought our faces close together. A bewitching scent reached my nostrils. She has been turning me on for two years already. I knew

GERHARD OBERRESSL

*her name was Vesna. I did not care about my great love any longer.
At the risk of being seen by Xanda, I went up with her encouraging
neighbor. We both looked at Xanda's door viewer when we flitted into
Vesna's flat.*

*Vesna was too impatient to go inside; she started in the anteroom.
Perhaps her son is on a visit, I thought to myself and I felt uneasy about
it. After the first surge she whispered, that her husband was sleeping
inside. I was taken by complete surprise. Was she insane? In the end she
succeeded in coaxing me to go to Xanda's flat.*

*In my office I learned that the young man I had seen before was
not her son but her husband. Earlier she had been married to a building contractor who left her for a younger thing. Her present husband
was not interested in consummating their marriage. But she had of
course known beforehand. He is not gay either. He simply has no interest in sexual activity. And he would allow her to take a lover. But she
did not think that she could bring one home to the flat. I did not go
to Syget that night. I wonder since, if Xanda has something noted or
sensed. I have no bad conscience. As from now on, my attitude towards
Xanda will be relaxed and noncommittal. I wonder for how long we
will be able to carry on this way.*

*Christmas Eve was demanding. Until one o'clock p.m. rushing
through shopping malls, and thereafter wrapping of presents. When
the dark fell, we started handing out of presents in Xanda's flat.
Thereafter the process was continued in my house and last at the
house of Xanda's parents.*

*The Christmas holidays were pleasant for the children as well
for the grownups. We spent some days skiing near Salzburg. We behaved like a normal family. The sparks of attraction between Xanda
and me flew as intense as ever. But the great love I had once carried
in my heart for her has faded away. Perhaps this is just normal? The*

thought makes me feel sad.

On New Year's Eve we returned from our skiing vacation. The evening we spent with the van Aanstryks. Besides the family circle they had invited other relatives and friends. All in all we were nineteen persons at the table. Some allusions were made as to when I was ready to marry Xanda. They were ignored by all who were privy to the real situation. But I observed Laurens and Marike giving signals by winking and faint shakes of the head, signifying not to drill ahead. At a late hour, actually shortly after the turn of the year when everybody waltzed to the strains of The Blue Danube, an elderly lady who obviously had not yet realized the signs of the time, blurted encouragingly into my ear: "May the New Year bring you marital bliss!"

"The only thing Xanda wants is to fuck; nothing more," I replied, clearly audible for everybody. We were all a little drunk and my vulgar remark seemed to cause amusement. At that moment I made the decision that I shall make use of the phrase in similar situations in the future. Maybe it can help us to get away of each other.

Later in bed Xanda tried to appease me with the ominous remark: "believe me, one day you will be glad we never married." So it was postponement not anymore but acceptance of the fate. She was so distraught that I, not for the first time, was convinced that Xanda had a deep secret that she was unable to divulge. I hugged her heartily and said nothing more. "I love you so much," she said fervently several times on the trot.

Wednesday March 13, 2002:

Last night Xanda was wrapping presents for Easter. Purely on a whim, or so she said, she wanted to surprise all her colleagues at the television station with a small present. For this purpose she occupied the whole sitting room suite. Everything was crammed with presents.

What was destined for her beloved ones was shrouded with dish towels. There were also finished parcels; and in addition there were sheets of wrapping paper, packaging straps and scissors. For this reason I watched television sitting in an armchair that I had put quite close to the screen.

Titus helped his mother making parcels. Xanda was scolding Titus because he let himself be distracted by the television. After a while, Selissa came in and sat onto my lap. She had already dressed for bed in a short nightdress. Her knees and more reflected in the frame of the television. "The way you sit one can see everything," said Titus. His remark was meant for Selissa. But the reaction came from Xanda. "Go and dress properly; you are too old for sitting on Mateo's lap!"

Selissa came back draped in her dressing gown and resumed her seat. "There is nowhere else to sit," she said.

I stopped at this point and walked along the lake. I had to sort out the names in my brain: Pauline, Selissa, Yanica, Xanda, Rita, Vesna, Aleva; my mother Tusnelda. What a collection of curiosities!

§21

St James's Park Lake

On Saturday morning I went again into St James's Park. Walking along the lake I was thinking about what had happened the day before; last night, when I walked along this path, I called Rita. First I had hesitated to call her and then I didn't know what to say. Her episode with Xanda which I had read about in Capota's account bothered my mind. But as soon as I heard her familiar velvety voice which so often before had bewitched my senses, I knew it was right to call her. She displayed concern about my wellbeing and her voice sounded so affectionate and loving, that a strong feeling of togetherness grew on me until my breast was full of happiness. Reassured, I had then slept well.

Today the weather was fine again, so after a while I sat down on a park bench and resumed reading the Capota file:

Thursday August 8, 2002:

Yesterday Xanda and I went to an apple wine tavern in Alfalfa for a snack. Typically she wears glasses and sometimes a bandana so as to remain incognito. When people started to sway to the music, I held myself back. But Xanda appeared like a modified person. She spurred me on and called me a bore.

Tuesday August 20, 2002:

We have just returned from a farm vacation. It was pure nature for five days. A neighborhood girl was allowed to come with us. She is a classmate of Selissa. Xanda was in the kitchen with the farmer's wife. She wanted to learn how to prepare a certain dish. I entered the little lounge. I had in mind to read, when the girls came in. Obviously they had followed me and had something in mind. They grinned sheepishly and adventurously at the same time. Before I knew what was happening, Selissa grabbed me briefly playfully but boldly. Looks of expectancy were in their eyes. Obviously they had planned to do this. Clearly they wondered what my reaction will be. The attack had been so unexpected; I managed only to bring out, "you know, you shouldn't; 'tis is inappropriate." I think I was more embarrassed than they were. I told Xanda nothing about the incident. She was not unlikely to put the blame on me.

Monday March 17, 2003:

This noon Xanda and I dined out. When we had finished eating and were sipping at the coffee, I felt completely contented.

"Mateo?"

"What is the matter, darling?"

"Of late you look so depressed; what's going round in your head?" said Xanda, looking at me with concern in her eyes. "I know of a teacher colleague from my days in school. He suffered from depressions for many years before he sought help. You know, it's the same with any disease; the sooner you accept treatment the better."

Indeed, I'm having problems with a client who makes me responsible for his having had a non-productive time in his plant for some hours. Time and again, thoughts haunt my mind and ideas of ways of proving that the failure of the computer network had not been my fault; that it had not been caused by one of my programs. But I had not assumed that this might show on my facial expression. I do not want to burden Xanda with my problems. Since the day she took the word marriage impostor into her mouth, I'm careful not to mention financial matters at all. If I mentioned that the guy has threatened to sue me, she is likely to suspect, that I want her to help me with money. Or might she even feel obliged to help me out with money? Nonsense!

"In my profession, there are all the little problems that want to be solved. Now and then there crops up a bigger problem that even causes a little head ache. But I am a problem solver. Don't worry, Xanda; I have no depressive illness."

"You shouldn't downplay it, when you are in trouble."

"Come on! Why do you have regular sessions with a psychotherapist? Why do you frequently see a clergyman? You do also not tell me about your problems. Why don't you confide in me?"

"Now you are harping on this again."

"But isn't it the same thing?"

A profound sigh from deep within was the answer.

"In sighing so deeply you are already half confiding."

"The day will come, when you will know. Believe me Mateo. And in the meantime you should be glad that you have only your petty problems."

I did not reply and changed the conversation.

There is no foundation of trust between us. Such discussions made me sad in former times. Why can't she tell me about her problem? Now I'm used to it. I have even lost interest in finding the golden key to Xanda's golden casket.

GERHARD OBERRESSL

Friday September 19, 2003:

Today was a fine day in late summer, sunny and warm. The four of us went on an excursion on our bikes. We were having a break in a pub garden where a band was playing and a few guys were dancing. While Titus and Selissa had a try at a jive on the dance floor, Xanda and I sat in the shade. Xanda didn't feel like dancing; this was alright with me. Xanda told me how, when she went dancing with Manfred, they used to have a bottle of sparkling wine in the car. Now and then they would go outside to have a sip. This way they avoided buying expensive drinks inside. On one occasion Xanda nearly suffocated because a tiny bit of tin foil from the bottle top had got into her wind-pipe.

Monday October 4, 2004:

The day before yesterday I took Xanda and the children out to The Golden Lion for dinner. We wanted to celebrate a little our anniversary in the inn where we first met five years ago. I had made a reservation. We all were in high spirits. For camouflage Xanda wore a blond wig and sunglasses. On the way to the Inn my car nearly lost a wheel. I had mounted my winter tires the week before; obviously one of the wheels had not been tightened properly. Luckily I noticed a funny noise in time when we were going at a moderate speed in urban traffic. Young people are quickly ready to discover the funny side of a thing. Even Xanda, who normally can be swift to take offence, laughed a lot. The dinner went according to my taste. The trip proved to be a complete success, until suddenly someone brushed against Xanda's wig, which got out of place. So she got up and went outside. When she returned to the table she had taken off the wig. Apparently she had also taken off her sunglasses and put them into her bag.

We were right in the middle of the main dish, when at a neighboring table a discussion broke out which got louder and louder. "Why should I shut up? I've waited long enough for the instance, to be face to face with this teacher whore and your brat of sin! She is the spitting image of her father."

"Really! Darling, you have known all these years; why are you so furious all of a sudden?"

"To know and to see so unexpectedly, are two very different animals. You said that she resigned as a teacher and went overseas. Now I can see that it is this television bitch. If this was a clumsy venture to acquaint me with them, it went down the drain. You couldn't have done it in a more abusive way. To take me unawares in this mean way ...". With the last words the strident lamentation transformed into a pitiable and inconsolable sobbing.

"Maude! What makes you think that anything was arranged? It's pure coincidence."

Xanda, who sat with her back to the brawlers and had not seen them before, got rigid. She sat thunderstruck and I took her hands into mine. I think she would have preferred to dissolve into thin air. Even Titus and Selissa sat like stones. The restaurant manageress offered for one company or the other, or both, to sit in an adjoining room. But the storm had ceased and the two companies at table melted into one. The former teacher colleague's group comprised also a son with spouse and their two little children. The teacher his son and I, we tried to keep clear heads. It was decided that at the next opportunity a meeting must be arranged.

We were then the first ones to leave. For the moment and in this place, our appetite had vanished. At least we had been lucky to nearly finish our main course, whereas the others were at the stage of starting. When we parted, Maude even hugged Selissa and apologized to all of us. When we sat in the car and ready to start, I suggested that we conclude the interrupted meal in a pastry shop. This suggestion was met with approval.

Driving off I cast a look at Xanda and put my hand onto her thigh. Her countenance reflected gratitude, relief and determination. I knew that she had in mind to make up for her failure; her failure to be truthful about Selissa's begetter. Selissa has only a fleeting memory of Manfred. She seemed to be the least concerned. Titus remained tight-lipped for the rest of the day and in the evening he went over to his grandparent's house for the night.

Monday October 4, 2004:

I must this make a separate and second entry for this memorable Monday. I'm determined, to do no stroke of work today other than reflecting on and noting down about the recent events.

Yesterday morning Xanda had to go to the studio. I had heard the buzz of the alarm clock but I had dozed off again. I was half asleep when I perceived Xanda's body to be very near to me. She rarely makes the first step; not spontaneously. She has a very subtle way of making me feel like desiring her. She is not the obtrusive type. I was therefore a little astonished when I felt her taking me into her mouth. I was still not fully awake and I enjoyed the event fervently.

When I turned around and uttered a sigh, I beheld through the open bedroom door how Xanda came back into the flat. She must have forgotten something. Involuntarily I held my hand over my bulging duvet. Had Vesna invaded the flat? I lay motionless for some moments, until Xanda left again.

I lay motionless a while longer. "Have you lost your senses?" I said eventually. When her hair appeared, I realized who it actually was. "Selissa!"

"Don't be angry with me, Mateo. I love you so. I have been picturing this situation for years. I am sincere with you. Mum is not as she

pretends to be." While saying this she had crawled out from under the duvet and rolled on top of me. She caressed my face.

An hour later I was packing my belongings for transfer to Syget. "We cannot start a relationship, Selissa. There are other persons involved. We are not alone on an island. We must be sensible. There are laws in this country. There is such a thing as a legal protection for children and young persons."

"I'm not a child! I don't want to be protected."

"I'm leaving today, and I shall never come back again. It's for the better for all of us. Please go over to your grandma and let me pack with leisure. We must nip this in the bud."

"Please do not leave — so we can at least see one another every day."

"Don't you see that first of all we must clear the air?"

"When you move out for good, can we then meet as often as we like?"

"I didn't say that I want to meet with you. I would be ruining your whole future if I started a relationship with you."

"We can go on secretly until I am of age. We are not the only ones. A schoolmate of mine is carrying on with her stepfather for two years now. Nobody has told on them so far; although her mother is probably wise to it."

"All I can say today is that we now need a few days to collect our thoughts. Don't you think? So please go over now. Titus is also there. Mum will come late tonight. You should stay there until tomorrow. I'm going to leave a message for your mum."

"Mateo, please, don't tell her."

"Don't worry, Selissa. I'm not going to tell her about us. There are other things galore to cite, for not coming back to this flat. You need only to think of yesterday's revelations."

"You're so right, Mateo. I see your point. I'm sure we will meet again soon; I'll be thinking of you day and night."

First thing Selissa had gone, I made myself some coffee; then I sat in the kitchen reflecting on what mistakes I had made. Should I have seen this coming? Should I have taken countermeasure in time? Had I secretly anticipated this to happen? Am I guilty?

About half an hour after Selissa had left the flat I became totally relaxed. An overwhelming elatedness came over me, when I started sorting out my belongings. In the five years of my detention in this flat, many things had accumulated which were of no use to me any longer. With every item I threw away, my mood increased by an increment. Eventually I was in a state of complete happiness. At last I had found a cause to leave for good. And the occasion couldn't have been more delightful.

In an extra fit of joyfulness I sat down and wrote with my fountain pen on a sheet of white plain paper.

Dear Xanda!

Thank you for the last five years. We both know that our time is over. Since yesterday's revelation I cannot trust you any longer. I cannot stay in your flat any longer. I need my own home and my peace of mind. This is my final decision.

I wish you all the best for your future life.

Mateo

I found an envelope decorated with floral ornaments among Xanda's things. I put the note into it and sealed up the letter. Then I lettered it with the words To Mrs. Xanda van Aanstryk and laid it onto the kitchen table. I imagined how she would get sight of it as soon as she came home. Habitually, first thing she enters the flat she goes into the kitchen.

I went back to my office. It was my desire to leave the baroque dining room in an immaculate state. Who knew better what to do than Xanda's cleaning woman? Her name was Meta. Xanda had sometimes mentioned it, because the woman does also the laundry and she irons my shirts. I found the name Meta on a list of numbers next to the landline telephone set. I tried the number in a haphazard way. And I was lucky. A woman's voice answered with a name that didn't sound familiar to me and which I didn't catch. I didn't know her full name. "Mrs. Meta," I said. "I'm calling from Mrs. van Aanstryk's flat. This is a case of emergency. Could you please come over as soon as possible? Sorry I don't know your full name."

She said a name which again I didn't catch. But she added that I can call her Meta. "My name is Mateo Capota, you know, Mrs. van Aanstryk's … um, well, partner." I shied away from using the word ex-boyfriend.

"What do you want me to do? Will it take long?"

"It's about the baroque dining room that serves … served me as an office. I'm moving out of it today and I don't want to leave a mess. I want to leave the room in the same condition as it was when I took quarters, five years ago."

"I see. This is no problem. I'm coming;" she said, "as soon as we have finished lunch."

"I'm sorry; I didn't realize it's already lunch hour."

"It doesn't matter, it's all right, mister Capota."

I felt relieved when she took it so calmly; with a cheerful heart I directed my efforts towards packing my belongings.

My three suitcases were nearly bursting at the seams when I carried them into the lift and rode down in order to stow them in my van. When I rode up in the lift a second passenger managed to dart in at the last moment. Besides greeting one another we smiled civilly. I hadn't seen her before. Obviously she was also going up to the top *floor. When after getting out of the lift she followed me to the flat, the penny dropped.*

"You must be Mrs. Meta. I'm so sorry. I only know you in jeans and with a bandana. It's very good of you not to let me down. I'm going to pay for your efforts as soon as you have finished. I don't want you to charge this to Mrs. van Aanstryk."

First thing she entered the flat she made for the kitchen. Same as Xanda, I thought. She put her handbag on the table beside the letter I had written for Xanda. Along with what I had said on the phone she seemed to know how matters stood.

Turning around and going to the dining room she said, "Is all this to be thrown away?"

"Wait, no; I must still sort out those things that might contain confidential information; certain data media and papers. Actually I didn't expect you so soon."

"OK, you sort and I stow. The good ones go into the pot, the bad ones go into your crop."

"Good. The dust bin is the pot; but I need also a crop. I have no suitcase left; I must borrow one of Xanda's. I shall bring it back as soon as I have emptied it in Syget; this afternoon."

I thought to myself: And then I will lock the door of Xanda's flat for the last time and throw the key into the letter slot.

I went to the spare bedroom. On top of the clothes cupboard were two suitcases, one above the other. When I was in the process of wrenching out the bigger case from beneath the smaller one, I almost ignored a small something which silently fell to the ground. But I had perceived a momentary glitter. I checked on the carpeted floor, but could detect nothing. Had my eyes been fooling me?

When we had begun filling the trunk, I mused that I had to go twice anyway. Borrowing Xanda's case and then bringing it back, or

returning with one of my emptied cases and fetch the rest of my belongings; it was all the same. So I placed the big trunk back onto
the clothes cupboard and then I put the smaller one on the very top.
Then I remembered that something had dropped down. I bent down
and looked and searched carefully once again. Sure enough, under the
wardrobe lay a golden key; the key for the tabernacle. Swiftly I tried it
and the sanctum opened. In one of the small drawers I found a memory
card and I discerned some letters. Skimming them I recognized them as
blackmailing letters.

Meta didn't get any of it. Quickly I unpacked my computer equipment which was still in the flat. I copied the data medium and scanned
the letters. I stored everything on my hard disk. I locked the shrine
again. I didn't know if the key had been under the big suitcase or on
top of it. I thought it safer to I put the golden key under the cupboard
from where I had picked it up. Should Xanda return unexpectedly, she
would not suspect that I had noticed it. I would then tell her that I had
taken down a suitcase but then returned it again. Meta did not become
suspicious in any way.

We filled the trunk and Meta went several times to the waste disposal unit. Meta had a delightful sense of humor. She was glib and
had a cheerful habit of mind. When I had packed those items that I
wanted to sift through more thoroughly at home, I wanted to say good
bye to Meta.

"Mrs. Meta, you will be gone when I return to fetch the rest. Here
is for your generous help," I said, and I handed her a banknote.

"Not on any account," the woman said in a matter-of-fact way. "I
do not want to benefit from your misfortune. You can go reassured to
your house. I will clean up and lock the door; and that is that."

"Then you must allow me to ask you and your family to dinner tonight. After all I've deranged your Sunday. Let's say in the steak house

over in the Avril Mall?"

"Is it open on a Sunday? We never dine out."

"It's open every day; tonight then, seven or eight o'clock?"

"I think seven would be fine."

I knew that Meta was not responsible for the bedrooms in the flat. But I feared that she might find the key nevertheless and try it herself on the tabernacle. So I returned to the spare bedroom and picked the key up and put it onto the cupboard under the big case.

Meta helped me with bringing down the computer and the scanner. I took the heavy trunk. Then I moved all my belongings to 'Hollywood' — my house in Syget. Immediately upon arrival and after unloading the car, I emptied my suitcases onto the table and onto the floor in the living room. Then I put the bigger case next to the front door so I would not forget about it.

At six o'clock I took the trunk and left the house and returned to Cyclamen.

My letter lay still on the kitchen table when I arrived in Xanda's flat. I packed the rest of my belongings into the suitcase. Then I went into the spare bedroom for a last inspection. The key was where I had put it.

Thereafter I picked up the trunk and — without looking back — I left the flat and locked the door. Then I held the key into the mail slot and released it, so it could fall freely. I went down by the staircase. I didn't feel like meeting somebody in the lift accidentally.

I drove my car over to the mall. I was ten minutes early. I remained in the van so as to await the arrival of Meta and her family. When by seven o'clock they hadn't shown up I got out of the car and went over to the steak house and peeked inside. I couldn't see Meta. I decided to take a seat and wait. Would they fail to turn up? There! A school-girl beckoned from a table in a corner. She sat with Meta who looked breathtaking. I didn't know that she had so beautiful black long hair. Was there no husband?

"My daughter and I constitute the whole family," she said when I had come near enough.

Monday May 19, 2014:

Meta and I married a few weeks only after we got acquainted with one another on the day of my relocation out of Xanda's flat. I forgot about the copies I had made of Xanda's secret. They were of no interest for me any longer. And they were none of my business any longer; if ever they had been. On top of that, her hidden dark mystery had been revealed on the day before I left her flat, anyway — I had thought.

A few months after I had left Xanda, I had inspected my hard disks for superfluous data. When I detected Xanda's copies, I deleted them. But a day later I became curious and I recovered them. And then I examined them briefly. Thereafter I saved them to several mediums. As time went by, I forgot about them again.

Yesterday we heard that Xanda had died in her sleep. Her passing away has stirred me up more than I would have thought possible. She had been out of my mind altogether. The recordings passed through my mind and I began to search for them. When I had found them I examined them; and then reexamined them; and then again. And again and again and again. So Xanda had had another shocking secret, after all. I felt certain, that somebody was responsible for her demise.

I saw now why she could not bear this burden of her horrible secret on her own and that she had to seek help from psychoanalysts and priests. This was the foul deed she could not tell me about. She probably had known that I was so addicted to her that I would not have told at the time. But she was so far-sighted to know that feelings may change and that one of these days my being in the know could become a threat for her. So it was missing trust from the beginning.

But she need not have feared. I would never have betrayed her. But would I have made a retreat? I can't tell today. But I would not have told to anybody and I shall not betray her now. Fraudulent concealment they call it, I think. But nobody will ever know I was wise to it. I'm not even going to tell Meta. Nobody knows that I had found the golden key. Even if Xanda's felony should become known, I'm not going to disclose anything. They will find the evidence when they search her flat, anyway. I'm so sorry for Xanda; I could never hate her.

The memory card contains a video. The recording shows a scene at a shunting yard, obviously taken from afar. You see a rail carriage run very slowly into a second rail carriage standing motionless. A railroad worker pushes another railroad worker between the buffers of two carriages the moment when they collide. Abruptly the video ends.

The murder victim is Manfred. You see his surprised horrified look when he looks his murderer in the face. Of the latter you see only his back. Could he be a fake railroad worker? Could it even be a woman? Who made the video?

If Xanda was in the secret before the cold-blooded murder happened, I ask myself did she do it herself or did she commission somebody with it. Or perhaps an admirer did it without her knowing and gave her the proof thereafter? Or she had an affair with somebody and they wanted to do away with the troublesome husband? Was the teacher colleague in it?

One thing seems clear to me. Regardless of how it came to that infernal deed; after the crime, Xanda wanted the widow's pension and the orphan's pensions. She was then an attractive woman of thirty-four. She had two children. The younger, the five years old Selissa was fathered by a teacher colleague. In all likelihood her husband Manfred was unsuspecting; or was he? A shiver runs through me when I think what poor Xanda had to go through as a penalty for her wrongdoing.

The blackmailing letters are cryptic. They contain few words and many allusions. If you had any doubt what it is about, you would not guess. But I know now.

I interpret the contents of the memory card and the letters like this: Xanda wanted Manfred's death and assigned somebody to do it. I can hardly imagine that the price was money. And if it was, she failed to pay. Howsoever, the murderer became embittered and blackmailed her. She did not succumb but turned the tables and blackmailed the murderer. I'm glad I escaped Xanda's affairs ten years ago and am no longer enmeshed in them. I think I wandered for five years on the brink of disaster on Xanda's side.

For heaven's sake! What must I do now? I jumped up from my bench and made straight for the Home Building. But after a few strides – slowly and gradually – the state of affairs became clearer to me.

This murder happened some twenty years ago. There was certainly no hurry. Probably not one damned person was present in the offices of Home Investigations, anyway. And if there were, it is only Etienne Friendly himself that I would speak to about this hideous crime.

So I turned back. Absorbed in thought, I walked along St James's Park Lake until I suddenly found myself in front of Buckingham Palace.

I knew I had left my mobile phone in the office, but automatically I reached for it, in order to tell Rita, where I was. When I realized that this was futile I gawked for a while. Then I walked away along the Mall. After some time I turned into Marlborough Road and then into Pall Mall.

When I was nearing Charing Cross I decided to avoid it and make a shortcut along Whitcomb Street. I had the feeling that in doing so, I could make it right to the back door of the Home Building. When suddenly I found myself in St Martin's Street, Pauline crossed my mind again and I decided to go and pay her a visit. She had been so nice. It didn't mean that I was going to cheat Rita.

When I arrived at the given number, there was no dwelling house at all, but a storage depot. I tried several doors, all were locked. The depot would probably be opened again on Monday morning. I verified the number. Pauline had the number distinctly printed. Even if I had my mobile phone on me; I didn't have Pauline's mobile number, anyway.

Nothing! My date melted into thin air. Perhaps it's actually not such a bad thing, I thought.

§22

Edelweiss Castle

On the morning of the Sunday it was raining. After my morning toilet I went into the office and continued reading the Capota file. This time I would read some of those sections that I had skipped on first reading. I had left out a chapter now and then, because I had wanted to come to the end quickly. Now with this murder in the past, perhaps I could find one clue or the other.

When I had read for three hours or so, Etienne came into the office with another guy whom he introduced superficially.

"You should have breakfast," said Etienne.

"Have you read the Capota file to the end," I asked.

"I haven't had the time as yet. But today I'm going to bury myself into it. How far are you?"

"I skipped some sections, of which I'm doing today as many as can accomplish. The account is so extensive. I'm glad I read the end yesterday. Listen up! In this script, Mateo Capota discloses the murder of Xanda van Aanstryk's husband Manfred!"

"His death in the shunting yard was not due to an accident? This happened more than twenty years ago. The woman was then twenty-eight or nine. Does he admit to having done it?"

No! Not he. But he found evidence, in Mrs. van Aanstryk's flat the day he left her, when he packed his things. He forgot about because for him, at the time, a new stage of life began; with his present wife. He inspected the evidence only now, when he heard of Xanda's death and that she had possibly been murdered.

He thinks, she must have been in the know about Manfred's killing; or she is even the instigator or even the murderer. On the video he found, you can't see the face of the doer, he writes."

"This blows my mind; absolutely devastating! As I said, I shall read the report today, at least what you can recommend to me. You too should apply yourself to the file very carefully. Don't forget to make notes. Tomorrow we go back to Goodland and have a talk with Mr. Mateo Capota."

Next morning, Monday, I was in Sara Lagoon's office, when I saw Pauline come in. She perceived me immediately and looked not exactly friendly. I raised my shoulders and showed my palms, a question mark on my face.

As soon as I had dealt with Sara I went over to Pauline. "I'm sorry Pauline," I said. "Something is wrong with the number you printed on the sheet of paper."

Pauline shook her head doubtfully and said, "You probably confused St Martin's Lane with St Martin's Place. I remembered, but too late. It's happened to me when I came to London."

"Are you not a Londoner? Where do *you* come from?"

"I came from Melbourne, only months ago."

"But I'm sure, that I looked in St Martin's Street, not Place. I'm very sorry. Come to think about it, I remember you said lane. But when I chanced to come into St Martin's Street, I was dead certain that this was what you had said."

"Good grief! I'm awfully sorry! It's my fault."

"It's a pity, yes; but it wasn't to be. Better luck next time! You have been very nice, Pauline. Thank you for everything."

Two hours later Etienne Friendly and I were in an airplane bound for Goodland.

"After having read Mr. Capota's notes, can you spot any suspects?" said Etienne.

"Not for Manfred's homicide, of course."

"Naturally."

"But for the Xanda case," I consulted my notes, "Xanda's friend Aleva has a motive. Although … after ten years? And if jealousy is a motive for murder at all, is depending on the mental condition of the woman. As a last resort we should perhaps look into her present situation and find out, what has become of her."

"Very good! Not so much jealousy, but late vengeance is to be considered, if the woman's alcohol problem has worsened," said Etienne. Who is next?"

"I think nobody can be left out. So I considered also the parents for a motive."

"You are right. But it seems that her mother still dotes upon her. And her father too seems free from suspicion. You are acquainted with Selissa and Titus, you said the other day in the Golden Egg?"

"But not good enough. You interviewed them. What do *you* think of them?"

"I have not crossed them out completely, but I would be very much surprised if one or the other or both were guilty in the placing of the honey. This is the impression I've got from my individual encounters with them."

"What do you make of the fact that Selissa has been in love with Mateo Capota? Do you think there might something be *there*?"

"This didn't take me by surprise completely. She herself passed a remark to me the other day. But she was fifteen at the time she adored him and was sexually attracted to him. True, she thought that Xanda treated Mateo meanly. Still, at the utmost, this could be one of many occasions that contributed to an accumulation of contempt; but not of hate. I think that Selissa is a woman that is capable of love but not of deadly hate."

"Well, from the beginning, Louise Chevrolet was my favorite. But she seems to be off the hook. Anyhow, there is no reference to her in the file."

"Oh yes. I think we need not go into this again."

"Very well then; now I think Mateo Capota, and more so this neighbor Vesna must be examined carefully."

"Are you serious? You think Capota gives away his notes when he is the culprit? And don't overlook the fact, that he has no grudge against Xanda; and he only achieved through her, detouring, his present state of contentment."

"And Vesna?"

"We must keep her in mind."

"What about the woman whose husband – the teacher – made Xanda pregnant, and then led his spouse to believe that the rival, together with her daughter, lives abroad?"

"You never know. But we can shelve this, I think."

"The fact, that Mrs. van Aanstryk did not have a lot of friends, seems to narrow down the possible set of perpetrators.

This brings me back to her father. I think he was not as blue-eyed as her mother was. He could have been fed up with the unscrupulous behavior of his daughter. Perhaps she had become too greedy."

"But there is no indication as to that effect in the file, is there?"

"No, there is none."

"Still; you have a sense of psychology. I also wonder, how I would feel if I had such a ruthless offspring."

"This woman, Xanda I mean, cheated and stole. But somehow, none of the suspects we have just perused seems to have sufficient motive for doing her in, I think."

"I think a real motive could be buried beneath the circumstances that led to the murder of Xanda van Aanstryk's husband. An investigation into this business can bring totally new aspects into play, and motives may come out into the open."

"Quite so!" said Etienne Friendly.

"I wonder, what's next."

After some minutes of silence, Etienne Friendly said, "You said before, Xanda had few friends. When you listen to her mother you'd think she was either at work or at home. Also her colleagues in the television station think so, because that's what Xanda told them. But in actual fact, the persons that were close to her never knew when her working hours began or ended. She worked early some mornings, then she would work for a whole day or only deep into the night; in short, she worked inordinate hours. With her deviousness she succeeded in deceiving anybody."

"Hello Mateo," said Etienne Friendly into his mobile "…

can I come and visit you today or tomorrow? ... ah, very good ... that would be great ... you drive into the castle yard and give me a ring ... yes, I come outside ... ok ... see you later!"

I frowned.

"We need not go. He's coming round in about an hour. We are lucky. He's on business in Cowford and will soon come through Edelweiss. It was a good thing to call him this evening."

"Without a hitch," I said. "This morning we left the Home Building, and now we are expecting to talk to Mr. Mateo Capota in Edelweiss Castle."

"Are you going to take a room in the castle?"

"Neither do I want to dwell in the castle nor with Rita. I have stopped by at the Fox and Hare for a short reunion with Rita. But I told her that I have taken up quarters with Nelson. Nelson's wife runs a bed and breakfast. It's only a few paces away."

"I see. You can go to your room then and relax until Capota arrives. I'll lie down a little myself. He said about an hour. But it can easily become two or three hours. I'll give you a ring as soon as he's here."

"Fine," I said and went over to Nelson's, which is behind the Castle Inn.

When Etienne rang, I had gone to sleep. I got up and went to the castle. When I entered the Golden Egg, Etienne Friendly and Mr. Capota looked up and Etienne waved me nearer and indicated a seat.

After explaining to Capota what my function was, Etienne said, "Mateo, have you any idea who the murderer of Manfred van Aanstryk might have been?"

"Oh shit!" said Mateo Capota. "Only after you had left last Monday I began to suspect that I had accidentally copied also the last entry from Monday May 19, 2014. But this was not meant for you. It is only my life with Xanda that I was prepared to let you read."

"It was your subconscious then that wanted to tell me the whole truth," cackled Etienne.

"Nonsense! You can't use this essay. I have only made it up. I told you that I do occasionally some scriptwriting. It is only an invention of my brain, a figment."

I drew breath. Etienne veered off and asked Capota how his family was. When Capota answered, Etienne listened very carefully.

When Capota asked Etienne about his family, Etienne said that he was away a lot because all the time people cheated, robbed and murdered. He sounded very pathetic.

Neither Friendly nor Capota spoke for a while. I was quiet anyway.

"On reading about the demise of Xanda you certainly did not compose a story about the murder of her husband," said Etienne eventually.

Nobody spoke.

"I appreciate when you still want to protect Xanda's offspring. But they know that she was no saint. The other day Selissa confessed in this very room that she was conceived illegitimately. You yourself write about it in your account. At the same meeting it became manifest that Xanda, when she was fifteen years old, was pregnant from her husband to be. But she did not tell him, but came to this castle and seduced the administrator in the belief that he was the lord. When she realized the error, she seduced the real lord, and planted the child on him. He sent her for one year to the Netherlands as an exchange student, where she was delivered of the child. Some years later the child was adopted by the lord's sister in law and lives in the castle since.

The administrator too thought that he was the father and had to live with a bad conscience for half of his life. Titus has now found a real brother and Selissa has found a second half brother. This was cleared up a week ago in here. So they know what devil the woman was. The only thing they might expect is recourse claims by the insurance company. But I think it is all over and done with. And if not, it wouldn't really hurt them. They both have a secure subsistence of their own."

"Agreed! Everything shall be dug up," said Mateo Capota, banging on the table after some hesitation. "I want to know who killed Xanda. I think that for all people involved, to have certainty is better than anything else. My wife will also appreciate it. But it must be clear, that I have hit upon the evidence only now. And what about the police; they must also have found it?"

"This is something I'm not so sure about. The forensics found not the slightest suspicious trace in the flat. So they had no reason to search the furnishings."

"I suppose that the hideout of the golden key that I hit upon was not the authentic, permanent one. Xanda may have put the key there ad hoc, temporarily, when she was caught off guard by someone the day before or something like that."

"What are you driving at?"

"Titus may have found the key in its secret stash. He might try to hunt the murderer down on his own."

"Do you want to speak to Titus? If not, I will."

"It's your case. I would prefer not to speak with either person of the van Aanstryk family."

"I think of speaking to them, but only after I have read and seen your evidence. You should hand over copies of everything you have. Then we can start going," said Etienne and looked at me and then at Capota.

"It's become late. But if you want to, you can come with me and pick up what I have. As a matter of fact, I would prefer it to sending it by e-mail."

"So would I," said Etienne Friendly.

So we accompanied Mateo Capota to his home in Syget.

"What day is it?" said the elderly male part of the couple at the breakfast table in the other corner of the room, distinctly. Apparently they were summer vacationists from some northern part of Germany.

"Here is the newspaper! Today is Tuesday the fifteenth of July 2014," said the female half of the couple, audibly.

This morning was the first morning of all my mornings in Edelweiss, when I woke up not in my room or in Rita's.

I had slept soundly, but before I opened my eyes I was already highly agitated, because the events of last night crossed my mind immediately.

I had not expected the profession of investigating could be so exciting.

Last night, Etienne and I went to Syget with Mateo Capota. He handed us copies of his secret documentation which he had abstracted out of Xanda van Aanstryk's tabernacle.

"And you are sure you don't recognize the person who

pushes Manfred van Aanstryk between the buffers of two rail-cars," said Etienne Friendly, in a reflective manner.

"Haven't a clue."

"It's getting late. Thank you very much, Mateo. We won't keep you any longer," said Etienne, and put the material into his breast pocket.

"It makes no difference," said Capota, and switched a computer on. "Let's quickly have a look together."

When we viewed the video, Etienne Friendly became very excited, but tried to mask the fact. However I watched him closely. I myself did not recognize the person; he or she had curly blond hair peeping out under a blue baseball cap and wore a reflective vest as they were in use by the railroad workers.

"You can't tell whether it's a male or a female," said Etienne, before we left.

However on the way home he got more explicit. "I think I know who it is," he said.

More he did not say. Only that he must first have blow ups of still images made of the video, to be sure.

While I stomached these happenings together with my breakfast egg, Etienne rang.

Gordon Aybesford had spoken to the district attorney of Cowford, Mrs. Melitta Stern. Forthwith she had contacted the chief prosecutor in Cyclamen City, Mr. John Younghenry, who promptly had fixed a meeting for the afternoon.

Chief Prosecutor John Younghenry, District Attorney Melitta Stern, Etienne Friendly and I were sitting at the conference table in the chief prosecutor's office, when a rigid blond gentleman was walked in by two persons in police uniform.

The prosecutor indicated to the uniforms to wait outside

and to the awkward one to sit down. Then he cleared his throat and said, "Special Constable Willie Dunstig, the evidence against you, which you so desperately wanted to screw out of Mrs. Xanda van Aanstryk's possession, has been found. What do you think about that?"

The sad stiff shape, sunk down in its chair, stared at the prosecutor like a little rabbit at an Egyptian cobra, with the only difference that Dunstig wore a pair of spectacles. Younghenry got up and went to his desk and pushed a button, upon which a secretary appeared who took a seat at one end of the table.

"Just in case the electronic recorder fails, we are taking down by hand everything you are going to tell, Mr. Dunstig. To make a clean breast of it all will be very wholesome for you," said the chief prosecutor, after switching on a recorder.

Willie Dunstig harrumphed.

"Tell us how you got involved. What is the first thing that springs to your mind when you think back?"

"It began when I found out that Dalia was gay. I discovered that she used to hang around with Xanda van Aanstryk. I began paying close attention to the doings of the two."

"Am I right in thinking that you are talking about Detective Chief Inspector Dalia Kalanda, your superior?"

"That's right, sir."

"And then it appeared to you that you could take advantage of your findings."

"No, not quite; not at all, in fact."

"But?"

"I think Dalia was afraid I could shed a rumor. For this reason she maneuvered me into a situation so she had something on me. That's how I saw it later."

"What did she do?"

"She stated categorically that she and Xanda were both straight; that they were closest friends only. She hinted that Xanda was crazy about me, in fact. I showed interest and she introduced us with each other."

"Xanda made my mouth water, but said she would not commit adultery. But if I'm serious, I must first help her, to do away with her husband, whom she despised."

"This prompted you to work out a plan to kill Manfred van Aanstryk."

"That wasn't my idea, but hers. I refused point-blank at the beginning. But Xanda had worked out everything. She had ascertained the best day and hour. She talked every day about it until I was ready to do it like a duck is ready to take to water. She had a spare high visibility vest and a cap and one day we did it."

"Was there also a certain amount of money that tipped the scales?"

"She said there was plenty of money to come."

"I have made inquiries this morning at the hospital. You were injured at the spine when the bump occurred; and your clothes must have been smeared in blood. How did you manage ... your departure from the scene of the crime passed unnoticed?"

"We had brought along clean garments anyway. While in pain I changed laboriously in the car. Then Xanda dropped me off at the foot of the stairs in front of the court building. Somebody found me and called the emergency ambulance."

"Did you know Mrs. van Aanstryk was filming the crime at the shunting yard?"

"Not at the time. She told me only later, when I claimed

my rights."

"Your wart in your neck has given you away. Although your hair was longer at the time, the jerk has caused your hair to reveal your verruca for the fraction of a second."

Willie Dunstig looked pitiably through his spectacles; but also relieved, in a way. He said nothing.

"This is not a trial, Mr. Dunstig. I've heard more than enough to seize you for the murder of Mr. Manfred van Aanstryk, though. There is no limitation for murder. Consider yourself under arrest."

Dunstig sat without moving or making a sound.

"Was Mrs. Dalia Kalanda in the plot?"

"We never talked about it. But she helped me to get the job of a special constable when I was no longer fit for full-fledged police work. I remained a handicapped person after recovery. "

"The blackmailing letters speak for themselves. Now will you please tell us: what gave you the idea to put a glass of poisoned honey at Mrs. van Aanstryk's door?

"I had nothing to do with this," croaked Willie Dunstig, barely audible because of his parched throat.

The chief prosecutor waved for a glass of water to be given to Dunstig. "As compared to your first crime, this second one is less grave. So why make your life more miserable by not spilling the beans completely, now that you are at it."

But Dunstig, who still was not able to speak, waved NO with his hand.

"Mr. Etienne Friendly here is an investigator from London and he found the evidence for your first murder. But he has also proof of your second murder."

Dunstig did not recognize Friendly, who had been in

disguise and had called himself Monsieur Fermat on their previous encounters. He remained firm and stuck to his denial.
On being shown the photos of the *lumberjack*, he displayed an
idiotic mien but there were no telling signs of guilt.

"Mr. Dunstig, do you know who placed the honey at Mrs.
Van Aanstryk's doormat?"

Dunstig shook his head. "No, I have no idea whatsoever."

"Do you think that Mrs. Dalia Kalanda, whom you de-
scribe to be gay, may have done it; perhaps out of jealousy?
We have evidence that Mrs. van Aanstryk was having a relation
with at least one other woman."

But Willie Dunstig, who seemed to be exhausted, reaf-
firmed over and over again, that he had no idea. But he admitted that they had downplayed the van Aanstryk case because
both, he and Kalanda had had reason not to come into the
limelight. In fact, they had suspected each other.

"So you suspect her still," declared the chief prosecutor.

Willie Dunstig shrugged his shoulders.

"But you are stubbornly insisting that you have no idea!"

"I have no evidence. I cannot simply denounce her."

Etienne arranged with the Aybesford family a meeting in
the Golden Egg for Tuesday evening. We must give an interim
report before unverified stories go around, had Etienne said.
In the morning of this day Etienne assigned me with contact-
ing Aleva and Vesna. I was to pose a series of interesting questions to them. I immersed myself into the task with vigor and
I was looking forward to presenting my findings in front of a
home crowd in the Golden in the evening.

When the time had come, the same people that had

attended the meeting ten days ago were again assembled in the Golden Egg. I sat to the left of Etienne Friendly. The audience was in very good spirits. Gordon was downright hilarious and urged everybody to help themselves. I thought he was even a bit tipsy. He spoke exuberant words of welcome. Eventually he handed over to Etienne Friendly. I ran my gaze over the crowd. I was in my element.

Etienne Friendly began like this: "Very few people ever have occasion to see a flock of swans in the air; not even in their lifetime. Last week Mr. Naran Dasgupta, we know him also as the ferryman, came riding home from the hills beyond the Holly, when he beheld five swans flying, not very high, along the river, downstream. His camera always ready, he managed to take a few snapshots of the incident. One of these photos may become world-famous because it shows the swan squadron flying directly before and above the castle. And the blue rock appears most spectacular at the time of the day when this happened and the picture was taken."

Wide eyes were looking at us. Friendly made a pause.

"Besides its magic, the picture showed something else, that made my blood go faster. If it turned out to be, what I thought it to be, it would considerably shorten my work on the Xanda case. In fact, it could contain the solution of it."

"Here we go," said Gordon and switched on the projector, while his son Nicholas dimmed the light.

"When I met Mr. Dasgupta this morning, he showed me a print of the spectacular image. When I noticed a yellow spot in the blue of the rock wall, I remembered what Melis had told me a week ago."

Everyone held his breath. I was no exception.

"She told me, that on the day before the general election, she had seen Mrs. Nadler go to the abyss and throw a yellow plastic bag away. Remember, this was the day of the interview. Mrs. Nadler was then already dressed for the evening performance. The bag must have got caught on some twig or a tip of rock.

"What of it?" said Mrs. Tusnelda Nadler, when all eyes turned to her.

"Can you tell us what you disposed of?"

"I had dressed early and I thought there was plenty of time to go and feed the gulls. I grabbed the next best plastic bag that I could get hold of in the storage room next to the garage. I meant to dispose of it in one of the wastebaskets in the park. That's what I always do, when I've finished feeding. When the bird food was nearly used up, I was just going to examine a false beard or something that was at the bottom of the bag, when a sudden gust of wind whipped everything out of my hand. I had not in mind environmental pollution, if this is what you are driving at."

"Tomorrow morning the volunteer fire department will get hold of the evidence," Friendly proceeded. "I predict they will find a baseball cap with long gray hair glued to the rear inside of it. An item made for carnival revelries. I wonder whose DNA will there be to be found on it?"

All eyes were on Tusnelda Nadler, my mother.

"DNA?" she said.

"Deoxyribonucleic acid," I explained.

"Don't stare at me like this, all of you. I did not plant the hibiscus honey."

"It was no hibiscus honey at all; just ordinary blossom honey," I said. What else should I have said?

Now I was the focus of everybody's stare.

"How did you find me out?" I asked, looking sideways at Etienne.

"You were a main suspect because you felt that Xanda van Aanstryk was a nuisance factor for your relation with your girlfriend. When I was shown the photos in judge Larissa Bennent's flat, I suddenly remembered that I had noticed a single long gray hair on your trousers, when we met for the first time on the day of the interview – when I was pretending to be Peter Dorset, a reporter from Manchester."

I nodded. "I see," I said. I was not proud of myself. Had I thrown away this carnival trash, I could have denied everything. I don't know what my facial expression was like at that moment.

Friendly went on: "I grant you that you did not plan the murder well in advance, and that you even tried to retrieve the honey; this was your reason for coming back, this time not in disguise. But alas! The glass was no longer on the doormat."

A murmur went through the crowd, as if in appreciation of my noble deed.

"This afternoon I paid a visit to your aunt Mitzi in her new dwelling. She told me that your deceased uncle was a chemist. He had a small chemical laboratory in their former house; the very house that you helped your aunt to clear out. When you found the cyanide, it gave you the idea to prepare a deadly mixture for the annoying person Xanda van Aanstryk. You had probably heard that she had acquired the habit of drinking a cup of milk with honey before going to bed. Howsoever, why not deposit a glass of poisoned honey on her doormat and see what happens?"

I listened fascinated.

"You couldn't be sure that nobody would see or recognize you in Avril Court. So you were in need of an adequate disguise. Some old clothes were easily to be found. Finding this carnival article, a baseball cap with long hair attached to it, was a piece of good fortune."

You could have knocked me down with a feather.

"I think after depositing the honey you changed clothes at the roadside. Later you disposed of the clothes in a rubbish bin or you threw them into the river Holly. For some reason you kept the cap with the hair; perhaps you thought you could have use for it next year during the carnival days. On arriving home a queasy conscience seized you. So you put the bag down in the storage room and went back to Avril 2."

On impulse I thought of trying to disagree with certain details of Etienne Friendly's remarks, but then I realized the futility of this endeavor.

"Where is the yellow speck?" asked Melis. "I see none."

"Do you think it was wishful thinking on my part when I had a thorough inspection of the photo this morning?" said Etienne Friendly.

I looked only over the heads of hair of the people that were staring at me, avoiding thus looking them in the eye.

I perceived how Rita was aghast. Shaking her head she looked at me; but I couldn't care less. My thoughts were with Pauline all the time, anyway.

CPSIA information can be obtained at www.ICGtesting.com
Printed in the USA
LVOW08s2344140815

450242LV00001B/223/P